KEIKO'S KIMONO

A DOLL'S JOURNEY TO AMERICA IN 1869
WITH THE WAKAMATSU TEA AND SILK COLONY

Historical Fiction By
Herb Tanimoto

To Barbara,
I hope you
enjoy my story
of Keiko!
Always,
Herb Tanimoto

Tanimoto, Herb

Keiko's Kimono: A doll's journey to America in 1869 with the Wakamatsu Tea and Silk Colony/by Herb Tanimoto. Create Space, July 2017

ISBN 13: 9781546334026

1. FICTION: Historical. 2. Immigrant. 3. Cultural Heritage. 4. Japanese-American. 5. California History I. Keiko's Kimono.

Library of Congress Control Number: 2016959695

Cover art by Donna Orth

Copyediting by Two Songbirds Press

Book design by Lisa Ham for Two Songbirds Press

Printed in the United States of America

Available from Amazon.com, CreateSpace.com, and other retail outlets.

For Okei and Henry

Table Of Contents

Acknowledgements

The dream of writing my first novel would not have become reality had not steadfast friends and wonderful professionals helped me in every step of this endeavor. I owe a debt of gratitude to Nancy March, Myrna Hanses, and my editor, Robin Martin, for their determined proofreading work. Robin especially helped add professionalism to a first time novelist's work. I also would like to thank Phyllis Ogata for helping me with Japanese customs, history, and translations. Wendy Guglieri's unfading enthusiasm for digging into the dustiest, most deeply hidden corners of historical research has been a constant source of inspiration for me. I want to recognize the spiritual motivation I got from reading Joan Barsotti's book, *Okei-san, the Girl from Wakamatsu*. Lastly, I want to express my appreciation to my fellow docents at the Wakamatsu Tea and Silk Colony Farm. One of the talented docents, Donna Orth, designed the fabulous cover art. Working together these many years, we have all become "honor and duty bound" in our dedication to preserving the first Japanese Colony in North America.

Preface

A series of fortuitous circumstances led to the writing of this novel. I was born of Japanese heritage. I am "sansei," or third generation, my grandparents having come to America around 1900. I was already a member of the American River Conservancy, a land trust and natural resource preservation organization, when its director and board decided to take action on an offer by the Veerkamp family to sell their historic farm in 2010. I had known a little about the story of the colony from my parents, who had attended a centennial celebration in 1969. I realized that an opportunity of a lifetime had been delivered and I hadn't even asked for it. I became part of a small group of people who work tirelessly to cut the weeds, plant the flowers, paint the walls, do historic research, lead the tours, and do a thousand other duties necessary to maintain and embellish what we lovingly call "the farm."

I soon began to wonder about the pioneers who had walked the halls and rooms of the old farmhouse and sweated in the farm fields on this land. What would it be like to have lived in their time and world? I found myself thinking about how their story had begun, how it had ended, and everything that had happened in-between. I felt that this was a story that needed to be told, and I soon became the instrument for its telling.

After 140 years of farming operations, the Veerkamp family was ready to end their agricultural enterprise. In 2010, the American River Conservancy purchased the farm, with help from the Sierra Nevada Conservancy, Natural Resources Conservation Service,

California Rice Commission, Japanese American Citizens League, private contributions, and bridge loans (much of the loan still remaining). Along with the farmhouse and land, came the story of Veerkamp family life over the many years and also the story of the brief time of the Wakamatsu Tea and Silk Colony.

Henry Veerkamp was nearing the end of his life when researchers began to appear at the farm inquiring about the Japanese ranch and stories they had heard about a Japanese girl who had been buried there. It was then about 1930, but Henry could still vividly recall those times in his youth when he knew John Henry Schnell and many of the Japanese colonists. He especially remembered Okei, whom he described to historians; "When she wore her kimono, she was very beautiful. She learnt sewing and cooking from my mother, who was very fond of her." (VanSant, J., *Pacific Pioneers*, 129)

We are blessed that members of the Veerkamp family gave us stories that were passed down from generation to generation. We also have many articles from pioneer newspapers such as the *Daily Alta* and *Sacramento Union*. We are, however, fortunate to know what little we do. Many pioneer immigrant stories have disappeared because no one had cared enough to save the memories. All of us have passed by those derelict old buildings, slumping further into the ground with each passing year, wondering briefly about the people who had once lived there. Who were they? Where did they go? Almost always, we will never know. Such total loss could easily have happened to the Wakamatsu story if not for the work of a small group of dedicated individuals. Many, such as the early historians who came to interview Henry Veerkamp, live on in the legacy of their research—work that has opened this window to the past.

Known facts can go only so far in the writing of historical fiction. Sometimes a small tidbit from hours of dogged research can be found to hang like a decoration to add a bit of color. More often, the color must come from imagination. Sometimes, even conclusions escape the notation of history. The fate of the colony leader, John

Henry Schnell, is such a mystery. By attempting to explain his disappearance in my story, I am not trying to fill in what history has left blank. My motivation was simply to tell a good story using what information that I had available.

Writing about Okei-*san* was not easy. Although she was the central human character in the Wakamatsu story, very little is actually known about her. There are no known photographs. Little is written about her family and nothing is known about their fate after the Boshin War. The majority of Aizu residents were forcibly removed from their own town, the Imperial government being wary of a concentration of enemy sympathizers. Okei's parents probably left their home also, never to return.

Okei's grave lies on a small hill on the Gold Hill ranch sheltered by a grove of oak trees. The lore, passed down from generations of Veerkamps, says that this was her favorite space on the 160-acre farm. She went there after chores, watching the sun setting to the west, dawning light on her beloved Aizu homeland where her family awaited, and darkening the new world where she now found herself living. It is said that she sang lullabies and children's songs as she watched the light fade. Her gravesite is on the National Registry of Historic Places, honoring her fateful recognition as the first woman Japanese pioneer buried on American soil. She was only nineteen years old at the time of her death.

Many have taken Okei's story to legendary status. A popular song about her filled the airwaves in Japan some years ago. There is a memorial in her honor on Mt. Seaburi overlooking her Aizu hometown. Many Japanese people consider her the embodiment of the Japanese spirit of putting honor and duty above oneself. Whether such feelings about Okei were deserved or not, I never intended to challenge this mythical vision of her.

In *Keiko's Kimono*, I have tried to be as accurate as possible with the use of historical facts, but I am a novelist first and did not intend to write a historical document to be used for research or study. *Keiko's Kimono* is my effort to bring to life a story of what it might have been like back then. Most of the characters in the story were real, but I don't pretend to know what thoughts were in their minds or know what their motivations were. They are actors on a stage that I created, working off of a screenplay that I wrote.

Still, every time I walk in the hallway or one of the rooms of the old Graner house, or stand before the giant keyaki tree, I wonder what the people who were there would think about my story. When I am at Okei's gravesite, I pray that I did not dishonor her in any way with my presumptions. I can only say to those spirits that I tried my best to tell their story. I have felt their kami still lingering in the air, still seeping from hallway walls, still in the rocks at Okei's gravesite. I found motivation for *Keiko's Kimono* during those times.

To help the reader, I have included an appendix in the back of the book with historical information about the places and characters in the order of their appearance. I have also included a Japanese glossary to help understand the Japanese words.

I hope that my story motivates you to visit the Wakamatsu Tea and Silk Colony Farm. Donations also help cover maintenance and public facility improvements, in addition to paying off the still large bridge loan. To participate in a tour, please call the American River Conservancy at 530-621-1224 and visit the website www.arconservancy.org for more information about the colony's history. Our docents would be happy to show you around the farm that all of us love. You might even get a chance to meet Keiko. She has an amazing story to tell.

All profits from sales of this book will go to the American River Conservancy, Wakamatsu Tea and Silk Colony Project.

CHAPTER 1
Tsuruga Castle

Konnichiwa. My name is Keiko. I am profoundly honored that you have decided to hear the story of the life journey that has been blessed upon this pitiful little soul.

I do not know where to begin as I am but a woeful and untrained storyteller. Perhaps an explanation of who I am would be a good place to start. Oh, *gomennasai!* Already I am being deceptive. *What* I am is probably better. You see, I am not a being such as you. I am not even alive. If one is alive, then one should be able to die, ne? I have been in this world for more than 145 years. Of course my mind isn't as keen or clever as it used to be. My eyesight and hearing have slipped considerably. I am getting older, but not by human terms. I guess it is because I don't have a body with heart and lungs and tissue that will wear out with time. My body is that of a doll. That is what my maker, Okei-san, put my spirit, my *kami,* into.

You have never heard of kami? It is a little difficult to explain to people not accustomed to oriental culture. Kami is the spirit that is in everything. A rock can have kami. If you throw a rock and it hits and injures someone, that is due to the kami of the rock, added to the kami of your own wickedness. The sun has kami. A storm has kami. A river. An ocean. A mountain. The smallest bacteria or grain of sand to the tiniest flickering star in the night sky has kami.

My maker, Okei-san, had a very strong kami. It was so strong and special that it became a part of my being as well. Of course, I was just a doll and only had a basic, simple kami to begin with. However, even before she had finished me, before the final stitches were sewn, I was already beginning to sense that I was very different because of her.

I don't know how she was able to do this. I just know that something began to happen even before the bits of silk, thread, and cloth were put together to give my body shape. Okei-san was a very special being. She had a special power, an ability, that very few on this world possess. I don't know how she came to have such a great gift.

I can remember the first day that I had felt existence. Out of the darkness, whiteness had appeared. It grew to envelop me in it, then, as I watched in awe, the whiteness became uneven, less bright here, more bright there. It began to take shape. Then there were corners and edges, straight things and things with curves. It was happening so fast, and I had no idea what any of this would mean to me. I think I felt much uncertainty, and also fear.

Then something magical happened that I would remember to my last days. I began to notice that the light was different on many things. There was a pleasing unevenness, not like the difference of light and dark. There were hues—colors. I could see colors! Of course I didn't know what the colors were. I had no vocabulary and no way to express myself. I only knew that the colors filled me with the awed sense of witnessing physical beauty for the first time.

I felt something. What could it be? How could I know that I had been touched for the first time?

Gomennasai, Keiko-chan. I am too tense. Breathe deeply, and let the air flow out. Feel my heartbeat slow. My hands must be steady because any mistake is permanent. The doll will live with it forever. Now, do the other eye in the same manner.

Suddenly another half of the world opened up for me. My vision was doubled! I could tell some objects were nearer than others. Some were so very far. There was a blur very near to me, almost touching me. Then I felt it again.

Now that you have two eyes, what can you see?

The object so near to me held something long and sharp. It was directly above what I was observing with.

I am brushing on your eyebrows, Keiko-chan. I mixed some sacred earth from the ancient burial grounds with the black block ink I used for your eyes. I am painting the lines at an angle to give depth to your face. It is only paint, but it will help you have the quality of life about you.

I felt the strokes, the same number on each side. The wetness of the paint on my skin was also a new experience for me. Oh, but I don't even know if I have skin! This strange new world was so confusing.

Ah, but you have no ears! You can read my thoughts, but you will need to hear to understand the world that awaits you. I will remedy my foolish oversight right away.

Very soon the world of sound was opened to me. Again I became frightened of new sensations rushing into me that I could not understand. My maker seemed to notice my uneasiness.

"Don't be afraid, my little one. All of this you will need for the journey ahead of you. It will be a wonderful life, Keiko-chan, full of adventure, mischief, and love."

Her soothing voice was the first sound that I had ever heard. I just watched with my new eyes, and listened with my new ears. I still could not understand what was happening. I had never experienced existence, so I had no sense of what it was like to be.

Suddenly a loud sound made me withdraw into myself. The sound was harsh and it continued, hurting my sensitive new ears. It came from somewhere beyond my maker.

"Okei! What do you think you are you doing?"

"This doll is a gift for Schnell-san, mother. I have told Jou-san that I would make this for little Frances, and I must honor my commitment. Right now Keiko-chan has no nose or mouth. She has no clothes. I cannot give it to Jou-san's little Frances like this."

She was concentrating on me so much that she didn't even notice her mother holding out her arms in exasperation. I could feel her soft hands grow more tense and harden as she quickened her pace. She left my side for a moment and I could hear the rattle of moving objects close by. In a long moment, my maker returned with a cup of orange liquid.

I watched as she pulled out a long glistening object. I sensed a great power in that object, but didn't know why or what that power was.

Do not watch this, Keiko-chan.

The silver object then seemed to merge with my maker, and I heard a guttural sound that I instinctively knew reflected pain.

"Forgive me, Keiko-chan. There is no crimson for your lips and I had to do something. My hand will heal, but now you will always have a part of me with you."

She steadied her hands and I could feel several long and quick strokes on my face. She placed the bottom of her hand on me and spent precious moments filling in with tiny, meticulous movements of her finest brush. My maker then held me out at arms length on the table and gazed at me. The smile that I saw on her face dazzled me with its brightness.

"It is done! Say something to me with your new mouth, Keiko-chan!"

I watched her lips move as she spoke. The sounds were coming from between them as they parted. I tried to follow her example, reaching into my thoughts to find the right connections to make my newly painted lips move as hers. But I could find no such connection. In fact, I could find nothing in my thoughts that could make any part of me move such as she moved.

How could I be so different from my maker?

She once again used the magic of motion to go somewhere farther away. She was out of my view and I could not turn to see where she had gone. I was but a few moments from panic.

I heard sounds coming from where she was, mechanical sounds that would have sent a shiver through me, had I the ability to tremble.

The sound made me uncomfortable. Perhaps something in me knew that what she was doing could be dangerous for us both.

In an instant, she was in my vision again, directly over me. I felt something behind me and then came an odd sensation of rising. It was only a few feet, but it might as well have been a few thousand. I was being pushed upward and the barrier above me was crashing down. I couldn't close my eyes to avoid seeing the surely coming catastrophe.

All at once, the motion stopped. It was then that I realized that my maker had somehow lifted me with something on my back. Her hand! It had the warmth of life and made me feel safe. She lowered me gently and I felt myself on something softer than the surface that had been at my back since I had awakened.

"You are naked, Keiko-chan. You only have the cloth-skin

covering that I had sewn for you and the remnant filled material within. But you are so lucky! I will make you a kimono of the finest silk that will make you feel and be beautiful."

Yes, to feel beautiful! I would like that very much.

As she folded some of the fabric around me, I could see flashes of its water and sky blue color. A tiny but sharp shiny stick came in and out of my vision. Again I felt apprehension.

Please be careful, Okei-san. I said this but of course my painted mouth could not speak the words.

It was then that I realized then that my maker's name was "Okei-san." I was Keiko.

Okei-san's hands moved swiftly, the silver needle darting in and out of the silk cloth as fast as it could move.

All the time there was much commotion about us. There were many rapid footstep sounds from somewhere nearby. Then I heard a sharp, piercing noise so loud that I might have jumped out of my cloth skin. Luckily, I could not do that, either. I felt my maker's thoughts.

Someone is still shooting. I thought that the war was over.

The second living being that I had seen in my life then appeared in my vision, gazing directly down as I lay still on the colorful cloth. This human resembled my maker, although appearing perhaps more aged. This was the creator of my maker, I somehow was able to recognize. She was Okei-san's *mother*, that was the word I had been searching for.

"Schnell-*sama* and Jou-san will be honored by this gift you have bestowed for their daughter. But the castle is over run by the Satsuma soldiers and the Lord and Schnell-sama are in hiding. I fear that you will not be able to get it to them."

"I am taking it to the meeting in the secret chamber, mother."

"Oh? I did not know of this. Why did you not tell me?"

"I am sorry to say that I could not. Matsu told me just this morning and swore me to absolute secrecy, even from my own mother."

"Then something is happening? Surely, they can look around and see that everything is hopeless. We are defeated and most of our samurai are dead, and there has been too much bloodshed already. What could they be planning?"

Even as Okei turned for a moment to look at her mother, her hands moved quickly to stitch my kimono. She had already finished both of the long sleeves and was placing the two-piece collar by my neck.

"No. No more bloodshed. It is not about a revolt against the Satsuma, but something else. I don't know, perhaps they are planning an escape," Okei said.

"Escape? To where? The Satsuma and Imperial soldiers control the entire land. There is nowhere to go!"

Okei's mother continued to look over her shoulder at me. She moved closer to her daughter.

"I learned today from Seichi that the great Lord himself suggested you when Jou-san needed help caring for her baby. You have brought great honor to our family."

Okei worked in silence for a moment. Outside the noise seemed to have lessened.

"You have done well, my daughter. Father is proud also, although he cannot bring himself to say it. But these ties to our Lord could place you in great danger now that we have lost the war. You must watch your step, and your back."

Yes, mother. I will be careful. She thought this but did not tell her.

Her mother left my vision and Okei concentrated even harder on her sewing. Moments more passed until she finally stopped.

"Eee. At last, I am done. Oh, you are so beautiful, my little Keiko-chan! Let me show you in the *kagami.*"

Again I felt the sensation of being lifted, although this time I did not have the apprehension. In fact, I felt a little giddy. Then my eyes came to the mirror glass on the wall that had been behind me. I saw myself for the first time.

Is that really me? Her thoughts swept into me.

See how beautiful your kimono is, Keiko-chan? My great grandmother spun the silk from the cocoons. She made a kimono from it that grandmother and my mother both wore for their weddings. It was to be for my wedding, also.

Okei stopped for a moment and even an inanimate doll could sense the trouble she was having with her thoughts. *You are beautiful also, Okei-san,* I sent in her direction.

The kimono was lost when oba-chan's village was burned down in the war with the Toshi. I was then just a child and couldn't understand. In the rubble all I found was a sleeve.

"It is lucky that you are so small, Keiko-chan, for I used all of it for your kimono."

I could not stop gazing at my kimono. There were designs

floating in the blue of the water and sky. Flowers of many different sizes and colors fluttered. Floating leaves of green and yellow were in the water, along with golden eddies. Birds flew in the sky that seemed to be a continuation of the water. Tiny fish swam in the river. Fishing nets with lines reflecting the hues of the setting sun completed the peaceful scene.

My maker wiped her eyes and I could see the glistening moisture still around them.

"Now that the world is upside down, it doesn't matter anymore. What matters is that my little Keiko is as beautiful as she can be. . . and you are."

I am!

"A hundred years from now, Keiko-chan, your kimono will be just as beautiful as today. The colors will not fade, as your life will not fade."

I would have shed tears had I known how.

What is life? I asked with my immobile mouth.

Her mother's voice spoke again.

"Someone is coming. Satsuma samurai! Quickly get your things! We must leave!"

More sharp and loud noises made me want to cover my ears, but my arms, like every other part of me, would not move. I could not turn my eyes or my head to see what was happening. Oh, the frustration! Then I heard my maker's voice so different than it had ever been.

"Satsuma do not have the right to be here! Please leave!"

A deep voiced laughter came from beyond my vision.

"Shut up, Aizu slut. Your slime Lord has been defeated by the great Emperor's army of destiny, and you cannot stop us from doing whatever we want!"

Just then a giant and hideous creature entered from the far side of my vision. It sprouted jutting golden horns on a shiny blackened head that seemed to flow down onto its incredibly broad shoulders. Scale-like plates covered every area from the neck to the hands. A large black plate covered the chest, and on its center was a painted double-lined circle surrounding a brush-stroked character.

I was more fearful than I had ever been in my extremely short life. Okei-san's voice came from my left.

"I am sorry, we did not mean to dishonor you or my Emperor's commands by my impertinent words. We were just leaving. Please allow us to go."

"Silence, slut! I am looking for that lowly coward, Matsudaira. We have learned that there is to be a secret meeting where treasonous actions against the Emperor are to be discussed. I want to know where it is. You will tell me!"

"We know of no such meeting. We are simple peasant laborers. We are leaving the castle to go back to our home. I beg for your compassion to let us leave."

I was amazed at how gentle and unafraid Okei-san's voice sounded. I saw her to the left of my vision. Suddenly, the monster reappeared to the right, gazing directly at her from very close.

"Did you not know that the castle has been under siege, and your pitiful Lord has capitulated like the coward that he is?"

My maker made a strange sound and put her hands to her throat.

"I did not know this. Mother, is it true? Did we surrender? What do we do? Where are we to go?"

The monster came closer to Okei-san.

"You need not worry, young girl. The war will be over before today's last rays of sun touch the earth. The Satsuma will bring order to this sinful country, and you can blossom into the beautiful flower that you surely are destined to become."

Although he was less than an arm's length away from her, Okei-san did not go back one step and remained standing straight as an unyielding bamboo shaft. She seemed to be less than half the size of the monster. Her voice was just as smooth and emotionless as before.

"Did you fight against our samurai?"

"Yes, indeed. I was in the first wave at Sugami Castle that we stormed so fast that we had time for lunch in the courtyard. I also helped defeat your Lord's prized Red Dragon brigade in the mountains just to the north."

"It cannot be. They were our bravest samurai!"

"Ha! Yes, they fought bravely, but they were like boys against men, so shamefully inadequate they were against us. I personally took the head of the commander who was in tears like a baby begging for his life. He was so pitiful that I didn't even bother to stake his head."

"You did all this?"

"I've been in many battles, young girl. It would take a lifetime to tell you of all I have done and all the Shogun's samurai I have cut down. But you are so young, ne? I would have years to tell you, if you wish to share those years with me."

They were now so close to each other that the monster towered over her and she was in his enormous shadow. She then had to arch her back to keep his body off of her.

"My name is Ashinobi Gambi. What may I call you?"

"I am Flower Dragon."

She said it with so little emotion that the monster only looked on with a puzzled expression. He saw the steel of the dagger in her hand and was able to turn just slightly as it sliced into his side armor. Okei-san had angled the blade so it found a thread-tied seam in-between armor plates. However, the samurai's quick reaction and shortness of the blade had saved him from grievous injury. He quickly turned at Okei-san.

"Foolish girl! Foolish! Now you die!"

It was then that I saw the first *katana* in my life. It was very long with a gracefully curved blade that glinted in the subdued light of the castle. He swung it behind his right shoulder as Okei-san watched with what seemed to be detached indifference. Even though I had only been in existence for but a few moments, I could sense the imminent danger to my maker. Eee, I did not want to lose her when my own life was just beginning. *Please move, Okei-san!* I wanted to shout out as loudly as I could. Of course, I could not. I did not have the ability. I could not do anything.

The katana, however, seemed to stay fixed in the air, held by the black plated arm and hand. I heard the sound of something moving quickly above me, like the air itself being sliced. I saw only a blur of whiteness. It was followed by a spray of moisture all about me.

It was then that I saw the figure behind the monster. It was bigger than my maker, but not as large as the monster. It also held a katana in its hand, which was now unmoving and red stained at its side. It did not wear the armor, and was simply dressed.

Something fell to the floor with a terrifying sound. I instinctively knew what it was, and tried to close my eyes, but of course I could not. Luckily, I was on my back looking at the ceiling and not the floor, but then the monster tottered into my vision, its huge hulk leaning precipitously, before slowly gaining momentum on its final descent. The shiny black helmet with the golden horns and iron and leather plates that had terrified me was gone, as was the head that had been in it.

CHAPTER 2
Secret Meeting With Lord Matsudaira

Matsunosuke Sakurai shook the blood from his blade as he looked over at the transfixed Okei-san. Her eyes were still staring at the place where the monster had been standing inches from her. The samurai returned the razor sharp instrument to the scabbard on his obi and came closer to her.

"Okei, are you all right? I was going to get you for the meeting with our Lord and your mother came running. He did not hurt you, did he?"

She reached to the low table to steady herself, and then eased herself to the ground with Matsu's help. Another Aizu samurai entered the room and the two men grabbed the corpse by the arms and legs and disappeared for a moment. I saw Okei's mother wiping the table and floor mat with a large cloth. She cleaned all around me, then picked me up and smothered me with another wet cloth. I panicked at first, but realized that the chore must be done. All the evidence must be removed. My face and kimono must be cleaned of the incriminating bloodstains.

Matsunosuke came back and was able to call in another Aizu samurai to take away the head in the helmet. It was only then that he noticed the bloodied sword blade still in Okei's hand. He pried open her fingers and took the knife. Matsu glared at her in disbelief.

"You stabbed him? A Satsuma samurai? What would possess

you to do such a stupid thing?"

Okei's eyes were still unmoving.

"He knew of the meeting, Matsu. He wanted to know where our Lord was, and I could not let him find out."

The Aizu samurai got down on his knees and held her hands.

"Didn't you realize that he would have killed you if I had not come?"

Okei slowly, deliberately, turned her eyes towards him.

"I knew that you would come."

Matsu opened his mouth to speak, but could not think of anything to say. Her gaze, unblinking and steady, forced him to look downward. When Okei's mother came back, he appeared to be kneeling in prayer before Okei-san.

Matsu finally noticed the mother staring down at them, and awkwardly got to his feet before she could make too much of this embarrassing situation. He reached down towards the girl.

"Okei-san, we must go to the meeting that has already begun. I will guide you if you are not steady."

My maker shook her head and stood, wavering at first then becoming steadier. She was wearing a simple light blue kimono with a white obi. I hadn't noticed until then how slim she was. Matsu, the samurai beside her, was twice her bulk but no taller than she was. He wore a gray pinstripe jacket over wide haori pants. His gray obi held his two swords, the long katana and the shorter wakizashi secondary weapon. His hair was raised up severely into a knot in the back, giving the appearance of a more youthful age than he truly was.

Okei-san picked me up and placed me on a large cloth towel. She finally started to move quickly.

I will need to wrap you, Keiko-chan, to keep you clean while you are in my carry sack. Little Frances would not like a soiled going-away present.

I thought about what I had just heard. I am to be a gift? I can no longer be with you?

We are going to a very important meeting with our Lord, and learn the fate of our domain. Schnell-sama and Jou will be there, and I can give you to them there.

She wrapped me in several layers of cloth and I watched my vision disappear. I wished that I had a better idea of my own fate.

As we left the room and entered the castle hall, the other samurai who had disposed of the monster's head caught up to us. Okei-san recognized him as we hurried along.

"Kuni-san, could it be you? You look just like a samurai! Is that a katana that you carry?"

"I thought you would not notice, Okei-san. Most of our samurai are gone and the great Lord called for those with courage and heart to help defend the castle, even carpenters like me. I have proven myself in battle, Okei-san, you would be very proud. I am honored to be a ninja in service to my Lord."

Okei squeezed his hand as they hurriedly turned into another hallway, just as two Satsuma soldiers were approaching. Luckily, they were preoccupied in conversation and were not looking down the narrow hall to see the stealthy figures that turned into a stairwell just in time.

We descended several flights of stairs before reaching the ground level. There, Matsu reached for one of the decorated screen panels on a wall and tugged at it. Amazingly, it slid open. It was a secret entrance to an underground chamber that was known to only the Lord's most trusted retainers.

A short flight of stairs that was dug into the ground and secured with footboards led to a small, rectangular room. Several lanterns revealed its dirt walls and stone-laid floor, with a wood floor path leading to the long end of the room where a small stage platform had been built of fresh lumber. Lord Matsudaira was seated on a stool on the platform.

Of course, I was covered in cloth and enclosed in a bag that Okei-san carried, so I could not see any of this. However, my mind seemed to be able to visualize what my eyes were blind to. Even though I was facing away from the Lord, I saw him as if I was looking from some place above and behind the group of people who were there. This ability was new to me. In the castle room above us, I had been unable to do this.

Lord Matsudaira was ornately dressed but in subdued colors. He wore a heavy broad kamishimo over his shoulders that partially covered a light-colored kimono embroidered with two large circular crests of the three-leaf hollyhock emblem of the Tokugawa Shogun. He wore broad dark hakama trousers and dark-colored tabi on his feet. On his head was a tall triangle shaped eboshi ceremonial hat.

His narrow face and tiny, slit-like gaze looking out from the wing-like kamishimo suggested much remaining youth, but lines around the eyes and cheeks gave a much older appearance. It had been a troubling and stressful time for Lord Matsudaira, the daimyo of Aizu Han. The castle and the war had been lost, but there remained much planning left to do. He cleared his throat to speak, but noticed that Schnell and his wife were discussing something in the far corner. A young samurai kneeling near Matsudaira rose to look back. He instinctively moved his right hand to the handle of his long blade katana.

"Silence! Our Lord is about to speak!"

Schnell, his wife, and the child that had been hidden behind them, proceeded to the front of the room and knelt down, a good sword length away from the young samurai. The daimyo gazed down at him.

"Nishijawa, we are among friends here. Please ease your anger and pain for we have much to plan this evening."

A faint smile appeared on Lord Matsudaira's thin face as he said those words. The young samurai removed his swords from his obi and placed them at his side, then bowed down deeply for the Lord's forgiveness. The daimyo turned his gaze to the few people who were in the room.

"I have called all of you together, the most trusted and loyal of my retainers and friends, to thank you for your meritorious service to Japan, our Aizu domain, and to your Lord. You have fought bravely, but the war has ended and we did not prevail. We must accept this outcome."

The young samurai again faced Matsudaira from his sitting position.

"My Lord, please do not talk about defeat! We should make a stand here and take a hundred Satsuma lives for each one of us! There are swords and spears stashed in the back. Matsunosuke, pass them out! We will die like samurai!"

When no one moved, Lord Matsudaira waited until the youthful samurai looked around at the still seated figures and finally turned back in his direction. He had a look of total dismay and frustration. He decided to sit again and lowered his head in shame for his disrespectful outburst.

"I need you, Nishijawa. I need all of you. I will not see any of you waste your lives for what would be meaningless suicide."

Lord Matsudaira then stood, and to the amazement of all those present, stepped down from the platform and walked out onto the stone-laid flooring.

"Of course, I do not minimize what has happened to all of us. We have no hope of recovery, no hope of mercy, and no hope for tomorrow. But just as our way of life has ended, I have brought you here for what will be a new beginning in a new distant home. Aizu will rise from the ashes once again in a new land."

No one moved. Okei looked around and wondered if she was the only one who had been kept in the dark about all this. Matsu, sitting with his legs folded near her, raised his head up slightly.

"My Lord, then the rumors that we have heard of going to California are true?"

"Yes, Matsunosuke. We have been planning this for the last month, ever since the Shogun Yoshinobu was exiled from Edo. I realized that not even the bravery of our warriors could keep the Satsuma forces away for much longer."

Matsudaira gestured towards Schnell.

"Hiramatsu, as have all of you, has fought bravely for our Han. Although he does not have the blood of our ancestors, over the years he has learned the ways of our people and has become indispensable to us. He helped us obtain firearms to battle the Satsuma. He fought bravely alongside Takemoto-san in the Ezo War, and after Takemoto's death, brought him great honor by bestowing his battle sword to the Emperor Meiji. He has been in many battles to try to stop the Satsuma advance."

"When he came to me with this plan, I was incredulous. To escape is not the way of the samurai. When hope is lost, we must commit seppuku to maintain our honor."

Matsudaira's right hand went across his body to the hilt of the short sword that hung below his katana. In an instant it was out and pointed outward from him, held by both hands. Even in the subdued light of the chamber, the Masamune sword gleamed in its lustrous steel splendor and balance of the perfectly spaced hamon tempering lines.

Okei let out a gasp. The others were looking up intently from their seated positions as Matsudaira stared out at the pointed tip of the blade.

"Seppuku has always been the way for the vanquished, to die with honor by one's own hand instead of the blade of the enemy."

Just as quickly, Matsudaira secured the blade back into its scabbard.

"We will not go away so quietly! We will go to this new land. We will flourish and the Aizu banner will fly proudly once more."

Matsudaira moved back to the small stage and sat once again.

A long moment passed before Schnell arose, bowed, and walked up to a position near the daimyo. He limped obviously, a reminder of the final Ezo battle alongside Takemoto that almost took his life as well. Immediately he knelt down on the floor so as to be lower than his Lord. In slow, deliberate Japanese, he addressed everyone. His voice was sharp, his diction flawless.

"I am honored and humbled to present myself before my Lord and the brave and courageous people before me. Unfortunately, the victory we had anticipated has not come to pass. Many of our people have lost their lives in the battles leading to this day."

Schnell bowed his head and for a moment did not make any eye contact.

"I have fought alongside many brave warriors during these last weeks and also in the times before. I was honored to be with Takemoto-san in the Ezo War. Even though he died gloriously, I thought then how much the world has been diminished by the loss of such a great man. As we were forced to retreat from Nagaoka, then Nihonmatsu, then Komine, I was thinking of loss again, of what would happen if the unthinkable happened and Aizu fell. There would be no place to go. The Satsuma would be brutal and everything that we had ever known and loved would be gone. All the effort would have been for nothing."

Schnell was dressed as a samurai, although he wore his dark reddish hair long and straight. He wore a simple pinstripe gray kimono and wide black haori trousers. On his light-colored obi he carried the traditional pair of swords. As for his face, probably his most notable features were the closeness of his eyes to each other, and the dark mustache over his small mouth. Except for the color of his hair, his features seemed more oriental than of his Prussian homeland.

"I remembered my stay in California before I came to Japan. I was there only briefly, but I was stunned by the enormity of the land. Houses were so far apart that anyone inside one could imagine himself being alone in the world. There were mountains and rivers, the temperature was fair."

"On my final day in that land, I climbed a hill and saw a valley spread out beneath me that was pristine, where there were no tracks across the grass. It was that place that I remembered when I watched our last Western castle being overrun. There would be a place for us to go and this was it. Today would not be the end."

Lord Matsudaira once again stood and walked near to where Schnell sat.

"I received a message from Hiramatsu many days prior to his

return from the Western battles. He said that they would continue to delay the Imperial army but that defeat was inevitable. He urgently wanted supplies stocked for this colony in California. I looked at the list: thousands of tea saplings, bags of rice, clothing, mulberry trees, silkworms. It was preposterous. How could we prepare all this during a time of war?"

"But it was because of this war that this had to be done. I sent my retainers across all of Aizu asking for these things, not believing that anyone would listen. Life had become harsh and uncertain for our people during this time of constant war. But soon these items began to appear at the castle gate. Tea trees and seeds. Mulberry trees. Citrus trees. Baskets of rice. Clothing."

"When I went to the gate and saw the many items being left, I was humbled. I asked some men unloading a cart why they were doing all this. To preserve our way of life, one answered. It gives us hope, another said. I immediately felt like I was stabbed in the heart. Had they misunderstood my message? They could not all go. Only a very few would be chosen. The rest must stay and face the cruelty and revenge that was surely coming from the Satsuma."

"An old man struggling with a bag of rice looked up and saw my concern. "My Lord," he said, "we are aware that we must remain, but to know that Aizu will live again in this new world shines a bright light in our darkest times. Those who go will carry the hopes of all our people. I am but a humble farmer who wishes to do everything possible to assure that the hope is fulfilled."

There was a noise from behind. Someone was coming down the stairway. Immediately the katana blades of Nishijawa and Sakurai flashed to point in that direction. Schnell, standing by Lord Matsudaira, held his hand on his sword hilt.

A woman dressed nearly like a man entered and immediately walked toward the daimyo. She was breathing heavily and didn't seem to notice the blades pointed at her. She shouldered a rifle and had a belt half filled with shell cartridges. There was a katana also slid into the belt. She wore a simple brown robe with decorations of white flowers on it. She stopped and knelt down before Matsudaira.

"My Lord, a procession of a hundred Satsuma soldiers is nearing the castle. There are carriages with men in gaijin clothing with them. I believe they are coming to take you and your family from the castle."

While Matsudaira stared at the female samurai before him, Schnell's wife went to her husband's side. Okei had no choice but to follow with little Frances in her arms. Schnell's face hardened upon learning the news.

"It's Torima. He has come for his revenge. We are all in danger because of me," Schnell said.

Matsudaira stood beside him still gazing at the woman.

"Yes, he has never forgotten the embarrassment and shame you caused him before the Emperor. But I think he comes for me. He wishes to end the inconvenience that Aizu has been for him."

Matsudaira then spoke to the female samurai.

"Yae-san, we need at least another hour to prepare our party's departure. Can you delay them for that long?"

The woman slowly nodded and arose with both legs together in unison.

"My Lord, I can only do my best. I will need help, if someone is available."

Matsudaira shook his head.

There was not a hint of disappointment in her eyes.

"I understand, my Lord. Be assured that you will have your hour and more."

She bowed from the hip and Lord Matsudaira nodded briefly towards her. Turning as she straightened, in a few steps she was gone as quickly as she had appeared.

Schnell stood transfixed for a moment, looking out towards the stairway after she had left. He was thinking of times past, realizing the deep anger that Torima still felt for him. It was the kind of anger that time would not diminish. The retribution, he knew, was only just beginning. Matsudaira saw Schnell's distracted look.

"You must prepare your party to leave, Hiramatsu. Yae is among our bravest samurai, but I'm afraid the hour will end very quickly. Torima will not be kind if he finds you here. The ship is being loaded as we speak, with departure set very soon after all of your group arrives."

Schnell came out of his daze and realized what Matsudaira had said.

"My Lord, are you not coming with us? The whole point is to restart in California what has ended here. You are the whole reason for my planning!"

"Hiramatsu, be assured that I will come on the next ship. I expect you to have the colony organized and properly functioning when I arrive. Perhaps you will have some home-grown sake for me as well, and California rice, ne? I have complete faith that you will be able to do all this."

There was only a hint of a smile on the Lord's face as Schnell bowed down before him.

"Hai, my Lord. The Wakamatsu Colony will be fully operational, and will reflect the spirit and resolve of the Aizu people. You will have your sake when you arrive."

Schnell resisted the urge to smile or shake Matsudaira's hand because years of living in Japan had cured his European ways. He watched Lord Matsudaira return to the platform, where he stood and looked into the faces of everyone who was there.

"I want all of my brave friends to come closer for this prayer that I wish to offer before your long journey."

Jou and Okei with the infant stood next to Schnell. Matsu and Nishijawa and Kuni-san were to their left, and a man they would later know as Dr. Matsumoto was to the right.

Okei hadn't realized how few the number of people were. She herself was not to be going, so that made the number even smaller. Matsudaira seemed to read her mind.

"Several more farm families and craftsmen will meet at the ship. In all, there will be more than twenty in number going to America."

The daimyo looked at the people beside him and composed himself. He closed his eyes. Everyone bowed their heads down as far as they could in their seated positions.

"For the many who remain in the homeland, now patrolled by the Satsuma, I pray to the great Amaterasu, goddess of the sun, and creator of this world. Bestow on those who stay here the courage and will to persevere regardless of the torture and deprivations that they must face. I pray to Susanoo, ruler of wind and storms, to be gentle to the brave pioneers before me, for they will face great challenges in this new land and should be spared troubles in their journey there. I pray to Kompira as well, to be benevolent and show them the correct path across the ocean. I do not know the kami present in this new world, though many must exist as they exist here in Japan. To those kami, I pledge that these subjects who seek life in your world come with pure and sincere hearts. These are worthy people who are honor bound to continue the true ways. They will live in harmony with all the spirits that they will meet, will not change the will of nature, and will daily worship the ancestral spirits. They seek no special treatment, other than to be given the opportunity to share life in your world. For this they have given their lifetime devotion to you."

Lord Matsudaira nodded slightly to a man who had been kneeling just below him. The man rose to his feet. He wore a monk's dark robe and collar and bowed low as he faced the daimyo. Turning to the small gathering, he placed his hands together and led them in the Buddhist gassho:

"Namu Amida Butsu,

Namu Amida Butsu,

Namu Amida Butsu."

I saw the Lord leave even before everyone had said the final of the three recitations. The others could only look in wonder towards the empty stool as they raised their heads, still holding their hands together.

The Lord's quick exit also impressed on everyone that time was short and there was much preparation to be done. Schnell went to face them as everyone began to gather their possessions.

"We will go as quickly as possible to the Yokohama wharf where my brother has stored supplies in his warehouse. A steamship for America will arrive early Friday, only three days from today. Imperial troops will be patrolling along our route and at the harbor so try to travel alone to avoid raising suspicion."

Okei watched from the back after placing Frances in Jou's

arms. There was so much commotion that she didn't know what to do. All these people would be going directly to the ship from here. They would not have the opportunity to talk to their family or friends. For them, it would be like vanishing from the face of the earth. In many ways, that was probably true. For all anyone knew of California, it might as well be on the far side of the moon. She was filled with trepidation for those who were going. Matsu had been a family friend since her elementary school days in Hinomata. She had known Kuni for years. She had known Jou even before the birth of little Frances, when the great Lord had appointed her to be the baby's caretaker. They would all be going away forever. Life had suddenly become upside down and impossible.

Through her confusion, Okei realized that her principle duty was still to her family. She picked up her bag and took a step toward the stairs when she suddenly remembered me.

I thought that you had forgotten.

I did not, my little Keiko.

Turning around, she spotted Jou with Frances standing beside Schnell. She was surprised to see Lord Matsudaira with them. He was holding a silk flag in his hands, so large that most of it was on the floor over his tabi. Schnell had grabbed one end, and had withdrawn back slightly to unfold the fabric to view.

Of course, it was the first time that I had seen the banner. It was made of fine gray-white habutai silk, with a gold circle design covering most of the center and inner circles within that circle. Gold tassels hung limply from the bottom and sides. There were designs at each corner that I couldn't comprehend with the limited knowledge I had at that time. After all, I was but six hours old. I was learning as fast as I could, but the world kept rushing at me at impossible speed. My poor little mind could only absorb so much at a time. I could hear Lord Matsudaira speaking to Schnell.

"You will raise our Aizu flag on the new land."

"I am honored, my Lord. I will proudly display it after I have made the land purchase, and it will be the first thing you will see above the farm when you arrive."

Suddenly the sound of gunfire came from around them. It was muffled and probably came from outside the castle walls.

Everyone stood for a moment, and then there was great movement as people picked up items that they would need for the departure. There was another gun sound, and a rush to the stairway began.

Okei waited while watching everyone leave. It was a strange feeling that she did not need to be in such great hurry as they were. There was a troubling sense of not belonging. Walking slowly, she began to realize that she had no plans for the remainder of the day once she found her mother. The Schnells and little Frances would be gone, so her afternoons of baby-sitting had come to an end. She thought of me in her backpack just as there was a rustle behind her, followed closely by a familiar voice.

"I regret that I had not talked to you earlier."

Okei was surprised to see Lord Matsudaira standing behind her.

"My Lord? You are still here?"

"I must urgently speak to you. I was able to meet your mother and convey to her the necessity of your presence in the colony. She understood perfectly. I am to tell you that your family will miss you greatly, but they are proud of the great service that you are doing for Aizu, your Lord, and all of Japan."

Okei stopped still on the first step of the stairs and suddenly her vision of the Lord seemed to dim. I was first fearful that she would fall and damage both of us. But also I could feel the great changes suddenly happening. My maker's future, and mine, had been forever altered by those words.

Lord Matsudaira saw Okei tottering on the step and reached out to hold her shoulders.

"I greatly regret that you will not be able to see your parents before you leave. Torima's troops are almost at the gate and you must go quickly by the underground passage."

Okei tried to talk but her voice came out strangely as though speaking from the depths of the tunnel that her life's path had just been thrust into.

"My mother? Where? I will be going?"

"Hiramatsu asked for you. Jou may be expecting another child in the new world. She would be overwhelmed without your help. If Hiramatsu must worry about this in addition to the welfare of the colony, then all their efforts could fail."

Okei tried to get her mind to work. It was hard to connect thoughts and make them into words.

"But, my Lord! You will soon be there to lead them. Another sitter can go to help Jou-san, someone wiser and older and more useful than I could ever be."

Matsudaira kept the faint smile that seemed so small on his very thin lips.

"I will not be going. I have prepared myself to surrender to Torima when he enters the castle gate. I fully expect to be taken away under armed escort."

Okei put her hands to her face.

"You must go to California, Okei-san. Hiramatsu's courage and bravery are well known, but this will be the most difficult challenge he has ever known. Perhaps there are others who could take care of their infant, yes, I know this. But Hiramatsu asked for you. I ask for you. For the Aizu Colony to succeed, your presence is needed. They will need the special abilities that you possess."

Okei desperately tried to plead to her daimyo.

"Your faith in me is undeserved, my Lord. I am just a simple girl whose only desire is to live a simple life here with my family. I have never traveled away from my home—would be of little use in such a far away and strange place."

Matsudaira continued gazing directly into her until she had to avert her eyes.

"Okei-san, I have known your family for many years. I have known of your different nature since you were a small child. I have watched you grow and witnessed your abilities grow. The simple life that you desire was never meant to be your destiny."

Okei finally was able to look him in the face. Her eyes were glistening with tears.

"My mother. . . my brothers. . . it's just. . . when I saw them last, I didn't know. I was never able to tell them goodbye."

Left unsaid: I will never see them again.

Her pleading eyes could not find Matsudaira's, which were cast downward as he stood with his head bowed. I could not read what emotions, if any, he was feeling.

At that moment, Okei took a deep breath and seemed to compose herself. Her eyes seemed to dry instantly on their own. It seemed that in this short time, she had willed herself to discard her previous life like an old familiar coat, no longer useful in her future world.

"Hai, my Lord. I will honor you as I honor my family and my Aizu homeland. I will do everything I can to insure the success of the colony in the new land."

In the shoulder pack, I could feel the tenseness leave my inanimate body. I wanted to let Okei-san know that she would never find herself alone. Our long journey together was just beginning.

CHAPTER 3
Torima's Wrath

Kotoshi Torima had lived an eventful life during his forty-two years. Born the son of a barrel maker in Okayama domain, he considered the proudest achievement of his youth to be the fact that he had never stepped foot into his father's shop nor had he ever helped construct a single barrel. Such menial work would have been a waste of the time and energy needed to rid himself of the burdensome confinement of his tradesmen class status. He never understood why fate had started him off on such a lowly rung. It only added more years of difficulty in his efforts to achieve the level of greatness that he knew was his destiny.

The major break in his life came when he began to do work at his neighbor's home. His father, dismayed by his son's lack of appreciation for his craft, had allowed him to repair storm-damaged fences and screens for their neighbor. It was fortuitous that his neighbor was also preparing to leave shortly for America and Europe. Torima had immediately sensed the change in his fortune. Despite the Shogun's ban on such travel, the neighbor would be joining thirteen other young men who would be smuggled out from the southern coastal city of Kagoshima in the Satsuma domain. That entire area of Japan had always acted independently from the Shogun's edicts. Arrangements had been made with an Englishman of some sort of religious principle to sponsor the men for schooling in England and America.

Torima jumped at what he knew was the opportunity of a

lifetime. One night, he left a note for his parents on his futon and departed his homeland on a steamship. From 1862 to 1866, he traveled with the students to London, then Boston and New York, and San Francisco. He became proficient in English and had diligently learned the Western cultures and manners.

He returned to Japan with all the tools that he needed to leave his father's cramped house and move to the capital city of Edo. There, he monitored the new political situation that had developed since the visit of Commodore Perry's Black Ships. The Shogun was seen by the Japanese people as having capitulated to the Americans and Europeans. A rallying cry of "Sonno joi" had instantly erupted across the populace; Restore the Emperor, rid the country of the foreign barbarians. By 1866 the heavily armed forces of Satsuma and Choshu began marching northward to ultimately surround Edo and take control from the Shogun.

Torima then made his strategic move from Edo to Kyoto to be near the Emperor's Imperial Palace. Confident that the Shogun's days were numbered, he immediately found work in the Emperor's court translating documents brought in from various vessels that had come into the harbor. Soon he was acting as interpreter for foreigners, gaijin, who wished for a meeting with the Emperor.

In a very short time he had become indispensable to the young Emperor Meiji, who in all appearances looked and acted like a late blooming teenager. As Satsuma and Choshu officials and generals gained more control of the court, Torima found himself working closely with them as well. Then American and European businessmen and politicians began arriving in large numbers every day. They wanted trade. They had money. All of them had to go through Torima to see the Emperor.

When the Shogun finally capitulated, Torima envisioned an era of modernization where Japan would need Western technologies and materials to catch up from the dark days of Shogun isolation.

But the Ezo and Aizu actions by die-hard Shogun supporters had considerably delayed that. A man audaciously calling himself the Last Samurai, Shigeo Takemoto, had rallied his supporters against the newly formed Imperial government. They believed that Torima and his people in the Emperor's court were giving away the country to gaijin foreigners. Takemoto warned that the old ways were being destroyed so that Western ways could take root.

Torima looked at the sleeves of his New York bought dark brown business suit as he waited in the carriage at the head of his troops. It was impeccable, and as handsome as any worn by the gaijin businessmen who sought him out. He felt like royalty. He should be royalty.

Unbelievably, another obstacle to his rightful destiny had soon appeared. John Henry Schnell had come to Japan as a teenager and had found his wealth by selling surplus armament from the American Civil War. Soon he had become a trusted confidant of the enemy daimyo, Matsudaira, the leader of the Aizu house and the last remaining supporter of the old Shogun rule. Matsudaira then had the insolence to send Schnell to help the Ezo rebels fighting the Imperial forces to the north. Incredibly, Schnell was able to integrate himself so well within the Takemoto camp that he had become one of Takemoto's most trusted officers. They would go on to fight side by side in several battles that would delay Torima's vision of a modern Western-style Japan and his own personal enrichment for many costly months.

Finally, the Imperial army was able to surround and cut down the remaining Ezo rebels with Western style firepower. Takemoto was killed. Schnell, though grievously injured, was able to recover. Despite Torima's best efforts to imprison the gaijin samurai, the Emperor would not allow it. Schnell then performed his most dastardly act by convincing the impressionable Emperor to dismiss the Overseas Treaty that Torima had spent months crafting with his American and European business friends. The devious Schnell had even presented the Emperor with the sword that Takemoto had carried in battle, knowing the young Meiji's fascination with the story of the Last Samurai.

Torima had tried to deflect the Emperor's attention. It was just a sword. Takemoto had been an outlaw and enemy of the Empire.

But the German had been more convincing. The Emperor's longing for the disappearing old ways outweighed Torima's insistence that Japan had to face the modern world with modern technologies.

"I cannot sign your treaty. I do not believe that you have the best interest of my country in your heart."

The embarrassment of those words from the Emperor had not been Schnell's last despicable act. He had the Emperor cut off Torima's stipend and eliminate the office that he had used to gain political power. Torima was forced to move back into his parent's home in Okayama. Still not finished with making his life nearly impossible, Schnell had returned to Aizu to fight again for Matsudaira.

The column of soldiers stopped within sight of the Aizu castle. Torima stepped out of his carriage to take in the scene.

Yes, it had indeed been a long road back to where he was now, mere yards from eliminating the last obstacle to his vision of a modern, industrialized Japan. At last he was able to put together the words in his mind that had been buried in his heart for so long:

I have come for you, Schnell-san. I have come to tell you that I have recovered, and now have more power and wealth than you can ever imagine within your limited mind. You were not able to keep me down, and now I am here to crush you.

As he gazed at the towering structure, a rifle shot rang out. The officer standing mere feet from Torima crumpled to the ground and then lay motionless in a bloody pool. Quickly the soldiers took shelter behind stone buttresses that lined the entrance to the castle. Torima hid under the carriage. The soldiers fired back a dozen or so shots until Torima waved for them to stop. The rifleman was obviously well hidden and would need to be tricked into exposing himself.

"The war has ended," Torima yelled out. "Your Lord is dead. Surrender and we prevent needless killing."

"You lie! Lord Matsudaira is well," came a distant reply, a female voice.

The Imperial soldiers began firing again toward the sound of the voice. It was several minutes before the captain of the forces raised his hand. It took more minutes for the rifle smoke to clear enough to again see the castle.

"We got her!" The captain rose carefully from behind a stone fortification. "What lowly people the Aizu must be to send a girl soldier. She did not last long against us."

The captain turned to smile back at Torima when suddenly a bright red spot appeared on his forehead, just above the line between his two eyes. The sound of a single gunshot followed an instant later. The captain, too, crumpled to the ground.

This was just too much for Torima. The best solution would be a massed assault. The woman sniper would not have enough time to reload her weapon. He yelled for the soldiers to charge ahead. At first they just looked at him, unsure of what to do. Torima yelled again, more emphatically. Finally he waved his hands frantically. The soldiers charged.

A number of shots rang out in rapid succession and quickly

two soldiers fell. More rapid shots and another two fell before they reached the bridge where another went down just before the castle gate. Torima gasped at the carnage that he had witnessed. He hadn't anticipated that Yae was armed with one of the new Spencer repeating rifles supplied by Schnell.

The second in command soon signaled that the shooter was gone and Torima finally began to walk towards the castle. The gates were already open, having been blasted by artillery on the previous day. Some Satsuma samurai, sent earlier to clear the castle's interior, came out to see what all the commotion had been about.

It was then that several people on foot and a palanquin appeared from around a bend in the interior of the castle. The soldiers pointed their rifles but did not stop the progress of the group. In the open palanquin was an ornately dressed figure in a brightly colored robe. The four laborers who carried the palanquin stopped when they reached Torima, lowering the carrier to the street. Still seated, Lord Matsudaira turned his head slightly to look at Torima.

"Torima-san, I am surrendering Tsuruga Castle to you. I am going to Kyoto Palace to relinquish myself to the mercy of the Emperor."

Torima, ears ringing and still rattled by the battle that had just occurred, was finding it difficult to believe that Lord Matsudaira, supreme daimyo of Aizu Han, the final obstacle to the ending of the Boshin War, was there before him.

Seeing Torima's confusion, Matsudaira signaled for the laborers to pick up the royal palanquin.

"Wait!" Torima almost tripped approaching the daimyo. "I order you to stop. You must surrender to me!"

Matsudaira looked disdainfully at Torima but Torima was unable to read his face.

"I, a descendant of Minamoto, will surrender only to the Emperor, direct descendant of Amaterasu, the Sun God. I am going to Kyoto."

Torima raised his arm but could do no more than point weakly towards Matsudaira. The entourage continued forward. The soldiers moved aside to clear a path in front of them.

"Where is the German Schnell? I must know where Schnell is!" Torima managed to yell out.

Matsudaira signaled to halt the carrier. Again he turned his head very slightly.

"What is the time, Torima-san?" he asked

Torima looked at his Western watch but was so flustered he could barely read the numbers.

"It is…four o'clock."

He saw a faint smile appear on Matsudaira's lips.

"Then he has gone, Torima-san. His ship will be but a speck on the ocean by now."

Lord Matsudaira signaled to continue his journey to Kyoto and pulled the curtains of the palanquin closed. Satisfied that Torima had believed his lie, he sat back in his seat. He wanted to keep that vision of Torima's troubled face lasting as long as possible in his mind to give him comfort on his longest journey.

The second officer came to Torima asking for orders of what to do next. By this time, the palanquin and the attendants were already well past the soldiers and had reached the main road to Kyoto. Torima pushed past the officer and stared at the castle.

"I want every centimeter of the castle searched for Schnell. I must know if he is in there!"

The officers and soldiers rushed into the castle grounds.

"Then burn the castle down! I want the town burned!"

Soon Torima stood alone on the bridge to the castle. Smoke was beginning to pour from the buildings nearby as soldiers ran from house to house with torches. He could hear screaming and the sound of running on the cobblestone streets.

He began to see fire in the upper parts of the wooden castle. It brought him little joy because he knew that Schnell would not be found inside. Finally starting to think logically at the end of a very trying day, he thought about the world outside of Japan and what influence he might be able to have upon it. He thought about the size of the ocean, trying to recall those times of travel in his youth. He thought about the effort that it had taken to cross it. Torima allowed himself to smile for the first time on this day.

Okei was thankful that Sakurai-san had shown her the location of the secret passage that led beyond the castle walls. Not having to concern herself with the way of escape, she began to go up the stairs to look for her mother and sister. It was a foolish thing to do, but her 17-year-old mind found it difficult to think of anything else other than to hug them for the last time. If her past life must be sliced off so sharply like this, she must have a fitting farewell that would leave her lasting memories of the people she had loved and had loved her.

Searching for the room where she had been was difficult because of great changes that had happened just in the time that she had been at the meeting in the secret chamber. Now the Satsuma samurai were everywhere, along with Imperial troops dressed in dark blue Western-style uniforms. All the local citizens who had sheltered in the castle were gone. She was the one who felt like she didn't belong. The soldiers looked at her as she passed them, but no one tried to stop her.

Finally arriving at the room, she peered in, trying to expose herself as little as possible. The headless Satsuma samurai was now lying on the table where Okei had worked on the doll just a few hours ago. A blue uniformed soldier was examining the body. No one else was in the room.

The soldier spotted her. He began to point his rifle but lowered it when he saw that it was just a frightened girl.

"Go away! Go back home!" he shouted. How could he know that this wisp of a girl was the one who had caused the death of this mighty warrior?

Just at that instant she spotted a familiar object in the corner just to the right of where the soldier stood. It was a cloth package tied with a familiar double knot. Her mother's knot! Despite her fears, she pointed at the package and the soldier looked down to his side. He looked back at her and gave a brief nod of his head. Staying low, Okei entered the room and retrieved the package under the soldier's watchful glare. Safely at the door, she bowed deeply to him in appreciation and scurried away. She clutched the package tightly to her body as she fled down the hall. She could feel some of the loose items bound inside. There was clothing. One or two kimono. When she felt the familiar shape of her hand mirror, tears began to flow from her eyes.

She could remember little of her exit from the castle. Even though she knew of the route, she had never taken it before and was sure to encounter problems that would make the journey more difficult. But it had been uneventful. The escape door was where it should have been in the far lower room. The path, though dark, was free of mud and moisture and she did not even stain her kimono. Once outside in the light, there were no Satsuma soldiers waiting to arrest her as she had feared.

She stopped as if trying to wait out the moments that had been gained by the unexpectedly swift exit from the castle. A voice so near to her that she could easily have mistaken it as her own called out to her. It came from the pack on her back. My voice in her thoughts.

The road to the left. Quickly! Someone might be following in the tunnel.

Okei looked just behind her at the hillside and panicked when she saw the little trap door was still open. She turned around so quickly that she made herself instantly dizzy. No one was nearby. She closed the door and hurried down the street to the left.

The road curved downward, half circling the castle, which soon was just above a street she was crossing. It was the main road up to the castle gate. On the bridge to the gate were columns of soldiers holding rifles. They were tucked tightly among large stone blocks that lined both sides of the road. There were several horse-drawn carriages just behind the soldiers and very near to her. Then something that had the sound of a very angry bee rushed by the bottom of her ear. An instant later came the loud sound of gunfire.

Okei fell down so fast that it looked as though she had been hit. It was then that she saw the man staring at her from his hiding place beneath the carriage that was nearest to her. He was somewhat rotund and dressed in Western-style business clothing. He had a mustache over his roundly shaped lips with a short beard over his ample chin. The beard reminded her of the style that Schnell-san had on his face. It did not seem to look as good on this Japanese man, however.

Although Okei lay unmoving on the open road, the man made no effort to help her. It was hard for her to sense what he was thinking. His eyes showed fear as he tightly clutched the wheel of the wagon. His mouth, however, was tightly clinched, the jaw muscles taut, showing the signs of both frustration and determination. There seemed to be a purpose that he had to complete that he was having extreme difficulty accomplishing. She saw him lean out slightly into the road.

"The war has ended," he yelled out. "Your Lord is dead. Surrender and we prevent needless killing."

"You lie! Matsudaira is well!" came a familiar female voice near the castle. It was that of the woman warrior who had come into the hidden chamber. "You will have your hour," she had assured Lord Matsudaira. There was more rifle fire.

Realizing that the danger to her was not as imminent as she had thought, Okei raised herself to her feet and gazed down at the man who was again cowering under the wagon. For an instant she had a vision of the same face in a different place, a palace, seething and helpless as he was now. Schnell-san was there, and the Emperor. She suddenly knew who this man was.

Okei reached back into her obi but suddenly noticed a column of soldiers coming up fast behind her. Her hand reluctantly let go of the hilt of the hidden sword. The soldiers would certainly have detained her. Getting to the ship was her most important duty and must override every other interruption. Once more she locked eyes with this man, who now seemed to be looking at her with increased curiosity. Okei turned and slowly began to walk away. She did not hasten her steps until the troops were no longer visible.

With every step forward she began to have a sense of foreboding for what she had just left undone. There was a hollow feeling inside her soul. The man's face had been a vision from the future as well as the past, she now realized. Most worrisome to her was the extreme level of dejection, insult, and hatred that seemed to dwell within him, barely capped and explosive. This she had felt just as he had started to realize her connection to Lord Matsudaira and to Schnell-san. In another moment he would have ordered the soldier's rifles to fire on her.

She talked to herself as much as to me within her sack.

"Eee. I am afraid we will have more to worry about in this new world than growing tea or the strange customs of its people."

Looking back once more, her expectation was to see soldiers running after her, the man from the bottom of the carriage following close behind, short legs pumping, yelling madly and waving his hands with frenzied emotion.

But no one was following.

CHAPTER 4
Journey To The New Land

I have never known a vastness like that of the ocean. Three days and two nights had passed since the long low silhouette of Japan had disappeared in the merger line between the sky and sea beyond our steamship's wake. The people on board no longer gazed behind hoping for a sight of where their old home had been. Instead, they congregated by the front railings, looking ahead where the vision of our new home would some day appear.

The mighty black stack above us billowed black smoke and the giant wheels on each side of the ship churned constantly to bring us closer to our destination. The power and noise of the steamship was a comfort when the unchanging nature of the ocean made it easy to believe that movement forward was nothing more than a hope-filled illusion.

I was held by Frances who stood beside her parents with Okei standing next to them against the front railing of the bridge. I supposed that Okei was no longer my master since I had been given to Frances as a gift. Many times now Okei stayed in a different room. I did not see her as often as I would have wanted. However, I never felt my ties to Okei-san diminished because of this change. I still felt what she felt every moment. I still knew her every thought. I had a more difficult time understanding Frances-chan. She only seemed to be thinking of things that her ever-searching eyes and ears presently sensed. Nothing about yesterday or tomorrow existed in her mind. Her thoughts were not very deep or lasting, as was to be expected for a child of just two.

I gazed out at the distant ocean horizon. That there was still no land in sight was both disturbing and unsettling. How far away could our new home be? Everything that I had known before I could imagine myself touching, had I arms that moved and were long enough. Walls had always been around me. I had seen the sky but still couldn't comprehend that it was anything more than an overhead cover just beyond my reach. I did not have any appreciation of the true vastness of the universe.

"I do not see anything out there," Jou-san spoke.

"We are only three days out," Schnell replied. "It will be nineteen more days before we will see the coast of California."

I tired hard to comprehend the length of time of nineteen days. I could not. My mind seemed to be like Frances's in this regard.

"What are the people like?"

"I don't know. Hard working, I suppose, like the people of Japan. They don't have the traditions that we do. They don't think as much about their ancestors. Where they came from is not as important to them as where they want to go."

"This is sad, ne? Ancestors ground you to the world and give purpose to life. How can they know where to go when they cannot remember where they have been?"

Schnell smiled and briefly hugged his wife. He quickly realized how awkward and unnatural it felt and let her go. Jou sensed it too. The old culture still reached across hundreds of miles of ocean to let them know that they were not yet in the new world. Adjustment was going to be slow and difficult, even for Schnell who had spent his youth in Prussia and had once traveled in California.

California had then just been a stop on the journey to his real destination, Japan. Twenty years ago when he had started out, very little was known about that island nation. The first Tokugawa Shogun, Ieyasu, had expelled most foreigners in 1603 and banned all travel to and from Japan. For more than 250 years, the outside world knew little more about Japan than the outline of its coast seen from passing ships. Reports by a few priests and Dutch sailors only added to the mystique surrounding the country like a blanketing cloak.

To John Henry Schnell, the temptation of adventure had just been too great. It was said that dragons existed there. Hot springs in the mountains added years of life after each visit. Beautiful dark haired and pale skinned women were masters of the ancient oriental art of pleasing a man's senses and satisfying his desires. There were ornately dressed warlords with armies of soldiers versed in the martial arts and carrying razor sharp tempered steel swords with a length longer than their bodies. They were called samurai. They lived and died by a strict code of honor, Bushido, the way of the warrior.

Once in Japan, he had to endure the persecution faced by all outsiders. It only hardened his resolve and he worked diligently to learn about the culture and language. As those around him slowly accepted him, his fascination with the world of the samurai had grown. What was it like to be duty and honor bound? He wondered if he could ever give his life for a feudal lord, or commit ritual suicide for an act of dishonor or failure of duty.

Now twenty years later, he was leaving Japan. Whether he ever returned would depend on his karma, the Japanese expression for undeniable fate. He accepted the probability that he would never see Japan again, and that ultimately the memories that he carried would become harder to recollect, someday becoming just faded dreams of no certain reality.

Testing his mind, he thought about his last meeting with Lord Matsudaira. It had occurred just after the final meeting in the castle, when everyone else had left. Only two people have this memory, he realized, making him think harder of the words that had been said.

'Schnell-san, a divide has come on the road that we have traveled side by side for so long.'

'Hai, my Lord.'

'The plan we discussed is that I will join you in the new land, but unforeseen events could prevent our paths from ever crossing again.'

Schnell had listened in silence.

'Therefore, I must convey to you my appreciation and the appreciation of all my people for your service to Aizu, to Japan, and to your Lord.'

'I am honored, my Lord.'

'It is sad to think that the ways we have known for so long could not endure forever. Perhaps if the Black Ships had never come, the Satsuma would not have had the conviction needed to defeat the Shogun. I have prayed for that day to be erased, so that our world could continue in harmony as it had for more than 250 years. Eee, but that water had already been spilled into the sea. The old world is forever gone.'

'My Lord, we will just make a new world in America.'

'Hai, I am confident that you will. You have never failed me.'

'Arigato, my Lord.'

Schnell looked into Matsudaira's eyes. His Lord seemed always to be in deep thought as retainers and subordinates would come to him continuously to obtain his edicts on every aspect of life in the domain. He had become increasingly introspective as the world of the Shogun disintegrated around him. It had to be bitter and heartbreaking to have seen so much disrespect for the 250 years of peace and cultural development that had come to Japan during the Edo era of the Tokugawa Shoguns. Yet this man seemed to harbor no ill desires for those who railed against him shouting their "sonno joi" battle cry. Perhaps it was his Zen Buddhist discipline that allowed him to accept inevitable fate. When he finally spoke, Schnell wondered if these were the last words he would ever hear from him.

'When I sent you to Ezo, I had not expected you to fight alongside Takemoto-san. I had made you a samurai to honor you for obtaining weapons from the American war. You were not a true warrior, Schnell-san, and I was fearful that Takemoto would think that I was showing him disrespect.'

'When I heard what you had done and the honor that you had bestowed to Takemoto before the Emperor, I could only think that this had to be the work of someone else. Then when you returned, I knew. You had learned the way of the warrior. You had truly become a samurai.'

Jou saw Schnell wipe a tear from his eye.

"Are you troubled, my husband?" she asked.

"No, not troubled. I was just thinking how each of us carry our unique memories for all our lives. The memories are part of us, and can't be conveyed or explained adequately to anyone who might ask."

"Even if I should ask, my loving husband?"

"Yes, even you, my loving wife."

"Then I promise to never ask."

✣

I recall that the storm came on the fifth day after our departure.

It met us in the middle of the ocean, a most unwelcome visitor that added hardship at a time when many on board were finally realizing the great magnitude of the journey that had been undertaken. It reinforced the growing fear that the new world was beyond reach and the dreams of a new life were prematurely conceived.

It began when the midday calm turned to whitecaps and increasing clouds by evening. The tranquil rocking of the previous days changed to a continuous pitch and roll of the deck that only continued to get worse. There was no sunset to gaze at and then an unsettling cover of blackness had brought the daylight to an abrupt end. The captain sent his crew out to warn everyone to stay in their cabins during the night and for the duration of the storm.

Some anxiously asked how long the storm would last.

It will clear by morning, the captain had confidently assured them. Once by the helm, he somberly gazed into the gloom of darkness and could not see the end of it for at least three days.

I lay on my back next to Frances as I had done the previous nights. She had been crying for several hours. I could not blame her, and would have cried myself had I tears to shed. Sometimes it was difficult to determine what was up and what was down. The walls moved from one side to the other. The ceiling and the floor seemed to converge and then widen apart at irregular intervals. First one wall then the other became the bottom floor of the ship, and it seemed only a matter of time before the ceiling would also become the floor.

Eee, was the sea above our heads? How would we know which way to go if water began to seep into the cabins? The constant noise of creaking wood beams and items sliding or flying in all directions was unbearable by itself. Worst of all were the sounds from outside our enclosure, the howling of the wind and the crashing of the sea trying to penetrate the wooden beams and sideboards of the hull.

What if the ocean began to come inside? Would I be able to float above the water? Would I sink to the bottom of the ocean, as far below the waves as the distance to our new world? Would I be lost forever? Would I die? What is death?

No one slept that night, but I was the only one to notice the small figure trying bravely to stand in the middle of the sleeping cabin. By the dim light, I saw it being tossed one way then the other down the slope of the pitching floor, somehow able to keep upright amid the upheaval. I knew it was Okei-san. She was beside the crib where little Frances lay crying her eyes out. She reached into the crib and I clearly heard my maker's thoughts.

Do not be afraid, little Frances-chan. Susanoo has become angry and has caused this terrible storm. It does not know who we are or why we have come. I will explain that we are refugees seeking safe passage for a better life. Then I will seek Kompira's guidance to watch over us for the remainder of our journey. The storm will be gone soon and there will be no other. I promise you this, little Frances-chan.

I watched Okei struggle to get upright, then for a moment lose her balance as the tilting floor continue to toss her about. With supreme effort, she began to make slow headway towards the door at the end of the cabin. Twice she nearly reached it before a rising swell on the bow sent her careening almost back to where she had begun. At last clutching the doorknob, she held on to withstand another forward swell. Before the next wave could come, she opened the door and was gone. Only a brief ray of yellow lamplight came in before the door was closed behind her.

I could have witnessed what she had done on the ship's deck, but I did not. It would have been an unbearable torment to see her out amid the wind and waves and not being able to do anything to help her. What if she had been washed over the side into the sea, and I had watched her hands and then her fingers disappearing into the depths? The scars from that vision would have haunted me like a restless trapped ghost for the rest of my existence. I worried and I waited. That was all I could do.

The sea began to calm just before morning. A faint glow began in the direction we were headed. I witnessed this as the door at the front of the cabin again opened and a lone figure entered.

I knew it was Okei although she looked like a skeleton. Her sleeping clothes clung to her like pale wrinkled skin and her hair hung straight and lifeless. Water dripped from every part of her body. Her eyes were nearly shut by the sting of the salt spray, and I do not know how she ever found her sleeping mat. Without toweling or removing her drenched clothing, she simply fell where she stood into profound sleep.

The rising sun seemed to push the remaining clouds from the sky. Although it was time for breakfast, the early breakfast was missed that morning. Even the two cooks who would have been deep inside the ship in the kitchen were on the forward deck below the captain's wheelhouse. The captain himself stood outside by the railing, along with most of the passengers on the ship. The black stack sent black smoke high into the air and the two paddle wheels tossed sprays of water out to the sides as they churned the water. Our journey to the new land continued uninterrupted.

A man dressed in the black robe of a priest walked out partly onto the bow, and soon many of the Japanese on the ship had knelt down in prayer. Many of the Chinese on board soon followed, leaving the others to simply bow their heads.

I was held tightly in Frances's arms. Had I lungs to breathe, I would have been in a panic, but I found her dependence on me comforting. I knew without looking at the faces that Okei had not come out of the sleeping cabin. I was not overly concerned about her for I knew that she needed the rest after such a night. That no one but a doll had been a witness would not have bothered my maker at all. She would not mind that no one thought of her in their prayers of appreciation for the ending of the storm. In the ways that she thought, it was enough to know that the kami had heard her and the people were spared. She could feel no particular joy for her success, for it was tempered by the knowledge of the horrible consequences if she had failed. She had been given no choice. She had merely done what had been her duty.

There were no more similar happenings for the duration of the journey. The second week went by, then the third. Clouds filled the sky on several of those days, but they seemed to be quickly frightened away and not even a drop of rain fell upon the ship. Otherwise, the ocean did nothing to impede our progress, allowing the pointed bow to slice its path towards an ever-closer destination. At the beginning of the third week, a tailwind developed that allowed the Captain to order sails set on two of the three masts for the first time. The three days calculated for reaching America was reduced to two, leaving the Captain scrambling to make plans for the traditional ship's dinner. That morning, members of the crew were sent around to inform everyone that the dinner was moved up an entire day and now would be occurring that very evening.

Jou went into a panic when she heard the news. She had planned to try on different kimonos tonight and allow herself time in the morning to make the final decision. Now with the dinner mere hours away, she found herself limited in her selections.

"I do not have time to experiment with different obi to find the best combination."

Okei was on her knees, rummaging through the large lacquered trunk that sat on the floor. The Schnell family's assistant normally did the task that she found herself in, but that person had been left behind so that Okei could come. Jou had protested but could not go against the decision of her Lord. That Okei was trained only as Frances's nursemaid added to Jou's aggravation. She did not have the time for on-the-job training of someone who knew so little about the ways that people of culture lived.

Okei did her best to help Jou-san, and was relieved when they had found a combination that seemed to please her.

"You are beautiful, Jou-san. The lavender and white is an excellent choice to bring out the whiteness and purity of your skin. No man at the party will be able to keep their eyes from you."

Jou gazed at herself in the mirror on the wall.

"Yes, this is indeed nice. Do you think the Americans will notice? I have always wondered if they appreciate beauty in the same way as the men in Japan. I have heard that they have no culture and care only about themselves."

Matsu was already facing difficulty in converting to the ways of the new land. When the notice of the dinner went out, he gazed intently at "7 PM," trying to find a way to convert to the system that he knew. Then came the most terrible problem of trying to decide what to wear. Schnell-san had distributed strange "dungaree" pants to the men and white flocks for the women. The pants were far different than the traditional hakama that almost every Japanese male wore. The hakama was loose and comfortable and almost skirt like. These dungarees were stiff beyond description, the coarse heavy cotton feeling like unsanded lumber against his legs. His entire lower body felt constricted and suffocated. Still, Schnell-san had desired that the men wear these barbaric creations. Matsu was not going to disobey just because he felt uncomfortable. After all, he was samurai, and knew well that suffering was only a state of mind. This would be just one more instance of suffering that he would have to endure for the sake of the colony.

When he left the room, the diminished light on the ocean told him the sun would soon be setting. He struggled to move his legs in the stiff dungarees. At least his upper body felt better in the light haori jacket that had been brought from Japan. The wool plaid shirt distributed by Schnell still lay folded on his bed. It was a time of transition, he explained to himself as he walked alongside the ship's railing. By tomorrow afternoon when they reached California, he will have made the complete transformation as Schnell required.

The door to the dining saloon was open and Matsu turned in towards the staircase that led up to the Grand Saloon on the above spar deck. The gong for the first class dinner service had not rung yet and only a few blue tunic clad Chinese servants were in the immense room. There were two rows of tables that reached to the back of the room and enough chairs for almost 200 people. Even the largest castles in Japan did not have such an elaborate dining area. At any rate, communal dining was not a Japanese tradition, and most shared their meals only with their families or closest friends.

His hand came to the large polished wooden dome topping the lowest banister of the stairwell, and then felt the smooth curved railing leading up to the Grand Saloon. He looked up the grand staircase, stopped momentarily by the thought of how each step he took, like the miles of ocean passing beneath the ship, was taking him further away from everything he had ever known, towards a future world of which he had no comprehension. Matsu began climbing.

A strange sound came to him from the aft end of the room as he reached the top step. There was a man dressed in a bizarre red and white square-pattern coat pounding his hands on a large rectangular box that stood on the floor. The sound, somewhat like bells, was coming out of the box.

It took Matsu a moment before he noticed the many people around him. Over the sound made by the box, someone was calling his name. He must have turned almost completely around before seeing Kuninosuke towards one side of the room. Whether from the spin or the surprise in seeing Kuni, Matsu suddenly began to feel dizzy. Kuni came over to him.

"Matsu, my friend, so glad that you have come to our party. What do you think of my Western appearance?"

Kuni was standing in a pose with one foot in front of the other and his one hand held up to the brown derby hat on his head.

"That is really you, Kuni-san?" Matsu couldn't believe the total transformation that appeared before him. A long brown woolen frock coat went from his friend's neck to almost the ground. The opening in front revealed a black brocade vest and a dark silk bow hung at the throat. A golden streamer went from the inner coat to a hidden compartment on the vest.

Kuni saw Matsu staring at the chain and pulled out the gold encased watch from the vest pocket.

"It is a timepiece, Matsu-san. The case is 24-karat gold, and it was made in Switzerland, near the home province of Schnell-san."

"How did you get all this? How did you know how to dress in their way?"

Kuni smiled and looked around the full room. There were perhaps fifty people in the Saloon. A dozen or so were Aizu refugees, but the others seemed to be of many different nationalities.

"I had no Western money," Kuni explained, "so I bartered one of my swords. I thought it was a good deal, so did the man I traded with. We both got what we needed."

"But we might need the swords if we have to fight."

"Matsu, my friend, you must stop living in the old world. It is time to let go of your ancient ways of thinking. Swords have no purpose where we are going. They use guns to fight and protect their women. That will be my first purchase in America when I get my first work payment. Then I will begin looking for a woman."

The piano music had stopped and people were turned toward the front of the room where the floor was raised to a platform. A man in a white uniform with stripes on the sleeves and wearing a maritime type of hat was standing and holding up both his arms. When some people in back continued talking, he pulled out a naval pipe and blew a shrill tone. After a brief burst of laughter, quiet descended in the room.

"Now hear this, I am Captain William Jensen, and it has been the pleasure of my crew to bring the great steamer, the China, across the waters to America. The Almighty tested us a few nights ago, but I think it was just to show that the Americas are not for the faint of heart, but for the spirited adventurers that you all are. You passed the test, and in the morning we will be going into the Golden Gate to your new home. I wish you success, and hope that you achieve the golden dreams you seek."

There was loud applause, to which Matsu and Kuni joined in at the last instant. Neither had the faintest idea what the Captain had said.

"As the Captain, it is also my blessing to shine light on some of the special passengers that we have on board. There is one remarkable man, Mr. John Henry Schnell, a trusted advisor to the great Tokugawa Shogun, who led a valiant resistance to the forces of the Mikado at the battle of Aizu. Despite sparse and belated help from my American government, the Aizu forces lost against an overwhelming Imperial army, forcing Herr Schnell and twenty of his followers to fight their way to Yokohama harbor and finally to the safety of our vessel. They have hopes of establishing a colony in America to start anew. They will call it the Wakamatsu Colony. To this dream, please join with me in wishing every one of these brave new pioneers great success."

The applause was prematurely interrupted with many gasps of amazement when Schnell came onto the stage in full samurai dress. A katana long sword and wakizashi short sword were protruding from his gray silk embroidered obi. The same gray color repeated in the narrow pinstripes of his full-length black kimono. The Tokugawa three-leaf Hollyhock crest adorned each of the shoulders. A pure white silk ribbon wrapped around the obi.

Schnell stood looking into the room full of people and a smile soon replaced the stern look on his bearded face. He brushed his hand through his long red hair. Hoots and cheers spread throughout the crowd. Matsu and Kuni looked at each other in disbelief.

"He wanted all of us to dress like Americans," Matsu said with exasperation in his voice. "Why else would he pass out the gaijin clothes?" He glanced down at his board-like dungarees and tried to feel his curled toes in the painfully confining black leather shoes.

Kuni began to laugh. Matsu glared back at him.

"He is just being a showman, that is the American way, Matsu-san. He is showing us that humility is a burden in this new world, and success belongs to those who cast off the ancient barriers that block the way to achieving our dreams."

Matsu shook his head at once again hearing Kuni's immature and irrational ideas. After all, being a samurai was the ancient way. Were they not supposed to dress and act as the Americans to insure their acceptance in the new culture?

"I am Hiramatsu Buhei," Schnell began. "Twenty years ago I came to Japan as John Henry Schnell, a teenage adventurer looking for new challenges. As you can well see, I have found it!"

The crowd clapped and roared. Everyone crowded to the front as the tables of food in the back of the room were abandoned to but a few Chinese attendants.

"I fought in the Boshin War. I fought in the Ezo Rebellion. I had the honor of presenting the sword of Shigeo Takemoto, the greatest samurai of them all, to the Emperor Meiji. I have been wounded by the sword and spears, and once near death. I have cut men to pieces by my blade, without regret or hesitation."

He scanned the room with his piercing vision. He momentarily caught Matsu's eyes, and Matsu could feel the steely coldness in that man's mind. Many warriors who had fallen had undoubtedly felt that also. Of course, Matsu himself was not intimidated in the least and returned the gaze with his own hard look. Many men have delusions of self-importance, he thought to himself. Schnell was not one of these to be deluded. Matsu could not agree with his methods of self-promotion, for that was not the samurai way. The great Tokugawa Ieyasu would have scolded him for his lack of patience. But he began to understand that there was a place for a man like this. This place was America.

"Can you swing that long sword, you know, like you were cutting off my head?" A man safely at the rear of the saloon shouted out.

A smile joined the steady unblinking eyes on Schnell's face. He turned in the man's direction, spreading his legs apart in a combat stance. In an instance the sword was out of its scabbard and held directly to his front. The crowd hushed in uneasiness.

"This could be a Muramasa blade, made by one of the greatest sword smiths in Japanese history. If it is so, the gentleman has made a grievous mistake in asking me to draw it. Legend says that it must be stained by the death blood of the enemy before it can rest again in the scabbard. A demonic curse can befall me unless I accomplish this deed, and I do not wish to be cursed!"

Schnell jumped forward with his last word of exclamation. Those in the immediate front jumped quickly back, forcing the next few rows back. There was a scurrying sound towards the rear of the room as the man hurriedly found the exit door and slammed it shut behind him. A mixture of subdued laughter and anxiety filled the ensuing void, Schnell continuing to stand with the sword's steel glint before him.

Once again Schnell smiled, and his eyes softened. He lowered his weapon.

"Fortunately for the gentleman, this is not a Muramasa sword." In a motion as instantaneous as he had drawn it, he returned it to the scabbard.

Schnell bowed low to a great round of applause.

Kuni clapped and pushed Matsu on the back when he saw his friend standing immobile. At last, Matsu brought his hands together to a slower rhythm.

"Yes, Matsu, now you are beginning to understand. Our old samurai world of humbleness and taking orders from Lords with big egos is gone. We will become rich and pursue the dreams that have been denied to us."

Matsu stared at Kuni but did not say anything. After all, his young friend would not listen to him and would need to find out in his own way. It was a pity that Kuni had not undergone the formal samurai training that would have taught him the discipline that Matsu found so obviously lacking. A true samurai would know that rewards in life only came after the hard work to earn it. It was always prudent to live and work hard within the established guidelines, and to honor those important in one's life by rectitude and sacrifice.

"We have a special treat for all of you," Schnell held his arms over his head. "No, I am not going to show you my sword fighting skills. There are samurai here who are far better swordsmen than I am."

He looked towards Matsu and Kuni as another smile beamed to the audience. People turned their heads to see the other great samurai swordsmen. Kuni smiled. Matsu looked down at his hideously uncomfortable shoes.

"Rather, I offer something far more pleasurable and elegant for your visual senses. My fellow ladies and gentlemen, passengers of the good ship China, I present in traditional Japanese dance, the beauty of my wife, Jou, and our friend Okei Ito."

Jou appeared from the back door. Sounds of rustling clothing and moving feet filled the air as people turned around and then made a path for her to the middle of the room. For a moment she stood motionless with one hand shading her eyes and the other holding a deep-crimson-colored fan. She wore a lavender tomesode kimono with only two small golden circular mon at the shoulders. When she began to walk towards the center of the saloon, the intricate yuzen kasuri and embroidery designs of a white and silver forest of trees could be seen at the hem with every step, alternately hiding and appearing. Small-winged golden cranes climbed skyward from the forest.

Jou's dark eyes and ruddy painted lips stood out starkly from a face made paler with white powder. Her hair, elaborately bunned at the top, bore golden tassels and silver combs and a host of other ornaments with gold fringes.

The piano player began playing the only Japanese song that he knew, Sakura.

Moving slowly and unhurried, she made graceful arm motions alternately with her free hand and the hand holding the crimson fan. She turned slowly to the music, bowing, bending, striding forward and back, all motions designed to show off the beauty of the kimono and her graceful lines in it. Then an older Japanese woman in a kimono appeared from the front near the staircase, holding a shamisen, a long narrow instrument with a square wooden body and long neck. She brushed on the strings with a large shell pick, harmonizing the sharp complex sound it produced with the continuing music of the piano.

Absolutely entranced with Jou's movements, no one noticed Okei appearing from below on the steps of the grand staircase. Jou froze in mid motion, her fan and free arm pointing at Okei. Everyone turned their attention to Okei who posed briefly at the top banister.

Okei's kimono was a furisode with long full sleeves that hung down almost to the floor. It was the color of akebono, the pink salmon red orange only seen just before the dawn of an especially beautiful day. Intricate kasuri tie-dyed flower designs in white and red climbed up on long branches from the hem to just below her white with gold brocade obi. Branches and flowers also decorated her long sleeves. Her hair, unlike Jou, was simply brushed back with but a single large yellow flower on the front right side.

Taking short quick steps, all that were possible in the tightness of the kimono, Okei came up next to Jou at the center of the saloon. They paused together for a moment, transformed into elegant still decorations that blended into the grand room of luxurious gold-leaf-edged wood panels, massive arched wood ceiling beams, and center pair of chandeliers that glittered with polished bronze and sparkling crystals.

Another Japanese woman who had stood to the side in a less elaborate kimono now held a small metal triangle and began to strike it in rapid, even beats. The sound was tiny, pure, and piercing. The piano stopped.

The two women each stepped forward with the right foot, then stopped and placed both hands and arms above their heads. The left foot then came forward, stopped in unison, ending again with both arms overhead.

The shamisen joined about half the rate of the rapid tingling of the triangle, which began to pick up the pace. The dancers quickly increased their tempo as well.

Right side steps came next, and the arm on that side came up, like a wave. It was followed by left side steps and arm waving. The right foot stepped sideways, along with the right hand following like a floating butterfly. When the legs came tightly together, the left foot slid to the left side followed again by the butterfly arm of that side. The legs again ended together. The right foot stepped forward, and both arms again rose overhead. The pattern was repeated faster and faster.

All the while the kimonos flowed with motion, long sleeves alternately trailing and leading, short steps magnified by the constraint at the hem. There was no beat to the music, but the wooden gettas they wore clicked on the floor in harmony with each step and each stop. The audience was mesmerized, seeing the pattern, the repetition, but not really knowing what came next because the number of movements was too numerous to comprehend at such a frenetic pace.

They made their way around a circle, the audience moving quickly to make a path as they approached. The inside of the circle filled with people, now clapping with the shamisen, far slower than the triangle sound that now was a continuous metallic clatter.

The two women and the music stopped just as the circle was completed.

When Matsu heard the roar of noise just then, he didn't know what to think. It seemed to him like the frontal charge of a full regimen of screaming samurai bent on frightening the enemy from the battlefield. He gazed around stoically, knowing that Kuni was watching his reaction. He showed no fear. After all, he was samurai.

Kuninosuke laughed and put his hands on Matsu's shoulders.

Matsu backed away, more aghast at Kuni's behavior than the sounds of the crowd.

"Relax, Matsu. It is the way they show appreciation in America. They are letting Jo and Okei know that they enjoyed their dance. They appreciate our culture, and our beautiful women."

Captain Jensen strode once again onto the stage in front as the noise finally settled.

"Wasn't that just Jim Dandy? One more round for the beautiful women of the Wakamatsu party!"

When the cheering and clapping had abated, the circle that the women had carved out in the crowd had filled in, and more people began to mill around at the food tables at the back of the room. The piano began playing soft background music. Some non-Asian couples began to dance slowly in the middle of the room, hands together in front, arms holding behind.

Kuni pointed to the paired dancing.

"What do you think? Too much display of affection for back home, ne? But I like it. I will enjoy this new world very much."

John Schnell had found Jou and they danced together in a modified form of what everyone else was doing, Jo adding long graceful arm movements to display the kimono's colorful sleeves. The tight kimono limited her foot motions to a tight circular pattern.

A young woman of European descent appeared out of the crowd in front of Kuni. He was trying to look over her at Schnell and Jou, not realizing that she was staring at him. Matsu noticed the startled look on his friend's face before Kuni was able to regain his composure.

"Monsieur samurai, would you please honor me with your

acceptance to this dance?"

Both men stood frozen as the young woman continued to smile. She wore a sky blue satin dress with a modestly full petticoat, her long blond hair was full of curls that bounded and swayed. Her eyes were startlingly blue.

Kuni recovered enough to return a small smile. "Dance" had been the only spoken word that he had understood, but it was good enough to start his legs moving forward. The woman put one hand into his hand with the other on his back to guide him out to the other dancing couples. Before he got too far, Kuni took off his long coat and handed it to Matsu.

It started out awkwardly as Kuni collided with her. She was the same height as him and stood unruffled, filled with even more merriment than before. Kuni looked around at the foot movements of the other men, and after a few seconds of study, nodded his head toward her. He moved her closer with his hand firmly on her back. He didn't miss a step again. It seemed that dancing, along with a whole host of other activities that would come in this new world, came to him very naturally.

Matsu was at first amazed, but a few moments of watching the attractive young couple floating among the other dancers on the saloon floor left him feeling a little unsettled. It was the second time this evening that feelings of inadequacy had crept into his mind. For some reason, he couldn't seem to help judging himself against Kuni. This feeling was ridiculous. He had fifteen more years of life experience than his friend. He had fought a hundred battles and cheated death innumerable times, compared to the two or three conflicts Kuni had endured. He had even saved his liege Lord's life by foiling an assassination attempt by Satsuma spies.

Matsu hung his head down for a moment, as if not wanting to meet other people's eyes. He had never been honored for his heroic deed to save his liege Lord. If fact, neither Matsudaira, nor anyone else, knew what he had done. It had been for the best that way. The assassin had been a friend of Matsu's family named Digoro who had an exemplary record in the clan, before being seduced by Satsuma promises to pay off his untenable debt. The error in judgment had been immense, but Matsu could not see such a noble service record being soiled by one moment of indiscretion. Arranging a meeting with Digoro, he had killed his friend and left the crumpled body on the blood-soaked tatami mat. Matsu spread a rumor that Satsuma spies had killed him after unsuccessfully trying to persuade him to assassinate Lord Matsudaira. A thousand samurai attended his funeral. His family's subsidy was substantially increased and his debts paid to make up for his untimely death.

He looked up again and watched Kuni with the beautiful gaijin woman. Certainly he did not feel so empowered as to criticize his youthful friend. Kuni was right that the old world mindset had to change to adjust to the ways of the new world into which they would embark tomorrow. Indeed, even the greatest swordsman would be no match for modern rifles and pistols. While Japan had slept in contented isolation, the rest of the world had leapt forward into the future and left ancient warriors such as him mired in the dust and mud tracks that they left behind.

Matsu gazed across the boisterous crowd that made him feel like someone from another planet, someone who didn't belong and was left out of the joys that they were feeling.

This is a place for those who dream big and know no limits, he lamented. An old samurai would be as useless as his steel swords would be against guns. The strict caste system of the Shogun was gone, too. Peasants would no longer grovel down on their knees to make way for passing samurai. From tomorrow onward, he would be at the bottom of the social order, a common laborer eking out a living with a hoe and shovel.

He was shaking his head when Okei entered his vision.

"Matsu-san," she looked into his eyes. "You look like an old tree in a young forest."

"I feel old. I look old," he tried to smile. "I see so much youth and laughter."

Okei stood at his side and together they watched the dancing and listened to the small talk and the piano music.

"Youth needs guidance, ne?" Okei had slipped her hand into Matsu's without him being aware. "Lord Matsudaira was very wise to ask you to guide us in the new world."

Matsu didn't feel like being placated, even by beautiful Okei-san.

"Schnell-san is our leader, I am here only because I am good at taking orders. That is all I have done all my entire life, take orders."

A big bright smile lit up Okei's face. Matsu immediately felt his resistance to her charms tumbling down over a cliff with no bottom.

"Schnell is a good man but sometimes not wise, Matsu-san. He will do things without knowing the consequence. You will give him the wisdom he needs to guide our people to happiness and success."

As Okei pulled him out towards the dancing couples, Matsu's hand and part of his arm disappeared into the long flowing sleeve of her kimono. Okei was unmarried and her sleeve had a very wide opening unlike Jou's kimono, which had a shorter sode that was knitted to leave only an opening for the hand. Matsu couldn't avoid thinking of this as he gazed up his arm to hers and saw some of the white fabric of her undergarment.

They were in the middle of the Grand Saloon room now and Matsu could see and feel the eyes staring at him. The samurai who had stood his ground innumerable times against charging enemies wielding swords and lances and firing arrows felt brewing panic inside because he didn't know what he should do next.

Sensing his unease, Okei raised the hand that held his hand high to the side. She took his other hand and with some awkward movements, placed in on the back of her shoulders.

"You must relax, Matsu-san. See how happy and comfortable everyone else is?"

"They are staring at me."

"No. Their eyes look at me."

Matsu scanned around and saw that indeed, most of the people were looking towards Okei. They didn't even seem to notice the samurai warrior dressed in the stiff pants, harori jacket, and uncomfortable shoes.

He followed their gazes to Okei and for the first time recognized that he was actually touching and holding her. She was touching and holding him. He was beginning to see what their eyes all saw. Okei was beautiful and radiant. It was more than the breathtaking akebono colored kimono and the intricate pattern of flowers and branches on her sleeves and hem. The girl herself was special in a way he had not realized before.

"Dancing is very simple Matsu-san. It is just four steps. I will show you. Just remember that most of the people around us also do not know what they are doing."

The piano music started, and this time the lady with the shamisen joined into the song. It was a classical European music that no one seemed to recognize. The musicians played freely and somehow it all sounded nice.

"Four steps: one, two, three, four. Right foot to the side and down, left foot following and down. Left foot to the side and down, right foot following and down. Right, left, left, right. One, two, three, four. . . ."

"I cannot, I cannot follow."

"One, two, three, four."

He was so busy looking down at his feet that he could not synchronize himself to the music.

"Matsu, look at me."

He saw the harmony that she had with the music. Her movements were effortless and graceful. The sleeves of her kimono swayed. She was looking at no one but him. He looked into her eyes. His feet began to follow hers. His motions copied her motions. They were dancing.

Matsu did not see Kuni and the young blond woman pass by occasionally. He did not notice the look of wonderment on his friend's face. Neither did he notice when Schnell and Jou came by and smiled in his direction.

Too soon the music and dancing ended. Matsu had been mesmerized watching Okei flow as one with the music. Others had been watching, also. Much of the clapping of the people around them came their way. Matsu's cheeks became the color of Okei's sunset orange kimono. She had once again left him amazed.

"You do this with so little effort. Someone must have taught you how to do this Western dance, neh?"

Okei gave him the look that he had become so accustomed to.

"I learned with you, Matsu-san. We learned the dance together."

Matsu could only slightly nod his head. This was a path that he had taken many times before with Okei, and still he had no answers, only the lingering sense of wonder of what the girl could do. How many times before? He had known her as a child because their fathers had been best friends. He had grown so used to her abilities that after awhile they had just become a part of her nature. Now she had grown to become a very special young woman.

Okei was not done yet and didn't have to beg Matsu to stay with her for another dance. That the music was faster paced and involved learning the new and more complex foxtrot steps didn't cause Matsu any great concern.

"Left forward, brush, back, back left, brush, together. Slow, slow, fast, fast," she told him. It was no problem. They were learning together. Kuni stopped momentarily to watch them. Schnell and Jou became part of the audience as well. They all clapped after the dancing was done.

CHAPTER 5
The Golden Gate And Beyond

The morning of May 20, 1869 was the most special one of my brief span of existence. I was in the arms of Frances, who was in the arms of Schnell-san. Everyone was crowded shoulder-to-shoulder and watched the great rock walls surrounding our ship open up and reveal a narrow path into a remarkable landlocked sea. A fort with giant iron cannons peered out between massive stone pillars on our right, and on the left small cabins on stilts rose spindly out of the water. Suddenly there were gasps from those to our right as the city made its appearance from a shrouding blanket of fog. Only the tops of the buildings could be seen, appearing like colorless floating squares and rectangles in a gray misty sea. There were no roads. There were no people.

"We are too late," Jou said. "They have all left for the Gold Mountain."

Schnell couldn't help but chuckle.

"My darling, you have no comprehension of time. The Gold Rush ended twenty years ago."

"Maybe they have never returned."

Before Schnell could respond, the fog lifted slightly to reveal the timber of wharves along the shoreline, and then roads climbing up into the hills beyond. There was movement on the roads; careful searching revealed the dark shape of wagons and horses climbing up and going down the paths.

More and bigger wharves came into view, some of them giant sheds jutting out into the water on thick log piers. Many ships were moored at the piers, with tall masts that looked like wooden skeletons. As we came closer to the land, more ships could be seen in every available inch of the waterfront. The docks looked like a forest of tall spindly trees. Some of the trees very near them came out of the water from submerged hulks resting on the bay's bottom.

Okei was startled to see the dark outline of a ship's carcass below the water.

"Did they just leave these ships?" she asked. "Were they in such a great hurry?"

Schnell was also troubled by what he saw.

"It was desperation," he reasoned to himself. "They looked around and saw thousands of others with the same dreams they had, and decided that there was no time to waste. I heard that some jumped into the water before their ships reached land. Even crewmen abandoned their ships."

The *China* rounded the curve of the peninsula and hundreds more piers and ships came into view. We were now close enough to view people walking alongside the water's edge.

Okei leaned against the railing. They didn't appear much different from many of the passengers she had seen and met on board the ship. She had been told that everyone in America carried guns, but no one seemed to be carrying large ones that she could see. Perhaps they had smaller pistols under their coats, ready to be pulled out if someone should say bad things about them.

Matsu was standing next to a Japanese man he remembered

seeing at the meeting in the castle. The man was shorter than him, his head only having hair at the sides by the ears and a small goatee on his chin. There was more gray and white than black in his hair, and Matsu guessed that the man was at least forty years old. He wanted to find out something about him.

"You are not from Aizu, are you?" he asked.

"No. I am from Aichi. I escaped to Aizu just before the Imperial army burned down my town. I only found out about this journey to America in the last week and didn't have time to pack. Even now, I cannot believe my good fortune on being on this ship."

Matsu looked quizzically at this odd appearing man, who was well dressed in a dark striped European-style suit jacket and slacks.

"You do not seem to be a farmer or carpenter, or samurai. Are you a friend or family of our Lord?"

The man smiled.

"Excuse me for my poor manners. I am Dr. Matsumoto Goro. I directed a medical clinic in Aichi before the Imperial troops put it to the torch. Then they started shooting at me and I ran. I had to leave everything behind. I never again saw my wife and children."

"I am Sakurai Matsunosuke from Aizu. Yes it is sad to hear about your family, but our Lord was thoughtful to include a doctor. We do not know what kind of medicine the Americans have, and it would be hard to trust any of it. It is good to have Japanese medicine for our illnesses."

"I lost all my supplies, my tools," he lamented, and then pointed to his head. "My only help to this colony is the knowledge that I have up here."

Matsu looked away from the doctor and saw that the ship had

slowed and turned towards a plank landing beside some rough wooden buildings. There were many people walking on the nearby street, and some were waiting for the ship at the landing.

"Still it is good to have you with us, Doctor Matsumoto. My understanding is that we have come to an ill-tempered world where life does not have as much meaning as in Japan. Most disturbing is that the fighting is not to protect family honor but for trivial matters such as personal profit. I have heard during their mad rush for gold, they would fight and kill for the right to dig a small hole in the ground."

"You have studied the situation here well. Twenty years has passed since the Gold Rush, but the change to civilization has been slow to come. They used to call this the Barbary Coast, after a place in Africa where pirates raided passing ships, raping and murdering, selling survivors to the slave traders for but a few ryo apiece."

Matsu had never heard of this before. Why had Schnell brought them to such an evil place? Was it possible that Schnell was seeking profit by selling all of them to work as slaves? He watched anxiously as the ship came closer to its mooring.

Sensing Matsu's uncertainly, Doctor Matsumoto tried to soften his language.

"Do not be concerned, Matsunosuke-san. The civil war just concluded here outlawed the practice of slavery. There was a great president, Abraham Lincoln, who believed that all men should be treated equal, regardless of where they were born or the color of the skin."

"Ah, he must be a great man to have this belief. I would like to meet this president Abraham Lincoln."

The ship docked and the giant ropes were wound around the iron moorings on the wharf.

Dr. Matsumoto gazed at Matsu for a moment then looked at the rough looking men securing the ship.

"He never saw the end of their civil war. He was killed by assassination two months before the last battle of the war."

Matsu was listening but had to think for some time before realizing what was said. By then, the doctor had left for the walkway into the new world.

It was the greatest moment of confusion and anxiety that any of them had ever faced. After struggling with their luggage and Schnell's several large trunks, they found themselves in the middle of the chaos of San Francisco's busiest wharf. People of many different appearances were going hurriedly in many different directions. Horse drawn wagons sped by without regard for anything in their path. There was shouting everywhere in a jumble of languages that mixed together to add to the unbelievably unsettled and cluttered scene.

Schnell had Frances in his arms with Jou clinging to his coat beside him. Others of the group stood close by, struggling to keep Schnell in their vision as a sea of people tried to rush not only around them but also through them.

Not knowing what to do but sensing he had to act, Schnell waved his arms and pointed to an area of bright sunlight at the end of a covered walkway. He shouted but no one heard him. He began to move and the others followed. Just as he was concentrating on what to do when he reached that opening, he felt Jou's tug on his arm to try to get his attention.

"Husband, some of the older people badly need to relieve themselves. Surely there are benjos here somewhere. What is it called in their language? It is a desperate situation."

Schnell turned and saw the anguished look on many of the faces. He saw Jou's pleading face. At the moment there was nothing that he could do.

Suddenly they were next to a wide street and away from the madness at the wharf. Schnell had just put Frances down and was flexing his aching arms when a man approached. He wore a gray suit and a white top hat. He had a notepad in his hand and a pencil in his mouth. The man removed the pencil and Schnell noticed the trail of saliva that followed into his hand.

"Herr Henry Schnell, I presume?"

Schnell stared at him with a blank expression.

"You are the Japanese party sent by the Mikado, aren't you?"

"Yes. Can you tell me where the toilets are? It is a desperate situation."

It took a moment for the man to understand. Finally his confused face gave way to a satisfied look of enlightenment.

"The long brown building over there, next to the ship. It has twenty holes, enough for your whole party. Men are to the far side."

Schnell pointed decisively in that direction. "Asoko!" he yelled out, his first important act of leadership in the new world.

In an instant, most of the group dashed off for the outhouse jutting out over the still bay. Jou, Frances, Matsu, Okei, and Dr. Matsumoto were the only ones to remain with him. At last Schnell was able to smile as he looked back at the man.

"I am Hudson with the San Francisco Daily Alta. We have heard of your group's escape from Japan and our readers are anxious to acquaint themselves with your heroic story. I understand that you have samurai warriors and geisha with you." Hudson just then noticed Jou standing beside Schnell. She was wearing the lavender and white kimono that she had worn at the Captain's dance. Her hair was combed down to naturally curly ends, and a white ribbon went around it at the back.

"Mrs. Schnell, aren't you very lovely? You have honored our city by wearing Japan's traditional silk dress, and a very beautiful example, if I may say so."

Jou returned a small smile after her husband translated the words.

Schnell watched the stream of wagons and people moving along the street and felt his mind finally beginning to focus on prioritizing the many tasks before him.

"Mr. Hudson, I am likewise honored by your interest in our endeavor. However, I must correct you that we are not a party of the Mikado, but rather were sent by my liege Lord, Matsudaira of Aizu Han, the last stronghold of the great Tokugawa Shogun. It is against the forces of the Mikado that we have waged war."

"Yes, thank you for enlightening me, Herr Schnell. The Alta has always strived for correctness and the truth, and in that light, I would appreciate some time with you and your wife at one of our city's finest watering holes. As I said before, your story is of great interest to our readers, and I intend to get to the bottom of it."

Schnell face broke into a wide grin as he began to realize the great opportunity that had just been presented to him. The thought of hundreds, perhaps thousands, of Californians reading about his tea and silk colony went through his mind. Even before he had purchased the land or planted a single seed, there would be huge demand for his tea and silk and he might even have to maintain a waiting list that would ensure success for years into the future. Of course, there would have to be a marginal fee for the privilege of being listed.

"Mr. Hudson, your kind offer is gladly accepted. First, I must make lodging accommodations for my people."

"I fully understand. I recommend the Hotel Fairfield, just up the street on Kearny, no more than three blocks. It is a first-class institution at a reasonable rate and should be able to accommodate your entire party. I will send a wagon to bring your party's luggage."

Schnell turned to Dr. Matsumoto and Matsu and began to talk to them in Japanese. Puzzled expressions gave way to nods of agreement. Remarkably, they learned Schnell already had been able to schedule a business meeting with a very important official of the city! This would lead to a purchase of fine farmland in the East, and fast, comfortable transportation to get there. Everything was coming together faster than anyone could have imagined and their wait to get to their new home would be short indeed. Matsumoto and Matsu quickly left through the covered walkway to gather together with the rest of the group. Hudson could only admire the diligent and studious expression on their faces and the pleasing appearance they had in their suits and hats and the women in nice light-colored frocks. He pointed to a place across the street and they began walking.

"Your people have a very dignified and cultured appearance, Herr Schnell. They are unlike the Chinaman, I understand, with whom we have long had dealings."

"Yes, Mr. Hudson, the Japanese are a very proud people. They will do whatever I ask, but do not take kindly to deceit and ill temperament. I have three samurai who are honor-bound to protect my family and my investment. They have razor sharp swords called katana, as do I."

Hudson had to smile. "That is all well and good, Herr Schnell, but we use guns here. Surely you don't believe knives can prevail in such confrontation?"

Schnell stopped in the middle of the busy street, momentarily startling the others who had been focused on hurrying across and dodging the onrushing wagon traffic coming and going in all directions.

"It does not matter, Mr. Hudson. They are samurai."

A freight wagon went by so closely that Jou dashed behind Schnell with Frances firmly in her arms. Hudson's white hat flew off and landed on the dirt and mud of the street, brim side up.

Matsu and Dr. Matsumoto went back to try to explain their present situation to the other twenty colonists. Their enthusiasm for Schnell's message was dimmed, however, upon seeing the concerned and frightened look on so many faces, and the barrage of questions that were shouted out at them.

Matsu began to talk in his usual voice, but no one was listening. Here was the first time in the new country that he needed to show his leadership skill and they were ignoring him! He raised his voice beyond anything he had ever done before. His ears hurt from listening to himself.

"We must find the Fairfield House where we will wait for Schnell-san. It is in the western direction, not very distant."

"Schnell has abandoned us here?"

"He is meeting with the leaders of the city. He is signing papers to allow us to go to our new home." Matsu didn't know of any document signings. Schnell had not mentioned anything. Maybe they were indeed being abandoned to slave traders. He would however do or say anything that would give him the appearance of knowledgeable authority. It didn't matter that Schnell had given him neither knowledge nor authority. They would need purpose and direction to survive during this uncertain time.

"Matsumoto-san, Nishijawa-san, you will take half the people up this side of the street. Kuni-san, come with me and the rest to go up the far side."

As they prepared to split up, Matsu had an afterthought.

"Does anyone know this language enough to talk or read signs?"

Everyone stared back with blank looks, as he expected.

"Ask them for the direction to the Fairfield Hotel. Ask them to point to it."

With that, they split up and went up Market Street.

Matsu was relieved to see Okei in the group crossing the street with him. She was wearing a white American style dress with a skirt almost down to her ankles. Although it was not a kimono, Okei looked nice in it. Of course, she would look nice in just about anything. Perhaps she could use her abilities to help them. Wasn't this a serious enough situation? Matsu shook his head and tried to dismiss the foolish thought. She was just a girl who had been able to beguile him with her charm, which indeed was considerable. This was a time for a samurai to lead them through this unknown country. He would not stoop to call on such a simple lower-class girl, unless, of course, it became absolutely necessary.

Someone asked how far they should go up the street. Matsu suddenly remembered that the reporter had mentioned "three blocks." He knew that "three" meant san in Japanese, but what were "blocks?" Were they like ri? Just then he stepped off a curb and noticed more buildings with signs to his right on the adjoining street. There were some people who looked Asian beside one of the buildings. He pointed to Kuni and the others to continue up Market Street and then began walking into the side street. Okei, an older couple with a small child, and Matsugoro, a carpenter with his wife, followed Matsu.

Approaching closer, he was disheartened to see that the people were all Chinese. His group would no more be able to get information from these people than by talking with one of the other natives here. The celestials wore loose white long shirts and baggy white pants and straw sandals on their feet. Several wore conical woven hats, while the rest wore skullcaps with the ends folded over. Long braids of black hair, queues, single or in pairs, hung down almost to the waist. All five were men of different ages. They had not noticed the group of Japanese staring at them because of a commotion from an adjoining alleyway that had their full attention. That noise had caused them to cower against the wall of the building.

Okei was the first to see the approaching group of men and gave a muffled shriek. Matsu instinctively reached toward his waist. There was no sword. There wasn't even an obi to hold it, only the thin belt on his stupid dungaree. Sensing his empty hands, he could only watch them coming closer.

Several of the oncoming men had been shouting but they became quiet and halted their advance upon reaching the street intersection. Some held pieces of lumber in their hands. Others had bricks or broken bits of concrete. The man in front held a long and pointed iron rod. They numbered nearly twenty and they wore nondescript clothing and a variety of different hats. They seemed to be of no particular nationality, and except for varying height and girth, all looked the same and all were very angry.

I was in Okei's hand and could feel her nervous moisture as her grip on me tightened. It was the same feeling I had when the monster Satsuma samurai had come to confront us. Danger had once again called upon us.

"We are the Anti-Coolie Committee," the front man shouted, holding the iron rod with both hands. There were other shouts.

"We are confederated patriots sworn to eliminate the scourge of heathens who have taken our gold fields and are taking over our cities."

"Next thing you know they'll be wanting our women!" More shouts.

Matsu stood closest to the frightened Chinese, only a few feet away. We were just behind him, with the other family just behind us. I could sense Matsu's silent urging for us to back away, but we were in each other's way, frozen in place like statues. This was an unfortunate situation that had befallen us. We should have stayed together on the safe main road when in a place so alien. I saw the regret all over Matsu's face. My mind raced round and round trying to find a solution for us. Eee. I am but a doll! I have no power to change anything, or save anyone. Then I felt the warm comfort of Okei's hands, no longer cold and sweating, and knew that there was hope amid such grievous hopelessness.

One of the men pointed at our group, and suddenly we had replaced the Chinese as the focus of their attention. Their looks of puzzlement at our appearance quickly turned to that of outrage.

"So lookie at the dressed up chinks. Just who do they think they are?"

It was true that we were all dressed in the American way. Schnell-san had wanted us to make a good impression on our first day out in this new land. Even Matsu was wearing a banded hat and well fitting dark jacket over his dungarees. I was the only one still wearing a kimono. I do not think that this was the kind of impression that Schnell-san had desired for us to make.

Why they did not notice Okei and me, I do not know. We were somewhat apart from the others where Okei stood straight and staring directly at the men. Not one met her eyes. I couldn't understand it. The white dress that she wore was simple and did not command attention as a kimono, but Okei certainly did not look repulsive in it. On the contrary, there was no garment made of any fabric on this earth that could dim the light that shown from inside of her. They did not see her, I reasoned, because she had chosen for them not to.

"You, chink, the little sewer rat in front, if you speeke English we just might be pleased enough to let you all go."

Matsu heard the angry words directed at him and knew that their lives depended on his ability to respond appropriately. In Japan, against overwhelming odds, it was best to keep conversing, using patience to lull the enemy, all the while searching for that one instant of weakness to strike. But he didn't have his sword. Neither did he know what the man was saying. How could he converse? He had to try something.

"No English. Japan! No China!" He couldn't believe how weak and frightened his voice came out. Had he already changed so much since stepping off the ship? He was samurai! They must know that he was samurai! He must show these American hooligans that they would forever regret this confrontation.

Matsu stepped forward, empty hands to his sides. A half-dozen men from the mob moved menacingly toward him, timbers raised, brick armed hands cocked behind. Somehow, I closed my eyes.

"Our Father in Heaven, by the grace of God I have come just in time!"

The men in front suddenly stopped. They were looking toward Matsu's left, in Okei's direction. Matsu didn't understand what was happening. He blinked, and then rubbed his eyes. They had lowered their timbers and other weapons! The leader however still held up his pointed iron rod.

"Hallowed be thy name, thy kingdom come!"

A man in a blue uniform slowly walked between the Japanese and the mob. He stopped before reaching the Chinese, and then did a military pirouette to face the men. Matsu continued to stare in disbelief, his empty hands still raised up to protect himself from the angry onslaught that had seemed inevitable. Where had this man come from? Who was he?

"I have obviously come upon a grave misunderstanding of the most supreme immensity."

Three golden rings adorned the ends of each sleeve of the man's uniform. A pair of large gold tasseled epaulettes hung from his shoulders. A French Napoleonic hat that sat on his head had plumes of feathers attached to the back. A long cavalry sword hung off an embroidered belt. He turned to look at the Chinese, now standing and staring with wide amazed eyes. He then gazed at the equally frightened Japanese, before looking forward once more.

"Know ye that I am Norton the First, Emperor of these United States of America and Protector of Mexico. Whom, I command, is wholly responsible for this despicable situation?"

The leader held up his iron rod with one hand.

"Go away old man. Do not interfere with the Anti-Coolie Committee. This is our fight!"

"You will be done!" Norton put his hand on the handle of the sword.

The face of the mob leader contorted in anger and he began to charge. Before he could take two steps, he was yanked backwards. Several of the men had grabbed his iron rod from behind.

"Damn you, let go! Let me finish the bastard. . . "

"That's Norton, Charlie, you can't hurt the Emperor. . . "

The leader continued struggling to free his weapon. "God, Christ, he's no Emperor. He's just a crazy old coot who's hoodwinked this whole city. He needs to be beaten to a bleeding pulp like the rest of the chinks."

"Not good, Charlie. You'd turn everyone against us. They won't let us have fun to hunt down chinks anymore."

He let go of the iron rod, turned and stood, breathing heavily.

"Are you all deaf and dumb? Are you all going to let this lunatic son-of-a-bitch buffalo you? I tell you he has no power to do anything! He's Emperor of nothing! He's just a damn nut case and you're all nuts to believe him!"

Emperor Norton continued to stand with his hand on his sword. The solemn expression on his face never changed the whole time.

"On Earth as it is in heaven," he said, "we are all God's children."

Some of men toward the back of the mob stepped back and began to disperse into the small crowd that had gathered to watch.

"Give us this day our daily bread."

Another row of men drifted away.

"And forgive us our debts, as we have forgiven our debtors."

Then there was only one left.

"And lead us not in to temptation, but deliver us from evil."

The leader had watched his entire crusade fall apart before his eyes. His arms reached into the air and he let out an anguished scream.

"This whole damned stupid city is as insane as he is!" The man knelt down to the ground and began pounding the earth with all the fury of his immense hatred.

My eyes opened once again. How I had closed them I cannot explain, since the brush strokes by my maker, Okei-san, had made them wide open and always seeing. That was unchangeable, so I had assumed, just as the powerlessness I felt to change the world around me. But I had not wanted to witness the bloody violence that seemed so inevitable. I had seen enough of it when I saw the body of the Satsuma samurai tottering to the floor, a shower of blood flowing behind it. I had willed myself not to see our destruction. What more was I capable of doing now, I wondered?

The man who had once been the leader of the mob was completely still when we came over his prone form. Okei stepped around, as did Matsugoro and his wife. None of us looked down at him. However, the Chinese men could not hide their feelings of contempt. Several spat down at him. Another kicked but missed and nearly fell over. Some shouted harsh strange words that were as meaningless to me as I'm sure they were to him.

Matsu was already before the uniformed man who had appeared out of nowhere to save us. He bowed two, three, and four times, even getting on one knee while holding his hat in his hand. If anything, Emperor Norton seemed perplexed by the attention. When we came and began to bow also, some of us speaking in our language that was strange to his ears, he backed away slightly and seemed ready to walk away. However, he stayed.

"You are Japanese," he said, the look of confusion on his face only slightly lessened. "As the Emperor of the people of the United States of America, I am honored to greet the ambassadors of the Mikado."

Matsu continued to thank him, more words coming out of him than I have ever heard before. I think he was extremely relieved that his ill-conceived decision to enter the side street had not resulted in any suffering for us. I found it embarrassing, but Emperor Norton did nothing to stop him, even though he understood none of it.

I was astounded by our incredible fortune of being saved by the leader of our new homeland. I knew that Japan had an Emperor, but did not know that this new country had one as well. Our Emperor back home was just a figurehead leader, however, who rarely appeared, spoke, or made decisions. It was comforting to see this ruler so involved in helping his people, even looking after poor new immigrants such as us. I wondered if he was also a deity, a direct descendant of the gods that had made the earth.

Matsu finally stopped bowing and began to shake Norton's hand. It was then that he noticed the brown stains on the sleeve's yellow stripes. There were a number of holes on the fabric of the arms. Some of the brass buttons on the front of the uniform were missing, and the silver handle of his sword was tarnished almost to black.

He hadn't looked directly at Norton's face before. On his chin was a twisted mass of graying and white hair that hung down to the collar of his uniform. His moustache covered the front of his nose like an unpruned bush. The sides of his head were covered with the same unkempt hair growth.

Matsu stopped shaking his hand.

Most noticeable of all were his eyes. When Norton looked

directly at him, one eye seemed to be looking at someone beyond Matsu's shoulder. Matsu initially turned to see who was there, but there was no one. Then Okei came up beside him and Norton's other eye turned to see her.

Okei also looked over her shoulder, and seeing no one, continued to smile at Norton. Then both his eyes came together when he saw the doll, me, in her hand.

"It is a beautiful little doll, Madam geisha," Norton squinted as if concentrating on keeping his vision aligned. "It is the exact copy of you. Did you make it?"

Okei continued to smile. Matsu decided that he needed to speak again.

"This is Okei. Okei not geisha." He couldn't believe that he was able to speak some English. How had he heard the words? Did Schnell-san speak it ages ago?

"I see. What is the name of the doll?"

Okei knew it was a question about the doll, but her mind went blank for an instant. Perhaps it was a sudden gust in the constant Pacific wind that caused me to move slightly in her hand.

"Doll name is Keiko. Yes, I make doll."

"Arigato, Okei-san. You are as beautiful as Keiko-chan."

Okei bowed her head as Matsu moved closer. "Emperor-san, Nihongo wakarimasu-ka?"

"Sukoushi-dake." Through it all, Emperor Norton kept his stern face and never smiled. He turned his attention from me to Matsu, and began to search the pockets of his blue uniform. He produced small cut pieces of paper that had printing and pictures on them and held them out to Matsu.

"I give you this as a token of friendship from the people of San Francisco and the Empire of the United States of America. It will help your people get a start here, and pay for your hotel room."

Matsu's eyes grew large as he accepted the papers. Okei was equally astounded.

"You give us money?" The paper felt smooth, stiff, and new in his hands.

"Please accept my apology that I do not have more at this time. If you are still here by late tomorrow, I should have more available."

Matsu was speechless.

"Arigato-gozaimasu," was all that Okei could think to say.

For the first time a hint of a smile showed from beneath the Emperor's scraggly mustache and above his protruding beard.

"I must bid you farewell," he told them, "as duty to my other constituents calls on me. I trust that your people will do well in our country. I pray you have a safe and pleasant journey to your new homestead in America."

Emperor Norton clicked his heels together and raised his right arm to his forehead in a salute. Without waiting for a response, he did a half pirouette and began to move away, walking faster until soon disappearing into the crowd of people on the street.

What a strange encounter this has been, I thought as I watched him leave us. Had my maker been the cause of this? As much as Okei-san had surprised me with her abilities, she seemed to have been as amazed by this man as the rest of us. I think she had only known that help was coming to us in our moment of need. She had not known that it would be the Emperor of America himself.

This was a good man, I thought reflectively.

"We have met a good man," Okei said in turn.

"Yes, for all his strangeness," Matsu answered.

Once again on Market Street, we only went up a few blocks before seeing the other half of our party. Dr. Matsumoto and Kuni were in the lead, eyes searching everywhere and with a look of desperation. Matsu kept his head down and stoically kept walking faster. Unfortunately, Kuni recognized him just as he was about to go past.

"Matsu! We could not find you! Did you get lost?"

"I did not get lost."

"Where did you go? What is that in your hand?"

Matsu hadn't realized that he was still holding the money in his tightly closed fist. He searched for a pocket where he could stash it.

"It is a gift from an American. He helped us avoid a confrontation."

"A fight? You were in a fight?" The colonists around them now listened intently.

Matsu wished he could walk faster. "He helped us avoid a fight."

"He was a great man," Okei chimed in. "The Emperor of America."

Matsu stopped and glared at her. Kuni looked from one to the other, in total confusion.

"You were helped by the Emperor of America? He gave you money?"

Matsu pretended to be looking at the signs on the buildings around them. "Fairfield Hotel," he muttered to himself. Of course he could read none of it. They might be standing right in front of their hotel for all he knew.

"Hontou-desu," Okei said.

"They don't have Emperors here," Kuni tried to get Matsu to look at him. "The man was lying to you. Tell him, Dr. Matsumoto. You have studied about this country."

"Kuni is right, Matsu-san. The leader is called "President," and he lives by the other ocean, 1500 ri from here."

Matsu wished that they could talk about something else. "Perhaps he is Emperor of San Francisco, or California. I don't know. All I know is that he was an important man."

"He was a good man," Okei stepped in front of Matsu. "He told us the truth."

Yes, a good man, I thought from Okei's hand.

Matsu's eyes continued to dart around. There were so many people hurriedly walking by that choosing someone to stop was nearly impossible. Then he spotted a man walking slightly slower.

"Sumimasen, excuse me, please. Where is Fairfield Hotel?"

The large man stared down with indifferent eyes, then pointed to the large sign on the building front where they stood.

Matsu gave a look of sudden recognition, as if the sign had just materialized. Even so, he would not have been able to read it.

"Ah! Yes, arigato. Fairfield Hotel."

The man curved his mouth in a disdainful expression, then brushed past without having said a single word. Matsu slumped his shoulders and motioned everyone inside the building.

They were all disappointed when they did not see Schnell and Jou in the lobby. Matsu especially found it disheartening. Once again he would have to deal in matters in which he had little knowledge or experience. He could only hope that the results would not be as disastrous this time.

"May I help you?"

"Please room."

"Name?"

"Matsunosuke Sakurai."

"For how many?"

"Niju nipon." Matsu couldn't look at the desk clerk's questioning stare. He pointed to the colonists in the waiting area and smiled. The clerk's stupid look didn't change. Finally, Matsu held out all ten fingers, raising them twice, and adding two more fingers.

"Twenty two?"

"Hai." Matsu held onto the ledge of the desk counter to keep himself steady. If he had his sword, this man would no longer have his head.

"You would need 10 rooms. How do you wish to pay for them?"

Matsu guessed correctly that he was requesting payment. He pulled out all of the neatly folded bills from the front pocket of his suit. He straightened out the creases before pushing them to the clerk. Matsu smiled again.

The man looked down at the bills, and then gazed back at Matsu. He did this several times. Matsu found it hard to keep smiling. The clerk excused himself and went into a back room. Another man came out soon after, taller, and better dressed.

"This is Emperor Norton's money. It is not real," he said without emotion.

"Norton is Emperor of America." Matsu was no longer smiling.

"You have been duped, mister." The man looked to his assistant who mumbled a few words.

". . . Suku Toma. Emperor Norton is only an Emperor in his deluded mind. He is a lunatic and a madman. His money is completely worthless."

Matsu only heard "Suku Toma" and nothing else. For the rest of the time that the man spoke, he spent trying to decide the quickest possible way to get the sword from his luggage case. The shorter wakizashi would do just fine for this one. It would be easier to clean it of the blood that was about to be spilled.

Just at that moment the front door burst open with a whoosh of air. Schnell, with Jou and little Frances, came into the lobby. Matsu was so deep in thought that he didn't turn to look. Sensing a need for action, Schnell immediately stepped to the front desk. Frances took the opportunity to run to Okei-san.

"This is my party," Schnell said cheerfully. "Mister Dooley of the Alta California assured me that all arrangements have been made for rooms at your fine establishment."

"Whom may I ask do I have the pleasure of this conversation?"

"Ah, forgive me. I have been away from cultured life for far too long. I am Herr John Henry Schnell of the Prussian Embassy of Nippon. I have been commissioned by the Shogun and the American government to establish an experimental agricultural settlement in California."

"Mister Dooley did not mention a large party of vagabonds."

Schnell fought to keep his cherry appearance. Unlike Matsu, Schnell did carry Jou's fourteen-inch long tanto dagger in his waistband.

"Mister Dooley did say that he would publish an article about our party and the splendid treatment that we will be receiving at your fine hotel. I told him that I would make a report to him tomorrow morning. I expect it to be a glowing report." Schnell's grin was about as wide as could be manufactured under the present circumstances.

The head clerk stood for a moment to digest the words. Meanwhile, everyone watched from the semi circle that they formed in the room. Kuni, Dr. Matsumoto and two families with children were to the right. To the left stood Jou, Okei holding a squirming Frances who held me, Matsugoro and his wife, and two young couples without children. Matsu had seated himself in a chair to the back, still trying to settle himself after his encounter with the clerk.

The head clerk didn't even blink as he stared at Schnell. "I shall take up the matter later with Mr. Dooley. In the meantime, Herr Schnell, your party will be assigned rooms 22 to 32. Pauli, would you kindly get the luggage and the keys? Good day, gentlemen." Quickly he returned to his rear room and slammed the door shut.

John Henry Schnell walked slowly away and at last allowed himself a moment of relaxation. Sensing the favorable turn in their fortunes, Jou and Frances joined him and they embraced in a not very Japanese fashion. The others, too, came up. Kuni hugged Okei. Each of the couples exchanged kisses. Even Matsu stood up and joined everyone. This had been a long day but finally they were in their new homeland. Japan had become a distant memory.

CHAPTER 6
San Francisco To Gold Hill

The days in San Francisco went by quickly after Schnell-san left in search of our new home site. I remember many outings from the hotel, going in different directions each time. Usually we were in small groups of six or fewer. I was always with Jou and Frances because that was my purpose in life, and Okei-san would be with us to tend to the infant's needs. Matsu and Kuni were usually in our group. It was comforting to know that the two samurai were always there to protect us.

Each evening we gathered together in the hotel lobby to talk of our experiences. One day Dr. Matsumoto surprised us by saying that he and Matsugoro had gone to North Beach despite Schnell-san's warning to avoid this lawless area where bandits lurked among the opium dens, bordellos, and innumerable drinking houses.

"Did you partake in the ladies of the night, Matsumoto-sensei?" asked Kuni.

"I must admit that I had a curiosity of what was offered," Matsumoto talked coolly. "However I saw nothing that compared to the ladies of Yoshiwara, and I politely declined all offers for their services."

Laughter resounded. All the men had glasses of a strange but fragrant dark drink made from fermented grape extract. They reached out to each other as they had seen the Americans frequently do, colliding their beverages with a sharp clinking sound, spilling some of the liquid onto the hotel's plush carpet, which was dark colored just for these incidences. They emptied their glasses.

"It was very smart of you, Matsumoto-san," Kuni continued. "I have heard that the whores here slip powerful drugs into your drink, and next thing you know you are on a ship to China."

There was a gasp.

"Nan ka? Why would they do this?"

As always, Kuni enjoyed the times when he had everyone's attention. He was going to savor the adventurous life of this new world.

"My friends, have you not heard of being shanghaied? They sell you to the highest bidder, and make you a slave on trading ships along the China coast. There is no escape. Your soul is lost forever."

"What about women? What would they do, say, if Okei-san, was shanghaied?"

Okei blushed as Kuni intently studied her. The wine glasses were held steady and the laughter subsided.

"I could not begin to imagine what fate would await a beautiful young lady."

I would have blushed too, if I could. It did not seem fair to put Okei in this situation.

"She would become a princess," Dr. Matsumoto finally said as he lifted up his wine glass. "The Emperor of China would lavish gifts upon her, and she would live the rest of her life in opulent splendor!"

Cheering erupted. More glasses of wine were drained.

I wondered if I was the only one to notice Matsu sitting quietly at one of the more distant tables. He did not have a drinking glass. He seemed deep in thought of matters of the future that all of us would soon have to be dealing with. Of course this was to be expected of Matsu and I did not find any concern. He had a great responsibility for all of us, and for the success of the Wakamatsu Colony. I would have been alarmed only if he had decided to join our joyful gathering.

More than half the group had retired to their rooms by nightfall. By the time the last wine bottle was emptied hours later, only six people remained. Of course I didn't count in that number, nor Little Frances, now sleeping in Jou's arms. Okei was here because of Frances. It was strange that we were present at such a late hour. Normally, only the men stayed to the closing time. Perhaps there was an understanding that our time in San Francisco was about to come to an end and the rest of our journey was soon to begin.

Suddenly the door flung open, letting in darkness and a man dressed in a well-worn dark suit. His white shirt was unbuttoned for several rows and in his hand was a rolled-up length of paper. His hair was long and unkempt. His eyes were wide with excitement, his beard long and unruly. Jou put Frances down and rushed into the man's arms. The child followed with quick jerky steps. Matsu, Kuni, and Okei, the only others still remaining, gazed on in shock and astonishment.

John Henry Schnell embraced Jou and scooped up his little daughter who grabbed him around the waist in her never-more-will-I-let-you-go grip. His smile was wide and brilliant when he saw Matsu, Kuni, and Okei. He raised the hand holding the rolled paper. His voice was unrestrained but hoarse from the dust of travel. He spoke a combination of English and Japanese.

"Ladies and gentlemen, my fellow refugees of a brutal and unjust war unleashed upon us all, I declare now that we are refugees no more! Henceforth from this day until forever we are Americans! We have land! We have a new home!"

Kuni stood up and yelled in happiness. Matsu stayed seated and smiled. Okei gazed around in wonderment. People of our group instantly began coming down the stairway as if they had been anxiously listening at their doors for this moment. In a short time, almost the entire group had gathered in the lobby.

"It is called Gold Hill Ranch" Schnell continued on. "It soon will be called the Wakamatsu Tea and Silk Colony Farm!"

There were shouts and clapping. It was as if the night had ended and the new day had just begun.

Schnell let Frances down and Okei came to grab the child's hand. The others were crowding closer to him and Okei moved further back in the crowd.

"How much land, Schnell-sama?" Someone asked, using the honorific reserved for only the most noble and significant statesmen.

Schnell was relishing every moment of their exuberance.

"Enough land for all our tea plants and mulberry trees, with plenty left for our rice and fish pond. It is good and fertile land, with a stream in the middle that runs the entire year. There is a substantial house that will be our headquarters. There is a barn to store our tools and animals. It is everything that we have dreamed of to start our new life."

Kuni raised his hand like a little schoolboy.

"Is there a machi nearby, you know where we can go after working hard all day?"

"Kuni wants to know where all the girls and sake are!" another shouted and there was a roar of laughter.

Schnell hugged and kissed Jou before looking at Kuni.

"Well, Kuni, they don't have sake here but they do have wine and whiskey. As for girls, you will have to earn that with hard work, very hard work. Wakarimasu ka?"

There was more laughter. Matsugoro had found a bottle of spirits stashed behind some drinking glasses on the cabinet shelf. It was a small bottle with a medallion insignia on the label and obviously had been saved by the hotel staff for a special occasion. Behind the bar were several small shot glasses. Matsugoro poured from the bottle for everyone near the bar.

Schnell lifted his little glass of dark liquid as did about a dozen others.

"Kanpai!" they shouted out together. "Kanpai!"

The glasses banged back down on the bar. Schnell tried to look into all the faces that he could see.

"It will be a long journey tomorrow. We have to board a riverboat that will take us to Sacramento. From there I will hire wagons to take us to our new home. With luck we will arrive at our new home by the following nightfall."

Schnell got up slowly, showing the wear of his long day of travel. Jou joined him at the stairs, followed by Okei carrying little Frances with me. Our people began to leave for their rooms to try to get some rest before the journey that would begin in the morning. I suddenly felt tired, knowing that I would be facing a day like no other I had ever experienced. Not often in life is one able to go home for the first time.

CHAPTER 7
Journey To A New Home

We gathered together in the storage shed that was attached to the back of the hotel. This had been our usual custom in the morning since our arrival in San Francisco. None of us could find any appetite for the asagohan that these foreigners, I mean native people, devoured each morning. Of the four families with us, one would steam enough rice in the hotel room for the rest of us. Daigoro oka-san brought down the community bottle of soy sauce that she had been entrusted with. We had used the last jar of pickled vegetables long ago so there was nothing to add to the rice but the soy sauce and some questionable meat that had been purchased from a street vendor.

We sat at the two long tables and passed the pot of steaming rice from one to another. The soy sauce and meat mixture was then handed around. There was a kettle of hot green tea brewing on each of the tables.

One of the seats sat empty and everyone looked around to see who was missing. It was Dr. Matsumoto.

"Did he not get back from the Barbary Coast place?" someone asked with concern.

"Let's hope he did not do something so foolish. Could finding a woman to lie with be so important at his advanced age? I hope he was not shanghaied."

A few laughed but the feeling of this morning was more subdued than the night before. Schnell and Jou had not yet arrived from their room. It was of no surprise that many eyes turned to Matsu who had been so quiet the past night.

"He told me that he was going to the Shina-machi," Matsu said barely above a whisper. He cleared his throat and spoke louder. "Matsumoto-sensei was concerned about the kinds of sickness that we might find in this uncultivated world. He wanted to find herbs and kusuri to have in case of sickness."

People ate from their bowls in silence for a moment. Another kettle of hot tea was brought out by the family oka-san.

"Matsumoto-sensei is a very wise man," one person commented. "I am glad that he is looking out for us."

"Hai," another said, and there were also many grunts of agreement.

It was only a moment later that Schnell came into the room and stood before the head of the main table that was reserved for him and Jou. He unfolded a large paper and used his hands to flatten it down in front of him.

"It is about us!" he proudly proclaimed. "This is going out to every town in California. They'll be reading about us from here to Timbuctoo!"

No one knew the precise location of Timbuctoo, but it was obviously a place very far away. Those sitting close leaned over to have a look while several people left their seats to gaze at the paper. Matsugoro put on his eyeglasses. No one could read the strange small lettering but everyone seemed to be impressed.

"Shimbun, ne?"

"Yes, but this is very much more. This is the Alta California, the biggest newspaper in the entire state! The reporter I talked to, Hudson, wrote a very nice story about us. This means we need to get our tea and mulberry plants in the ground as soon as possible. The orders will be coming almost before we are able to unpack."

Now even more fascinated, everyone continued to stare at the small printed letters.

"Read some of what the words say, Schnell-sama."

Schnell lifted up the paper and twenty-two pairs of eyes followed up and focused intently on him.

"It says the Japanese are very proud people. They are well dressed, dignified, and believe in the value of hard work. They do not take kindly to mistreatment, and it is an error to treat them like the Chinese."

"Yes, we fight back!" came a shout from behind.

"We lop off their heads!" Kuni said with a laugh.

Schnell was scanning down the long column before stopping for a moment to read and comprehend what it said. It was about his wife, Jou.

"Herr Schnell's wife is as attractive and dainty as ever it is possible to be. She is dressed in a fine and colorful native silk garment called a kimono. It is of such splendid and brilliant colors that it brings to mind visions of the most exquisite dawns and dusks, every bit as beautiful as anything in the natural world." He translated as much as he could to Japanese.

Jou demurely turned away as faces turned to gaze at her. Schnell gave her a fond hug that kept her from dashing away. Some even clapped their hands in the American way of appreciation.

Jou's face was crimson.

John Henry Schnell folded up the paper. Suddenly he brought his fist down sharply on the table. The noise caused everyone to jump, except for the three samurai, Matsu, Kuni, and Nishijawa.

"Ladies and Gentlemen, we have been refugees from our homeland for too long. It has been a long journey to get here, but we have endured. Tomorrow we are going to our new home!"

"Banzai! Banzai! Banzai!" Everyone cried out in unison.

Our entire group, except for Dr. Matsumoto, gathered in front of the hotel to wait for the wagon that would take us to our ship at the wharf. For me, this was the first time to see everyone at once. What an impressive and large group we were! Every person was dressed in their best Western clothes. In addition, there were the bags and boxes that each of us had, along with a small mountain of luggage piled next to Schnell-san and Jou.

At that moment, I could not help but feel grateful to the Buddha for our safe journey thus far. I felt great optimism that we would be successful in this strange new world. Why would I not? We had brave samurai to protect us, capable carpenters to build our shelters, and experienced farmers to plant and care for our crops. We had families to nurture children, a physician to cure our ailments, and John Henry Schnell to lead us. We had everything we needed to overcome any challenge that could possibly arise.

We tried to ignore the people who stared at us as they walked by, except for Kuni who returned a broad smile to each of them. Many would then crinkle their noses and walk away even faster.

Finally a wagon stopped before us. It was a very small wagon. Eager to commence our journey, everyone stepped forward before suddenly stopping. The tiny-wheeled vehicle was no larger than a handcart. Only two people could sit on the front seat, and there were no seats at all in the small luggage space. After a moment of staring in disbelief, Schnell-san took charge by ordering all of our luggage placed on the back. He then helped Jou up to the seat and followed her onto the wagon. Okei handed Frances to Jou.

"You will need to walk to the wharf," he said. "It is at pier 13. I will hold the ship as long as possible, but you must go quickly." With that, the Schnells and the wagon left the twenty-two colonists behind. Some stepped out into the street to observe the departing wagon but had to quickly jump back onto the boardwalk when a following wagon almost ran over them from behind.

Matsu did not even turn to watch them disappear into the distance. He continued to stare into the empty air where Schnell had looked down upon them. One by one, the eyes of the colonists began to turn to him.

"So desu," he said after a moment, at last turning to the east. "Ikimasho."

Eee, even my legs were aching when we finally arrived at the pier. Of course, I was stashed at the top of Okei's backpack and hadn't taken a single step. But I had felt Okei's efforts as if they had been my own. Even though the distance was not great, having to hurry across the innumerable obstacles in our way had been a great challenge. Each of the many buildings along the street had a raised board walkway that had steps ascending and then descending, like going up and then down a mountain. Often steps were missing or broken. The walkways were full of holes where previous footsteps had crashed down to the earth two or three feet below. Weaving around these many obstacles at least doubled the distance we had to cover. Going out onto the street had not been an option. The brown, gray, and black sludge on the entire traveling surface reminded us too much of the scum of the open cesspools that overflowed into the river back home. The smell was also very similar.

Schnell-san was happy to see that we had found the boat and ushered us up the small plank walk. Once we were onboard, his face broke into a broad smile and he waved to the wheelhouse where the pilot was watching.

"Matte, Schnell-san," Matsu ran up to him after he had been the last to board.

Schnell's smile began to fade as he looked anxiously at him.

"Doctor Matsumoto went to the China town. He has not returned."

Schnell's puzzled expression demanded more explanation.

"He told me that he wanted to get Chinese medicine. There are diseases here that we do not have in Japan."

Schnell began to frantically wave at the wheelhouse. No one was there. He ran to the walking bridge and grabbed it as the deck mate was about to cast it out. Just at that moment, Dr. Matsumoto walked onto the plank carrying a large canvas bag in both his hands. He didn't seem to be in any particular hurry, even though the walkway was untied and beginning to angle away from the boat.

Schnell had to grab onto the doctor's coat to help him step over the opening chasm between the plank and the boat. A split second later, the plank splashed into the bay below.

"Arigato," Dr. Matsumoto said down to Schnell, who had landed on his hands and knees on the deck. The doctor headed into the boat cabin with his bag, not the least concerned about helping Schnell back to his feet.

Our journey resumed once again. This segment upriver to Sacramento was only 125 miles. Our small steam powered paddlewheel boat sped up the bay and into the river channel. As the river narrowed and the current became more forceful against us, our travel pace slackened. The black smoke from the boiler stacks became thicker and the paddlewheel pace quickened. Still, we barely seemed to be moving against the current.

The slower pace was a welcomed development for many us. Perhaps the long stay in San Francisco had lulled us into believing that the journey was complete. After all, we had traveled 4800 miles across the Pacific Ocean and only a tiny fraction of that distance remained to reach our new home. Many of us had found comfort staying in San Francisco, knowing that our old homeland was no farther away today than it had been yesterday. If life in the new land proved to be too difficult, or the desire for the homeland too great, return was only a ticket purchase away. Now that we were moving east again, further into the depths of the new land with many more twists and turns in-between, the possibility of a return seemed less likely.

In many ways, we were like the river that was beneath us. On the surface, it was placid and pond like. There were no waves and the water made very little sound. But one look at the shoreline revealed the immense current that our little boat was fighting against. The entire earth that we were on seemed to be receding downward to the ocean, and only the boat's churning paddlewheel and overworked engine kept us barely ahead of the abyss.

Inside, like the river, we were tormented.

"It is quiet, but not quiet," Okei said to no one in particular as she gazed at the barely moving shoreline.

Matsu was the only one close enough to hear her words. He walked closer to her before stopping a few feet away. Okei was not referring to the natural quiet of the river journey, he knew, but instead was commenting about the quiet that had descended among the people on the ship.

"So desu. We are beginning to understand the hard nature of our task."

Okei continued looking at the passing shoreline. Mostly there were scrubby trees along the naturally cut embankment. Once in a while, wooden posts and a pier stuck out into the river. A road would lead up the slope to trees partially hiding immense white mansions, bigger than any home ever built in Japan and larger than many castles.

"We will never return to our homes," Okei said.

"That was never our purpose."

"Lord Matsudaira will not be coming here, and the people of Aizu will not be following us. We are alone."

"If they do not come, it is not a bad thing. We will still make a new Aizu here."

A boat that looked like the one they rode on passed by going in the opposite direction. Carried by the current, it was but a blur as it quickly disappeared around a bend behind them.

"What will our American neighbors be like, Matsu? What will they think of us?"

"I do not know. Schnell-san says that they appreciate those who work hard to succeed. If we work hard and succeed, they will appreciate us."

"How can you be so sure? I have only heard how uncivilized and wild this land is. I don't know if there is a place for me in it."

Matsu stood closer, their shoulders almost touching. Trying to get her to look at him, he found that she would not.

"Okei, you will find your place here. More so in the darkest places, sunshine is always welcomed."

Okei at last gazed into his eyes and their hands touched.

The afternoon began to feel much warmer on this clear spring day as the many hours on the river passed. Kuninosuke was at the rear of the boat where the cloth overhang stopped just short of where he was sitting. He shaded his eyes and finally wrapped a piece of cloth around his head. Still he felt too warm. He took off his over shirt, and then his undershirt as the temperature continued to climb.

Dr. Matsumoto, who had been seated in the covered shade, walked over and sat in the seat next to Kuni. Kuni pretended to be asleep so he would not be disturbed. Normally, he would relish any kind of conversation, but his mood had also soured since they had left San Francisco. How could it not, with everyone on board clammed up in retrospection? Let them worry themselves silly, he thought to himself. There was nothing more to be done than to face each challenge as it arose. He would concern himself about tomorrow in the morning.

"Kuninosuke, I was hoping to share some delightful conversation with you."

Kuni opened one eye and turned his head towards Matsumoto-sensei.

"There does not seem to be much delight this day," Kuni said.

Dr. Matsumoto laughed. "You and I are too crafty to be so downcast, ne? Life for adventurers is always challenging and never boring. We can't wait to see what the next day brings."

Kuni had to smile. He was beginning to feel better already and stretched out in his seat. Dr. Matsumoto poked him on the side with his elbow.

"Okei-san is at the front of the boat. You know that she cannot see you here."

Kuni had to engage his mind for a moment to understand what he was talking about.

"Oh, my shirt! Oh no, Okei, no, she was not on my mind. I was just hot."

As Dr. Matsumoto laughed again, Kuni noticed that the doctor was wearing a heavy long sleeve shirt and full-length dungarees. He also wore a wide brim hat.

"You are not hot? Back in Aizu, there is probably snow still on the ground. Already this climate is like our summer, still a month away."

Dr. Matsumoto leaned closer to him and spoke in a softer voice.

"Yes, I am hot also, but there are hidden dangers here that we might not be aware of. For now, I suggest covering your skin as much as you can."

Kuni lifted himself up and did not even notice that he was itching the back of his shoulder.

"Ah, you are worried about the American women! Yes, they might not be able to control their desires the first time they see a shirtless Aizu man!"

As Kuni put his shirt back on, he noticed that Dr. Matsumoto smiled but was not laughing as he was. He patted his friend on the shoulder.

"I will seriously consider your suggestion," Kuni told him. "I know that you are always thinking about our health and safety. We are fortunate to have you with us."

Kuni bowed low and the doctor bowed in return.

An hour before arriving in Sacramento, the boat stopped at a place called Walnut Grove that was the first established community that they had come upon. A church with a tall white steeple marked the beginning of the town and another at the far end marked the end. In between, there was a school, a post office with the town name boldly written on the front, and several smaller white painted buildings.

The passengers had a brief time to examine the settlement as crewmembers began bringing firewood from a large pile next to the river. Further up on the street were vendors selling various kinds of fruits and vegetables, many different types the colonists had never seen before. John Henry Schnell went to each vendor with a sack, purchasing pears, carrots, and tomatoes. One vendor was selling the juice squeezed from oranges, and Dr. Matsumoto stood in front of it imploring the colonists to drink the golden liquid.

The sun was setting as their boat at last docked in Sacramento. Each of the colonists stopped abruptly just a few feet from the end of the landing platform. There were carriages and wagons going off in every which direction and no one knew which way to go. John Henry Schnell, carrying several heavy sacks, was still struggling to get off the boat.

"Migi ikinasai" Schnell shouted when he saw the backlog of bodies on the docking platform.

Everyone was exhausted. Several colonists had reddened skin from the sun exposure and many were furiously itching rashes of insect bites sustained on exposed arms and legs.

Schnell stopped a passing wagon and got the driver to take our luggage to the closest hotel. The group trudged along together, not even caring about the many curious spying eyes. Many slept without dinner that night.

The next day's travel was the final one of our long journey from Japan. Schnell-san hired three freight wagons and a driver. Matsu and Schnell would be the other drivers. We started early, hoping to arrive before dark.

The sun was high overhead and barely casting any shadows when we finally stopped for our first rest by a small grove of oak trees. Brakes were set and the colonists slowly made their way to the trees. Blankets were set down and many sat or laid prone to ease the aches caused by hours on the hard rutted road.

Okei used an iron ladle to scoop lukewarm tea from the barrel on the side of the first wagon. In her hand she held the small porcelain teacup with pink flowers that she had found in the satchel that her mother had left in the castle room. It had numerous chips acquired from years of use and washing, but the lip was still smooth and it was one of the most treasured items she had retained in this new world. A vision of her mother began to form in her mind before she could shake her head and stop any more of those thoughts from taking root.

"I am not a farmer," she heard someone talking loudly from underneath one of the trees as she sipped the sweet, tepid tea. "I should have slipped away in Yokohama and returned to my family. I pray to the Buddha every night that they forgive me for the foolish and stupid decisions that I have made."

Okei walked away from that tree, hoping to find a more restful place to drink her tea. She began to hear another voice from nearby.

". . . should have come here ten years ago during the rush for gold! We could have become rich and returned to Japan as aristocrats! Eee. The gold is all gone! We are too late. All hope is gone. We will never make enough money to return to our families."

There were no more trees under which she could peacefully lay. Okei sat out in the sun. She unwrapped more of the paper around a small rice ball and was nibbling on it when she noticed dust coming from the direction their horses and wagons were pointed. Everyone stopped to see what was happening.

A rider was coming fast on the road toward them. Matsu was already at the lead wagon holding his sheathed sword in his hand. Henry Schnell reached into the adjacent wagon and grabbed a pistol from the floorboard.

Without time to think, Okei was fearful that an Imperial soldier was approaching to intercept them. It hadn't occurred to her in that instant how unlikely that would be, now that her old homeland and the dreaded Satsuma were thousands of miles of ocean water away.

The rider wore all black clothing and was mounted on a large black horse. On seeing the party of people grabbing for their weapons, he came off his horse and momentarily stood still. He held his arms up and forward, open hands pointed outward, and slowly began to approach the colonists.

Henry Schnell walked out to meet him with the two samurai, Matsu and Nishijawa, close behind with hands on their sword hilts.

"I am a man of peace and a man of God," the man spoke in a clear deep voice. "I came to see the party from Japan that everyone is talking about."

Schnell was momentarily stunned by what he had just heard. Matsu and Nishijawa stared at him for a clue of what they should do.

"You come from Gold Hill?" Schnell's voice stammered. "They know about us?"

"Of course," the man in black answered. "You are the talk of the whole region."

He reached out his hand. Schnell came closer, then shook it with his left hand as his other was still holding the pistol. Seeing the pistol, he put it awkwardly back into his waistband. The two samurai and the others who had watched tensely finally began to relax.

"I am Reverend Peter Cool. You have a fine looking group of people, Mister. . . "

"Herr Schnell. John Henry Schnell."

Schnell led Reverend Cool to the shade of the oak trees where the other colonists stood. The man was half a head taller than Schnell and was an impressive sight for many of the Japanese who gathered around him. His dark coat had a white frock collar and the white sleeves of his shirt shown at his wrists.

Jou stood with little Frances and Okei as Schnell introduced them to Reverend Cool.

Before Schnell said any words, the Reverend's eyes met Okei's. As he stopped before her, Schnell involuntarily steered him toward his wife. The Reverend's eyes then turned to the child between them.

"A little sister is on the way, I see," he said as he stooped to look at Frances, and looked back at Jou. Frances smiled at the strange, giant man. Jou put a hand to her face. "Her name will be Mary, like our blessed Virgin."

Schnell kept his composure but was clearly startled by the

Reverend's observant eye. He had only learned himself just prior to the meeting with Lord Matsudaira. How had the Reverend known?

"We expect it to be five months," he said after a moment, looking around to see if any of the others had understood what was said. "We haven't even thought of a name. . . "

The male colonists seemed to be clueless, but Okei had her eyes fixed on Jou's stomach. She then put her hands to her face. Okei realized that she had also known. Soon others were looking at Jou and talking and smiling.

Reverend Cool recognized that his observation had caused quite a commotion and tried to remedy the situation.

"As I said, I am a man of God. To serve Him faithfully, I have become good at learning about people by what they look like, or what they say. I hope I have not offended anyone by giving out unexpected news."

Schnell, realizing the error in keeping the secret to himself, was heartened by the sight of the colonists gathering about Jou to give her congratulations. It came to his mind that he hadn't seen so much happiness since they had left Japan. For once, he also felt a hopeful spirit rising above the turmoil of these last few months. He saw that the Reverend was also smiling.

"Reverend, you are the bearer of only good news," Schnell said with the first smile he had shown since San Francisco. "There is so much we want to know about our new home. Please honor us by sharing some of our food and spirits."

"Oh, no spirits, I'm afraid. But I have heard much about the delicious food of the Japans."

They spent far more time in that grove of oak trees than they had planned. A rejuvenated Schnell asked Reverend Cool many questions as the other colonists watched, and the Reverend answered as best as he could. With Schnell too absorbed in the conversation to translate, however, the others were left to only speculate on what was being said. Many decided to spend their time gathering belongings under the trees in preparation for the final part of their journey.

Okei was stacking together the small lacquered trays of her lunch box when the Reverend sought her out. Surprised that he had come to see her, she could only think that he was still hungry. She offered him a nori wrapped rice ball and a cup of tea. He gladly accepted, and motioned her to a place under one of the oak trees.

She hesitated and suddenly felt an overwhelming need to avoid this man. The feeling confused her, and only slowly, reluctantly, she followed him.

He squatted down while eating the rice ball and Okei also lowered herself out of politeness and respect.

"You understand English," he said to her. "Wakarimasu, ne?"

"Yes," her mind answered without thinking. Had he really spoken Japanese, to further confuse her? Had she answered him with "yes?" It hadn't occurred to her until now that sometimes English and Japanese sounded the same. It was as if the thoughts being conveyed crossed into her mind even if her ears could not decipher the words. How could that be possible? Her abilities couldn't possibly be growing, could they? She only wished to remain simple and humble, bound by honor and duty to her Lord and her family, free of unwanted burdens and responsibilities.

"You are very special," he said, raising a long finger toward her.

A look of shock and surprise filled her face. She shook her head and stood up.

"No. I am simple girl. Baby sit for Schnell-san." The English words came out of her with hardly any thought. How could he possibly know about her? Was his God so all seeing?

Reverend Cool stood up and towered over Okei. He leaned down with his hands to his knees to try to make her look at him. He knew that he was making her uncomfortable but at that moment he was more concerned about learning as much as he could about this uncommon girl.

"I knew about Herr Schnell's wife just by looking at her face, and when I saw you I got a feeling that you did, also. God gave me this ability so that I can help him spread his message in this world. Your God, the Buddha, I think, did the same for you."

Okei could not look into his searching eyes.

"No! Not true. Not special." She was getting more and more confused by the minute. She had to get away from this man before he made her learn too much about herself.

She started to walk back to the wagons hoping to find a moment of solitude in which to think, but Reverend Cool followed beside her.

"I have felt this before," he was saying to her. "There are others like us across the land. Not just preachers like me. I speak for the Lord but there are common people like you, doing deeds to help his children."

"I did not know of Schnell-san's wife as you did." Okei saw people staring at them from the wagons. "I only knew after you told us."

Reverend Cool did not want to keep arguing with her. "It's not our place to know everything. The Lord only lets us know when we can be of His service."

Okei did not add that she had quickly sensed Jou's pregnancy after Reverend Cool had mentioned it. She also had known that it was a girl.

In the far distance, in another world it seemed, Schnell's voice called for everyone to return to the wagons. A moment later, Matsu called out her name, having seen her and the Reverend still together in the oak grove below.

"You are here to help your people," the Reverend spoke to her. "The Lord did not mean it as a burden, but as a blessing. One day you will realize that this is true."

She looked directly into his eyes. She didn't know why she reached out to touch his face, but she did. Immediately she cast her gaze down and ran to the wagons. She passed by a startled Matsu without saying a word.

The sun had set many hours before when we crested the last hill blocking the view of our new home. The sky was indigo blue and the world was visible only in different shades of gray.

"We are here!" Kuni called out when the wagons stopped, but it was difficult to make out any details of the scene that surrounded them.

With only a few hushed words, we disembarked from the wagons and began to untie the ropes and canvas that covered our belongings. The plants and tools in the other wagons would be left until tomorrow. The door of the house was open as we entered, each of us seeing the broken windows and feeling the coldness of the dark interior. Brooms were used to sweep the dust and broken glass in the main room and sleeping futons were unfurled on the bare floor.

As tired as we were, it was hard for anyone to get much sleep that night.

CHAPTER 8
New Day At The Wakamatsu Tea And Silk Colony

I was awakened by a most peculiar sound. As my ever-open eyes began to fill with the sights around me, the sound happened again. It seemed to be a voice and I tried to understand what it was saying. However, it did not seem to be a human voice. It must be an animal, I thought. Could it be dangerous to us? Perhaps it devoured only cloth and was only a threat to dresses and dolls!

There was a rush of sound in the larger room where most of the men had been sleeping. The front door opened and slammed closed two successive times. A commotion was happening right outside the wall of the house. Okei sat upright and listened, ready to jump to her feet if required. I tried to bury myself deeper into my wrapping blanket.

The door slammed once again and someone entered. Okei rose as others came from different parts of the house. Kuninosuke's voice rose above all the other voices.

"This rooster will not be waking us in the morning any more!" he said in an excited, high-pitched voice. He held up the dead bird by its talons, its head swinging freely because of its broken neck.

Kuni started to approach Okei, but stopped when she backed up in revulsion. Instead, he handed the bird to Matsugoro's wife who, unfortunately, was standing close by. "Chicken teriyaki for lunch, ne? I am ready for some meat!"

That was how our first day in the new world began.

The sky that greeted us when we went outside was vivid blue and cloudless. Many of the colonists stopped on the expanded front porch and gazed at it in wonder.

"I do not remember it being so blue in Japan."

"Uso. It is the same sky here as at home."

"This is our new home!"

Schnell-san appeared from where the wagons were left and motioned for everyone to follow him to the back of the house. In his hand he appeared to be holding a long stick or pole.

At the back of the farmhouse, one of our men was using a shovel to dig a hole. It was Matsunosuke! Many stared in disbelief. A samurai was doing peasant labor! This was undoubtedly proof that the old values had been left thousands of miles of ocean water behind. In the old world, farmers and merchants and common people bowed deeply with their faces to the dirt whenever a samurai would pass by. Being even slightly tardy could result in losing one's head. Here, samurai shoveled dirt.

"It is deep enough, Matsu," Schnell tapped him on the shoulder and Matsu nodded and stepped aside. The people of the Wakamatsu Tea and Silk Colony gathered around as Schnell turned to face them.

"Yesterday, we concluded a long journey," Schnell began. Uncomfortable for once, he cleared his throat and scanned eyes of the twenty-one people before him. He had to clear his throat again.

"We left Japan on April 25, 1869. Last night, Thursday, June 7, we arrived at our new home in America."

Schnell tried to keep his voice slow and controlled, but it was obvious that he was having difficulty due to the emotions that he was feeling. Many eyes were cast down, not wanting to see their leader enduring so much discomfort.

"It has been a long journey for all of us. I have seen this moment in my dreams many times. I've seen the same hills and the same land."

His voice was fading with every word. Schnell took a deep breath, wiped some unseen irritant from his eyes, and forced himself to continue on.

"I am sorry to say that I had my doubts. I questioned if I were worthy enough to ask for so much sacrifice from all the brave people before me. Even now, I am still not sure. All I really can do is continue to ask for your sacrifice, and pledge to you that I will always do my best and never let you down."

The leaves continued to rustle in the wind, again the voice of silence.

"Today is Friday, June 8," he gathered himself and was able to speak forcefully, causing everyone to suddenly look up. "We will know this date forever as the first day of the Wakamatsu Tea and Silk Colony!"

He raised his arms high and the others did so in unison. "Banzai!" some shouted. Others clapped, or shed tears. I could do none of these things.

Schnell picked up the stick that he had placed at his feet. It was not a stick but one of the sapling trees that had been brought from Japan. There were nearly a thousand tea plants and half as many mulberry trees in the wagons. They had also brought gomma trees, citrus trees, and one keyaki tree. It was the keyaki that he held in his hand. Some of its tiny leaves had already begun to show. He raised the sapling before him.

"A thousand year old keyaki grows at the heart of Aizu. Many generations have passed under its sheltering limbs. It has been the symbol of our way of life, lasting when everything else has fallen."

Schnell stopped and looked above the colonists at the land and the mountains in the distant west. Perhaps he was trying to see the Aizu country in the new land. His eyes returned to the colonists.

"When I was leaving, I had to go through the center of our town that the Imperial troops had burned. Everything seemed to be destroyed, until I turned a corner and saw the keyaki tree, still standing in the middle of smoking ruins. "

Schnell stooped down and held the small trunk between his fingers as Matsu shoveled dirt into the hole. Matsu packed the ground encircling it. The little tree stood straight and lofty at the height of Schnell's waist as he rose.

At that moment, a small wiry older man the colonists only knew as Tanaka came to stand beside Schnell. To our great surprise, he wore the black robe and cap of a Shinto priest. All along, we had assumed that he had been a fisherman because he did not seem to be blessed with any other notable talents.

Tanaka-sensei placed his hands together, cradling a bright orange prayer bead. He chanted softly for a moment then bowed at the waist towards the little tree. Everyone else did, also. Tanaka then slowly retreated behind Schnell.

A wind came up and rustled the leaves of the nearby oak trees, the only sounds in the encompassing silence.

"A thousand years from now, our descendants will come here and see the keyaki," Schnell continued, as he gazed around at the colonists. "They will remember us and what we have done. Ganbatte!"

"Ganbatte!" came twenty-one other voices into the wind.

Most of the people went back into the house to begin the process of cleaning and repair. At midday, Okei left me to play with Frances and found a pail that she filled with well water. As she went outside to water the keyaki tree, I knew that she had also noticed the three men who had been watching us from the small hill to the west.

The new people came up until they were standing beside her. Okei put down the pail and bowed low in a formal greeting to strangers.

"Ohayo-gozaimasu," she said automatically, and then realized that they could not possibly understand her words.

Two of the men attempted a short stiff bow. The younger man seemed confused by the ritual.

"Guten morgen," the older man replied, standing straight and towering over Okei even though he was no more than average height for an American. He was heavy set with grey hair tinged with black, and a large wrinkled face with a streaked beard. He wore a wide brim light-colored hat, as did the younger man.

"We come to see if we can help fix up the house," the one who seemed to be the father of the others explained. "Old Graner, he has been gone a long time and he left the place to run down. It is no way to start a new life."

That she could comprehend what he said no longer came as a surprise to her. She did not know every word, but it didn't diminish her understanding. Thoughts of talking to the Reverend came back into her mind. Confusion returned. She felt frustration as she tried to smile at the new people.

"Dad, you're talking way too fast. Our language is as foreign to them as German is to me. Let me try." The other son, taller and leaner than his father and clean-shaven with long dark hair, bent down slightly to make eye contact with Okei.

"We are here to help, do work." His smile was what Okei noticed the most.

"Wakarimasu," she answered. Had she spoken in Japanese or English? She had no idea. She was still trying to deal with her confusion when she saw Schnell-san and Matsu-san approaching from the backside of the house. Relieved, she pointed towards them.

"Schnell-san will talk with you. He is boss. We appreciate you help for us."

The father turned to the approaching men but the younger man's eyes lingered on Okei. He continued to smile. Her eyes were locked to his and she found herself powerless to turn away. Finally with all the strength she could summon, she was able to move her head slightly down. She hurriedly tried to remember what she had been doing before this interruption had occurred. Her mind went blank. He was still smiling!

Okei watched as Schnell and the older man shook hands and patted each other on the back. Schnell introduced Matsu who took his hand off the hilt of his sword to shake his hand. They were exchanging words, but she couldn't make out what was being said, not even in her mind. It seemed to be a friendly conversation. Some of the words seemed to be from their common German homeland.

The handsome dark-haired young man was still smiling at her!

"That's my dad, Francis Veerkamp. My name is Henry. We are

your neighbors, over there." He pointed to a white painted house just visible among trees at the foot of a large hill.

"I am Okei," she was able to say. She followed his finger and could see the color of some fruit trees in blossom near the house.

"You are farming?"

"Yeah, we try, anyway. Right now the only thing we seem to be good at is making our family bigger and bigger."

Okei couldn't stifle a giggle.

Henry's admiration for her was growing by the second.

"Okei, I find it hard to believe that you understand English. I bet you never took no schooling for it either, did you?"

Okei was set to answer when she realized the truth of what he had just said. Of course she had not studied English. She hadn't even heard a single English word until she began baby sitting for Frances a year ago. What was happening was just too improbable to believe. Perhaps all this was a dream, and she was really back in Japan, drinking tea and laughing with her brothers.

Henry noticed her hesitation and seemed to be trying to read her mind. Just at that moment, a small one-horse wagon approached on the narrow little road that reached out from the distant house. Henry saw it and recognized the driver.

"Ma must've finished baking the stuff she had in the oven. It's our present to our new neighbors. Let's go down and get some before she gives it all away."

Henry took Okei's hand hoping to guide her to meet his mother, but Okei instinctively withdrew it. He tried not to show his feeling of surprise.

"Oh, I'm sorry. Just being an uncultured fool, I guess. I forget they probably don't do that in your country."

Okei nodded to him and side-by-side they walked down to the wagon that had stopped at the front of the house.

Louisa Veerkamp was a slightly shorter version of her husband, with a serious taut face that belied the kind heart that beat within her stout frame. With the help of her husband, the two unloaded three large red linen covered baskets and took them into the house. A table was retrieved from the barn. Mrs. Veerkamp had even brought a starched white cloth that raised dust into the air when it was unfurled onto the table. Plates appeared from somewhere and were set on one end of the table.

A couple of hungry young colony men were already in line. Then Louisa and Francis lifted the red coverings from the baskets. It was hard to tell which traveled faster, the aroma through the air or the vision of the hot, fresh baked biscuits. Immediately the remainder of the colonists started coming from every which direction to crowd into the lengthening line.

Louisa positioned herself at the end of the table with a small metal tub filled with butter and another with wild berry jam. She was using a short spatula to show them how to slice the biscuits to put in the butter and jam.

Okei and Henry had come the farthest from the side of the house and their tardiness meant that they had to share the last remaining biscuit. Henry split it in half on his plate and put butter and jam on each side.

As they were going back outside, another wagon stopped in front of the house. A young man and a boy jumped off, each carrying a long bottle filled with dark liquid in his hand. They stopped when they saw Okei and Henry, and each did a painfully polite bow.

"My uncultured baby brothers, Egbert and William," Henry introduced them. "This is Okei-san."

"Konnichiwa," the older of the two said.

"Itadakimasu," Okei answered.

The young man and boy quickly left to go into the house.

Francis took the bottles they had brought then realized that they didn't have any cups. The Japanese understood the situation immediately and soon were showing up with various teacups that they had brought.

He watched as they tasted the liquid.

"Juice from apples," he said, seeing the smiles as the sweet taste made a favorable impression.

Francis took the last bottle and found Schnell in the master bedroom. A double-sized bed was the only furniture in the room, so Schnell was sitting on the bed and reading the papers that Francis had brought.

Francis took out a couple of small glass cups from his coat pocket and gave one to Schnell. He poured the dark liquid for both of them.

"It is from my own grapes," he smiled. "The world hasn't found out about our vintage yet, but I promise you that it soon will."

Schnell took a sip from his glass. The sweetness of the wine did not help the sour taste in his mouth.

"This is $1000 more than we had agreed upon. You know that I will have to build a canal to get water to our tea plants."

"It is good land, John. Ja, there is some initial expense, but with the wonderful workers that you have, you will be able to recoup it in a few years. Why, next year alone, you will have made several thousand in profit."

Schnell crossed his arms and laid the papers aside. He ran his fingers through his hair.

"I am not the businessman that my brother, Edward, is. I am only trying to do what is best for my people, and I just want to see that they get a good start on the life here."

He got off the bed and went to the window at the south end of the room. The panes were broken and he felt a slight wind in his face. He could see the little tree that they had just planted.

"Things have changed so much. When I was there, in Japan, I never thought that it would all end. I led troops into battle. I fought alongside the greatest samurai of them all. One day I even had an audience with the Emperor, and made the American ambassador rewrite a trade treaty. It was not that long ago. . . "

"You will find success here too, John, I know this. You will become the father of the silk industry in California. Your tea will be sought by everyone in America. You will sell your fruits and vegetables from here to San Francisco."

Schnell smiled before he turned around and picked up the papers on the bed. He wetted the ink and signed his name on the two sheets.

Francis Veerkamp took the papers and shook Schnell's hand.

"My sons and I will help you get things started. You will have nothing to worry about."

After he left, Schnell went to look at the broken windowpane.

He was thinking of measuring it when he noticed the folded banner that had been unpacked and placed on a small table. At the same time he remembered the long pole that he had seen in the barn. He was going out the front door as Matsugoro was coming in. Matsugoro's face brightened when he saw the banner. Other workers also stopped in their tracks.

"There's a pole in the barn," Schnell told him. As Matsugoro quickly left and Schnell waited, he felt a tug on the bottom of his pants. Gazing down, he saw something dark on the stair by his foot. Instinctively he kicked out his leg and contacted something furry that was sent flying to the earth several feet below.

Not until it stood glaring back at him did he recognize it as a cat. It didn't seem to be hurt except for a bit of wounded dignity.

"Sorry," Schnell spoke down to it. "I thought there was something dangerous down there. Obviously, there is not."

The cat, dark with white legs and forehead, sat on its haunches and now stared instead of glared.

"Neko o mite" came Okei's voice, and Schnell turned to see her and little Frances standing a short distance away. Frances was giggling as she pointed her arm at the animal. Okei tried to keep her hand from getting too close.

"Where did it come from?"

"It suddenly was by my boot," Schnell shrugged. "I thought it was a wild animal and kicked it away. Lucky for it, I didn't have my sword or pistol."

In an instant Okei was kneeling and petting the cat. Before Schnell could warn Frances to be careful, she was petting it also. The cat pushed its head into their hands in return.

"It is not wild," Okei told Schnell.

"Obviously."

As Frances held me, the Neko came and sniffed me, recognized me, and rubbed against me as well. It was as if our souls had connected again after a long period of separation.

Schnell was watching all this so intently that he hadn't noticed Henry Veerkamp and Matsugoro in front of him with the long pole.

Breaking out of the spell, Schnell showed the two men where he wanted the pole. Matsugoro left to get a shovel. Henry noticed the cat, now in Frances's death hug. The cat didn't seem to be minding the affectionate attention, however. It limply let itself be engulfed into the girl's arms.

"Well, Holy Christ," Henry smiled. "The Graners must have abandoned him when they left two months ago."

"Nani? It lived here by itself for two months?" Okei asked in mixed English and Japanese but Henry had no trouble understanding this, or anything, that Okei said.

"I suppose so. None of us have been over here in that time. He's one tough or lucky little fellow, that's for sure."

Okei had knelt down to the level of the cat and was rubbing faces with the animal. The cat's eyes were blissfully closed.

"Well, now we have our designated rat trapper," Henry smiled broadly. "There's a mess of them in the garage that he can start feasting on."

Okei got up and the cat continued looking at her and Frances in turn. Its capacity for absorbing and giving love hadn't been completely satisfied even yet.

"No rats, Neko will live and eat as one of us," Okei said firmly, looking into its contented eyes. "Be assured that you will have no more troubles in your life."

Frances clapped her hands. The cat purred noisily.

The banner was tied to the pole and the pole hoisted. The ground was packed. Slightly angled into a breeze, it fully unfurled its entire gold tasseled splendor.

Matsu, now dressed in American style work clothes, was the first to stop before it. He gazed down, then bowed formally from the hip. The young samurai, Nishijawa, then came and knelt beside him. Kuninosuke, farther away near the barn, saw what was happening and came as swiftly as he could move in his leather shoes.

Matsugoro and his wife stood behind the three men, as others appeared beside them.

Schnell stood for a moment, and then dropped to the ground with Nishijawa. Matsu and Kuni then knelt, also. They bowed deeply with their palms to the ground. Those still standing lowered their heads and bowed.

It only lasted for a moment. No words were said.

Matsu and Schnell remained standing together as everyone else departed for their duties. The movement of the flag's elegant silk fabric in the wind seemed to hypnotize them.

"Many died for this flag," at last Matsu said softly. "They died valiantly in battle, but for a lost cause. It was all just needless suffering."

The flag continued to flutter in the wind.

For the first time, Schnell placed his hand on Matsu's shoulder.

"I promise you that we will rise from the ashes. Our people will be great once again."

Henry Veerkamp and Okei-san had been watching from a distance. Henry approached the flag after Matsu and Schnell had left. Okei followed behind him. The cat followed after them.

"It is beautiful," Henry gazed in admiration. "It is the flag of Japan?"

"Oh, no. It is the symbol of the Tokugawa house. This flew over our castle before the Satsuma came and burned our town."

"Your people lost the war, that is why you are here."

Okei could only nod her head.

"I'm sorry. I had no idea."

Henry had his arm on Okei's shoulders, but she didn't seem to notice. Her mind was far away, half a world away, a little girl, once looking across the ocean, from the other side.

"It is my karma," she said at last, and leaned her head into his strong body. The cat rubbed against their legs.

✾

CHAPTER 9
A Time For Celebration

It was hard to believe that summer still had not arrived. The days were long and warm with hardly a cloud in the sky. With help from the Veerkamp's four strong young sons, the old farmhouse was made livable within one week's time. Windows were repaired. Rotted boards on the siding and floors were replaced. The house received new shingles on the roof. The carpenters made rough tables and chairs to be used until better furniture could be bought or built.

Jou and John Henry Schnell had the master bedroom in the main level of the house. Okei stayed with Frances in the next-door nursery room. Dr. Matsumoto would live in the bedroom by the family room. Upstairs, Matsugoro and his wife had the largest room, while Matsu and Nishijawa shared another room. One room was left open for guests and for storage.

A few days after they had arrived, John Henry Schnell looked out from the house and saw the thousands of tea and mulberry plants still in the barn. The workers, however, were still trying to finish building the several small structures that would be their living quarters. The job was harder because the Veerkamp sons who were trying to help them had no comprehension of the Japanese building technique of fitting wood together. The colony's carpenters, in turn, were mystified why anyone would waste scarce iron nails just to construct buildings. John Henry Schnell saw all this and for the first time became enraged. The leader of the Wakamatsu Tea and Silk

Colony ordered everyone out to the fields to plant the trees. Even the small children were not spared.

With hard work, the planting progressed rapidly, but half way through, a late spring storm came into the mountains. The deluge was at night while the workers slept outside in their bedrolls. Of course their living quarters still had no walls or roofs, having been neglected in order to do the plantings. The soggy and sorry-looking colonists came to the door of the house, waking Okei in the nursery room. Okei gasped and hurried to awaken Schnell, who grumbled as he went to the door and was astounded by the sight that he saw.

"Gomenasai," he bowed and apologized, watching them file in one by one carrying their soggy bedrolls with them.

The living quarters were finished within the next two days.

By the late summer of 1869, life on the farm had settled into a familiar routine. The tea plants and the mulberry trees were growing rapidly in the broad field across the main road from the farmhouse. Already some tea leaves were being processed for tea. Meanwhile, the silkworms were voracious and were fed as much as possible, but enough leaves on the mulberry trees had to be left to insure their growth.

"If we had more silkworms, we would not be able to feed them," Schnell said as he walked along the rows of trees with Matsu. "The trees need to become big if we are to have a profitable silk business."

"We will need to get more silkworms later," Matsu nodded. "We lost many on the journey because there was no cool place to store them."

"I have confidence in Lord Matsudaira," Schnell said. "He promised me thousands more on the next ship in late fall. I expect more mulberry trees and tea plants, also. Perhaps it was good to start slowly and establish our procedures with what we have."

Okei and Frances were coming up to the small rise where the two men were standing. The little girl, getting bigger, was walking at a frenetic pace to keep up but was laughing and enjoying the venture. There were also a half dozen workers scattered along the broad field that was bordered by oak forests on three sides and the farmhouse to the east. Some workers were digging trenches to bring water to the trees. Others were pulling weeds or plucking leaves from some of the small tea plants.

Okei wore a straw hat to shade her face from the hot sun, while Frances had on a small bonnet.

"Is she better?" Schnell asked about his wife as Okei reached them.

"Doctor Matsumoto gave her different herbs. She was then able to eat some rice, and did not throw up this morning."

Schnell leaned down and pinched his daughter on her ample cheek. "My little Frances didn't cause so much trouble." She giggled and pushed his fingers away. "Matsugoro's wife seems to have less problems with this than Jou."

"Matsugoro's baby is not due yet for another month," Okei reminded him.

Schnell nodded and turned his vision from the workers in the field to the large mountain called Thompson Hill looming beyond the Veerkamp's ranch house to the west. To the east was their own farmhouse, sheltered behind two sycamore trees. A small column of smoke rose from the small metal chimney of the wood stove in the kitchen. With the solstice, the sun was high overhead and signaled that the time for their lunch break was close at hand.

"We are doing well, Schnell-sama," Matsu said as he followed the leader's gaze. "Everyone has worked hard and with no complaint. They have brought much honor to our Lord and our

Aizu domain, and to you."

Schnell's gaze returned to the field workers. They were all men, unlike in the beginning when the women and children had helped with the planting. Later, with the start of tea leaf harvesting, the women would help to insure that only the best leaves were picked. Women were more selective than men, which resulted in better tasting tea.

"Yes, Matsu, I am pleased," Schnell said, finally looking at him. "It is time for the world to find out about us."

Matsu was dressed in a plaid-pattern long sleeve shirt and light-colored cotton pants, more comfortable than the dungarees he tried to wear as little as possible. He carried a trenching hoe in his hand, as he had been helping the workers when Schnell had called on him. He heard Schnell's words and gazed at him with a curious expression.

"There is an agricultural fair next month in San Francisco. I plan to reserve a table for us and display our tea and silk. I want you to come with me."

Matsu smiled. "Ah, so desu."

His smile turned to concern as he thought about problems that they would face to be prepared on such short notice.

"We don't have much silk, Schnell-sama. There is no finished product for us to display."

"Then I must borrow a kimono from my wife," Schnell said, not concerning himself with how he was going to accomplish this. "We must make a good impression so the newspapers will carry a good story about us."

A rider was approaching the farmhouse on the road from

the Veerkamp ranch. Schnell recognized Henry Veerkamp and found himself looking at Okei, who was holding little Frances's hand. He motioned the child over to his side, and then picked her up in his arms.

"Ikinasai," he told Okei. "I will take my little Frances back to Jou."

Okei gave an embarrassed smile and bowed, then headed down the little hill to the house where Henry would be waiting.

In Japan, it is considered impolite, even rude, not to acknowledge an act of kindness. Perhaps that is why gift giving has evolved into such an elaborate art form. Every time a gift is received, there is set in motion a feeling of overwhelming obligation to give a gift in return. Over time, the original act of kindness becomes lost to the sense of indebtedness in the gift giving. But that is the Japanese way, and the Japanese mindset.

Thus, it was no surprise that many in the colony felt the need to repay the kindness of the Veerkamp family. The cloud of uncertainty of starting in a new world was clearing now with the steadiness of the farm routine. Much of the improved outlook for the future was due to the Veerkamp's unwavering support from the very first day they had arrived.

The idea for the festival came from Kuni-san. Over the months, he had become good friends with two of the younger Veerkamp sons. Kuni even mentored them in the art of Japanese carpentry. One evening, when the boys had gone home after helping him shore up some siding on the barn, he felt the feeling of indebtedness more than ever before. He brought the matter up to several workers as they shared a bottle of wine on the back porch of the house after a long day. They sat on high-back wicker chairs as the last rays of the setting sun cast long shadows of the picket railings onto the broad wooden floorboards.

"We need to thank them with a gift," he said as he watched the wagon carrying the two boys heading back to the Veerkamp homestead. "We need to show them that we appreciate all that they have done for us."

"Eee, they could do all my work, it would not bother me," Kintaro groaned as he sank into his chair and stretched his sore body. Kintaro was one of the younger workers, only nineteen. He was a true laborer in every sense of the word. He had no samurai background. He was not even a tradesman, and before he came here, didn't even know if seeds needed to be planted right side up or not. He always was assigned the toughest and most menial work that had to be done at the farm.

"I am very serious about this, Kintaro," Kuni admonished him, pushing the young man's chair and delighting in the panic as he started to fall backwards. The wall behind Kintaro caught his descent before any damage was done.

"I think that we should have a festival and invite the entire Veerkamp family. We will have food and dancing, with lanterns and drums. It will be a celebration of our arrival and our success. Yes! We are the pioneers; the first Japanese colony in America!"

The others sitting around all nodded their approval.

"Hai. We can use the last of the sake that we brought from Japan. It will be symbolic, ne? We have indeed achieved our independence from the homeland."

"Our own rice fermentation is ahead of schedule. We can drink this grape juice in the meantime."

Okei was walking in front of the house when the round of laughter caught her ear. It was natural for the workers to get together to relax after a day in the field, but their celebration was not usually so cheerful or energetic.

Kuni motioned her over with a hand wave. Okei cautiously approached them, uneasy about how much sake they might have been consuming. She knew that there could not be much more left.

"We do not bite very big," Kintaro assured her. "We are more like the mosquitoes, just taking a morsel here, a morsel there. It is not enough to be of any concern to a pretty lady such as you."

Okei glared at the young man, but could not withhold the half smile that appeared on her face.

"Schnell-sama will withhold all your wages if he sees you like this," she admonished them.

"Do not hold it against Kintaro," Kuni grinned, trying to separate himself from the others that shared the porch space with him. "Kintaro is just a lowly worker, all brawn and no brains. All that he knows is pleasure and pain, and he complains that all we have had from the hard work is pain."

"It is time for celebration," Kintaro quickly added. "We have worked like slaves every single day since we got here. We will have our first harvest soon and it is time to give thanks for all the blessings that we now enjoy. This is the Japanese way."

Kuni kept starting at Kintaro, not quite believing that so many words had come out of the young man's untrained mouth. He turned to the more pleasing sight of Okei-san.

"We need to thank the Veerkamp family. We have a debt to them that every passing day makes harder to repay. We must show them our appreciation in a way that only the Japanese can do."

Okei felt the cat at her feet and stooped to lift it into her arms. She stroked its soft fur, for a moment enjoying the attentive stares of the men who probably longed to trade places with the animal.

"I see. So you suggest a festival? Perhaps it can be a Hana matsuri, ne? The summer is almost gone, but we were too busy to celebrate the blooming of the spring flowers. Or maybe we can do the Obon, to honor our families and ancestors back in Japan. The time is not right for that either, however."

"It doesn't matter what we call it," Kuni responded. "We are now in America. We are probably the only Japanese in this entire country. Let's just call it the American Matsuri. It will combine all the festivals from home with dancing, drums, and Japanese and American food. We will invite the Veerkamps and all the farm families around us. It will be a memorable event, unlike anything that has ever happened in America."

More of the workers were now crowded by the porch post and leaning on the railing looking at Okei. She felt her enthusiasm rising as well. A celebration would be good for everyone's spirits and give them a chance to reflect on the journey that they had made. The dancing and the music and food would also bring back fond recollections of what life had been like before the Satsuma-led rebellion had turned their world upside down. Also, such an achievement would be the greatest affirmation yet that they had truly made California their new home.

"What is it, Okei-san?"

She hadn't realized that her smile had faded away. She was able to bring it back with some effort.

"I was just thinking about the old days, back in Japan. . . "

Kuninosuke understood her feelings more than the other youths with him. "That world is gone, Okei-san. Thanks to the Satsuma, we can never go back. That's why it would be good to bring the joyful memories we remember here to America with a festival."

"Hai." Okei was then silent for a moment but the others

continued to stare at her. She brought more brightness to her smile. "My family would want me to be happy in America."

Kuni stepped off the porch and hugged her briefly. The others applauded in the American way. Now there was only one more thing to do and Okei felt that responsibility welling up inside her.

"I cannot ask Schnell-sama directly," she said as she thought of different plans in her head. "I am only the babysitter. I will need someone to help me. Matsu, perhaps, might be able to talk to Schnell-sama."

"Yes, go ask Matsu!"

Okei nodded. Suddenly, the plan for the festival did not seem like such a wonderful idea after all.

"A festival?" Matsu responded, not looking up as he stooped to examine the nose of the plow that had caught on something submerged deep in the ground. They were in a field far to the north of the tea and mulberry trees that other workers were tending. This field still needed to be tilled before anything could be planted.

"Hai." Okei wanted to continue but stopped. She knew she had caught Matsu in one of his less agreeable moods.

"Don't you see there's hardly enough time for planting and harvesting? Already some of the tea leaves are scorched, and the Chilean miners are diverting much of our water. We cannot waste time for such foolish and irresponsible amusement."

Though her ears ached from his words, Okei took a deep breath and was able to summon more courage.

"We have all worked hard since we came here. It is time to appreciate what we have done and. . . "

Matsu suddenly straightened up and walked to the horse. He grabbed the halter and made the animal back up a couple of steps.

"It is not time to appreciate anything," he said, still avoiding looking at her. "We have accomplished nothing yet."

An undaunted Okei walked briskly to where Matsu now stood.

"You are wrong, Matsu-san," she spoke as loudly as someone of her low class could talk to a samurai. "We have left Japan. We have come to America and made a new home. We have done a great deal even if you cannot recognize that."

Matsu stood for a moment, and then brushed by Okei to go back to the plow handle. This time Okei did not follow, instead remained and kept staring at where he had been. With his hands on the plow handles and the plow firmly stuck in the earth, Matsu found that there was nothing to do. He had to look at Okei. Slowly he found himself walking back over to her, then looked down to the ground to summon the courage that was always within him.

"I have many responsibilities and sometimes get carried away," he said to her, as this time she was the one who tried to avoid his eyes. "I do not mean to demean the work that has already been done. I know that it has been very hard for everyone, especially you."

Okei was finally able to directly face Matsu.

"You have never complained," he continued on. "Fate and duty made you leave your family and the only world that you had ever known. All of it, you endured like a samurai. I only wish those back home could know how heroic their little Okei has become. They would be so very proud."

Alone together on the north field, Okei and Matsu embraced. Tears in Okei's eyes were to be expected, but uncommon was the sight of the damp glint around the eyes of the samurai. As no one else was there to bear witness, it can be said for the record that this matter did not occur. Matsu untied the horse from the plow and together they walked back towards the house.

"A festival? You have seen how tired everyone is, Matsu." Schnell stumbled on the foot of the chair in his cramped room to get to the side window. A makeshift desk made out of raw boards occupied one side of the room, while a wide bed took up all the other available space. Though the window did not look out into the field, Schnell could see workers coming and going from their small residence shacks. Normally, Jou would be in the bedroom but he had sent her to the next-door nursery room with Frances. He could hear their voices softly in the background.

"Yes their bodies are exhausted," Matsu spoke from the hallway entrance, unsure if he should enter into Schnell's private room. "I am most concerned about their minds and spirit. There has been more drinking lately. I have heard some say that joy is absent in their lives."

Schnell had to collect himself for a moment to understand what he had just heard. Of all the people at the colony, Matsu was the last one he would have expected to be sharing in such idle complaining.

"We all knew that farming in America would not be an easy business," Schnell said firmly, leaning on his desk and staring at Matsu. "We still have to finish our first crop harvest. I am already late on the loan payment and up until now we have not yet made a single dollar in profit. At this point, we do not have any reason to celebrate."

Matsu stayed quiet for a moment. In the samurai way, it was not in his nature to challenge the wisdom of his leader. He would bide his time and let Schnell vent out his frustrations before renewing his request.

John Henry Schnell continued staring at Matsu, waiting for him to reply. Only after a few moments did he realize that none would be forthcoming. In the meantime, as Matsu had anticipated, Schnell's own feeling of uneasiness was beginning to grow. Indeed, he was well aware that he had been pushing everyone very hard since they had left Japan. There just hadn't seemed to be any other way to proceed. Even though the plan to journey to America had arisen from him, he had no firm ideas of how to proceed in the new world. Would their crops grow? How would Americans treat them? Could they adapt to a culture that many Japanese felt was decadent and valued selfishness above honor and duty?

With so much uncertainty, he had thought it best to discard unnecessary conveniences and be totally dedicated to the goal of making the farm successful. So be it if a certain amount of suffering was the result. In the long run, everyone would benefit from the hard work that they were now enduring, and they would eventually become grateful for his firm leadership. It did not matter for now whether some thought him a stubborn or arrogant leader. He was on the right path and would not waver.

Schnell looked up and Matsu was still standing quietly in the doorway.

"Is there something else?" he questioned.

"Yes."

Schnell's eyes were so focused on the samurai that any sunlight would have burned right through him. "What?"

"The Veerkamp sons have worked tirelessly alongside our workers."

"Yes, I know. The family has been very helpful to us."

"Without their support, our progress would have been

most difficult."

"I am well aware of this."

"We must show them our gratitude. It is the way of our people."

Schnell lowered himself down at his desk. It was troubling that he had to be reminded of the Japanese etiquette about indebtedness. Having been in Japan since a teenager should have ingrained every aspect of Japanese life into his being. He considered himself a Japanese. Even more so, he was samurai. He knew the ways of the warrior, as well as the equally important ways of politeness and selflessness.

He went back to the rear window, hiding himself from Matsu's view. What he found worrisome was that all this might indicate a change in his way of thinking. Could coming to America have changed him so much already? Little by little, was he losing the ways of honor and duty for the ways of profit and greed?

"You are right, Matsu," he conceded in a quieter tone of voice. "I have neglected my duty to recognize the assistance of others. We need to do something for them."

"Perhaps a gift," Matsu suggested.

"We brought very little with us," Schnell became thoughtful. "There is nothing in America that we can purchase that the Veerkamps do not already possess."

"It is a difficult situation."

Schnell's mind seemed to come around in a full circle. The solution was so simple that he didn't know why the thought hadn't come to him before.

"We can perhaps invite all our neighbors for food and music.

Jou can play the shamisen. We can have dancing." It didn't occur to him that his emerging ideas somehow had a vaguely familiar tone.

"Yes," a smile shown very briefly on Matsu's face. "We will show them the Aizu Bandaisan dance."

"They will like that," Schnell had the scene already pictured in his mind. Okei and Jou would be beautiful in their kimonos and be the envy of all the American men. He had already forgotten than Jou was far too pregnant to be able to do any dancing, or even play the shamisen. At the moment, it didn't seem to matter.

"Our women can prepare Japanese traditional dishes," Matsu continued. "The neighbors can also bring American food as they wish."

Schnell then had a vision of hundreds of people crowded into the small already filled house. Matsu seemed to read his mind.

"Okei-san has told me that there is a small hill north of the house that she walks to every evening. She says she can feel the spirit of Japan reflecting from the sun at sunset. We can have the celebration there."

"Yes, Okei's Hill. She has told me about it. There are no trees, but we can put lanterns on poles. We can put colored ribbons between the poles."

"It would be a celebration just like in Japan."

"It would be good, wouldn't it?" John Henry Schnell, once a teenaged world adventurer, a samurai warrior, arms merchant, confidant of the great Aizu war lord, leader of the first Japanese colony to settle in America, could not bring himself to recognize that Matsu had been able to carefully craft the thoughts that were now in his mind. What he knew for certain was that he hadn't felt this good about anything in a long time.

"We have been working hard," he said in reflection. "Perhaps it is time to appreciate our new life in America."

Except for that one small smile, Matsu was able to maintain the stoic samurai expression on his face.

CHAPTER 10
American Matsuri

What kind of being am I? I think I am living because I have an awareness of the world around me that seems like life to me. But why am I so different from everyone else? How could it be that I was not born, but stitched together from bits of cloth and silk, like a shirt or coat, or bed cover? Do those things also have awareness and the mistaken belief that they are living beings?

When I first came into this world, I perceived my maker, Okei-san, as a god who could create life from nothingness. This seemed to satisfy my need to explain my existence. But she lifted me up to her face and let me know that she was no more special than her mother, or brothers and sister, or other common human beings.

"I cannot stop the winds or the waves," she had told me then, a premonition long before that stormy night at sea on the *China*. "I can only pray for guidance. You always had the soul to understand, my little Keiko-chan. I only helped you realize how special that soul is. You then made yourself to be what you are."

Yet my uncertainties only grew. Why didn't I have the usual necessities of life within my small body? I had no heart or the blood for it to pump. I had no lungs to breathe the air. I was given no stomach to digest food for nourishment. Perhaps there was no room for these frivolous things. Then the question of my purpose came to my mind. Surely there was a reason that I had been brought into existence. Will I be left to always wonder what that purpose is?

I asked Okei-san if all things in this world have awareness as I have. She explained that many people in Japan hold to the Shinto belief in spirits, called kami that inhabits all things. There are eight million million kami just in Japan. Like people, these spirits need to be treated with consideration and respect. A vengeful kami can cause accidents or worse. A well-treated kami can be of assistance in life's journey, sharing in your joys and laughter, consoling in your times of pain and suffering.

Before we came here, we didn't know if America would have the same kinds of kami as Japan, or for that matter, any kami at all. Would it just be an empty, spiritless place? But thankfully, there were millions of kami here as well. The Americans did not notice them as we did, or chose to ignore them, but to the Japanese it was a good omen that proper worship and living in harmony with the land would ultimately bring about the peace, prosperity, and happiness to which we aspired.

All of us must have treated the many kami very well by the late summer of 1869. The great Buddha must also have been pleased. The first ever American matsuri was both a celebration of the success of our hard work, and a show of respect and gratitude to each of the kami and to everyone who had helped on the long journey to where we were now on Okei's Hill. This included the families left behind in Japan, their ancestors, and the ancestors of their ancestors.

We had even more to be thankful for. Schnell-san, Matsu-san, and Kintaro had returned from their trip to the San Francisco Horticultural Fair. The men were all exhausted from the long journey but still had enough energy to jump off the wagon and spread the good news to the rest of the colonists. Their exhibit of tea and mulberry plants, silkworms, oil and paper plants, and citrus fruit had been the most popular in the entire fair! Jou's kimono display had attracted visitors like a magnet. Some of the wealthiest men in California sent buyers to ask if they could possibly purchase it.

"A San Francisco tycoon placed a stack of gold coins in my hand for the kimono, but I had to refuse," Schnell beamed as he hugged Jou beside the wagon. He then gave the carefully folded kimono back to her and kissed her openly.

"The next day we were on the front page of the Daily Alta, alongside stories about President Grant and the Transcontinental Railroad. We were rewarded with the Best Exhibition prize medal and a twenty-dollar gold piece."

Schnell showed off the medallion hanging from its red, white, and blue ribbon. He held the gold coin in his other hand as the colonists crowded closer to see them. "We have put Gold Hill and the Wakamatsu Tea and Silk Colony on the map!"

Cries of pure joy erupted and people rushed off to tell the others far out in the fields. Within moments, the distant workers had heard the good news as well, smiled their approval, then continued their duty of tending to the plants.

The memories that I have of the ending of 1869 are of the best of times. The acceptance of our work at the San Francisco fair inspired everyone to work even harder. The harvesting of the early tea leaves went well and those who had tasted the first brew were confident that it was as good as anything grown in Japan. Many of the silkworms had begun to cocoon and the first silk spinning would soon begin. Then we heard of the story in a San Francisco newspaper that a respected kimono designer would be commissioned by the Japanese government to come to the colony to head the fabric-making operations. By the end of the next year, we would be making kimono and other luxury fabrics in America!

That fall, the sun was nearing the low slope north of Thompson Hill as John Henry Schnell poured a cup of tea for Francis Veerkamp on Okei's Hill. Though the two men continued to be suspicious of each other's motives, they would not let the mistrust spoil this evening of happiness.

"To your good health, John," Francis raised the small ornate teacup.

"And to your good health, Francis." Their cups of fine China clinked lightly with a bell like chime.

"Your farm operations have progressed as well as I had imagined," Francis continued after draining his cup. "The article in the Alta about your San Francisco display is a guarantee for success."

Schnell smiled and leaned forward with his elbows on the long table.

"It is a result of hard work and the good friends who have helped us here. We will always be thankful to the Veerkamp family for welcoming us to our new home."

Several wood tables, some chairs, and bales of hay were set up on Okei's Hill. There were long poles along the periphery strung with twine from which paper lanterns of multiple colors gave a soft candlelit glow in the fading evening light. A wagon filled with food that had been cooked at the farmhouse had just arrived and several people were busy placing the items on the serving tables. A wagon from the Veerkamp house had arrived earlier with food that Louisa had spent the night preparing.

There were ranchers from across the Gold Hill valley seated at the tables and standing in the serving lines along with some of the older Japanese such as Dr. Matsumoto and Matsugoro. Notably absent were the Veerkamp's sons and the younger colonists. Without the rancor and silliness of younger hearts, the atmosphere was subdued and relaxed.

"We have much to be thankful for," Matsugoro said as he sat back in the only padded chair that had found its way up to the hill.

His pregnant wife sat behind him on the less comfortable bench seat of the table. "It is very thoughtful to have this celebration to give appreciation to all the spirits that have helped us to be successful."

Dr. Matsumoto sipped on elegant wine that had been brought from the Veerkamp's cellar for this occasion.

"Hai. Things have gone very well, indeed. There have been no serious accidents and no illness. Jou Schnell-san is due any day now. Her akachan will be the first Japanese born in America."

"A girl, you say?"

"That is what the Reverend Cool has said. His God seems to have given him special powers to foresee these kinds of things."

"Hai, so desu." Matsugoro noticed the Reverend helping the older women setting plates on one of the long dining tables. The Reverend seemed to have no problems communicating with the women, occasionally causing a round of laughter even though none of them understood English. Apparently, he spoke an easily understood common language.

"How about your wife?" Dr. Matsumoto asked, turning to the woman behind him. "Will it be a girl or boy?"

"I did not ask. I have no need to know." The wine and the laughter, with thoughts of his family's addition, lifted Matsugoro's spirits. He remembered how hard things had been in the beginning.

"Our people do not have the fever anymore," he said, noticing that the doctor looked at him with a brief smile on his face. "Many were sick when we first arrived, and I was certain that there would be many deaths. We should be thankful that the Buddha has looked after our health."

"Ah, so desu, ne." Dr. Matsumoto tried hard not to show his

great feeling of satisfaction. Belief in the Buddha was a fine thing, but he was a practical man working in the real world filled with real problems. He knew that it was the Peruvian bark powder that he had bought in San Francisco that had stemmed the miner's fever. Ever since they had arrived, he had mixed it into the medicinal tea that everyone drank each morning. His only regret was that several weeks had been needed to adjust for the proper dose, causing needless suffering. Still, he was thankful to the Buddha for allowing him to be here to help his fellow countrymen. Also he should not forget the kami of the trees that had sacrificed their bark so that the medicine could be extracted. The practical world he lived in and the spiritual one could coexist after all, Dr. Matsumoto reconciled to his satisfaction.

A single distant booming sound seemed to come from all around them. People were looking in every direction to find the cause.

"Kaminari?" Matsugoro soon realized that there was not a cloud in the sky. Also the sound did not have the sharp crackling of thunder.

"Odaiko," Dr. Matsumoto said, turning to face the southern direction where the dirt path came from the farmhouse. Now the air was pierced by the soft but sharp sound of bell chimes. The rhythm of smaller drums could be heard, and then flutes weaving their melancholic melodies between the drum sounds.

The marchers appeared in the distance, moving slowly and deliberately. The rise after each step could be seen, everyone in unison, then they would stop briefly before starting again with the other foot.

A samurai in formal old world dress with wide winged shoulder ornaments was at the front. It was Matsunosuke. The hilts of his two swords projected from the solid gray obi at his waist. His hair was swept up and back and knotted at the top in the traditional way. The white tabi socks and wooden getta clogs could be seen beneath his wide black harori with each footstep. Women pointed and men stared at him. Had it been so long since a Japanese man had been seen in real Japanese attire?

Nishijawa was likewise dressed behind Matsu, except he had kept his hair long in the American way. He carried the Tokugawa banner on a shortened pole before him, its heavy silk fabric unwavering on this windless evening. From somewhere farther behind, the odaiko drum boomed again.

A splash of color that reflected the glow of the setting sun soon appeared. Okei and the young wife of the apprentice carpenter moved slowly together in matching motions, both wearing persimmon-colored kimono with dark-plum-colored obi. Their faces were barely seen in the shadows of their half moon shaped amigasa hats that accentuated their coordinated head movements. Three young men wearing only loincloths followed, marching in crouched footsteps to the slow beat of the drums behind them. Like the two women in front of them, they moved their arms from side to side, waving their hands, occasionally clapping in unison. A man and women playing flutes followed, and an older woman with a stringed shamisen added to the parade music.

The still unseen great drum boomed three consecutive times. There were three successive hand claps from the dancers, and the smaller drums began to beat a fast-syncopated rhythm. All those in the parade shouted loudly, the women's higher-pitched voices carrying the farthest. The dancers jumped forward together and the pace quickened considerably.

The great drum finally appeared, carried on a freight wagon drawn by two of the Veerkamp's largest draft horses. Two men in loincloths and white headscarves stood holding thick wooden sticks in their hands. Red paint covered the curved boards of the drum, made from the sides of wine barrels and the top covered with cowhides stitched together. The two men twisted and cocked their arms overhead. Their sticks pounded down in quick triple, repetitive booming beats with rapid single beats in-between. Two men marched behind the wagon, beating counter melodies on smaller drums strapped to their waists.

The parade split as it approached the hilltop and began to encircle those watching from the tables. The wagon with the great drum halted in front, while the other drummers, musicians, and dancers continued around in a circle.

Francis turned in his chair and smiled as he pointed to his little boys, William and Egbert, behind Okei and just ahead of the drummers. They were both struggling and giggling trying to match hand motions with the flawless dancing of the two kimono clad girls in front of them. Five-year-old Egbert seemed to have a better understanding of the rhythm than did his older brother, who seemed to be totally clueless.

Behind the drummers, the Veerkamp brothers Frank and Henry moved confidently holding flower design paper fans in their hands. They held their arms and hands close to their bodies, reasoning that less movement meant less chance for making errors and fools of themselves. They also did not crouch like the other male dancers were doing, making them stand out even taller among the shorter Japanese.

The music and drumming stopped when the circle was closed and shouts of joy flowed into the darkening evening. Many of the marchers rushed down to get to the front of the food serving line.

Matsu had ended up at the very top of the hill and turned to see the parade dissolving below him. Okei was the only one coming up to where he was. She stopped just beneath him and took a minute to admire the handsomely dressed samurai.

"Yoku mimasu, ne?" she said as her eyes took him in from his topknot to his tabi and gettas. Of course she noticed the protruding hilt of the sword that had cut down a threatening monster to save her in another world, now immeasurably distant and an unbelievably long time ago.

The proud samurai felt a flush in his face and was flustered when he could find no immediate words to describe his feelings for her. Before he could react, they heard a shout and saw that it was Henry waving from in front of the crowded food tables. Okei excused herself with a formal bow, and then half ran back down. Matsu watched in silence as the two met and held hands just below the hilltop.

"You are beautiful," Henry said as his eyes recorded the graceful shape that she gave to the enchanting kimono she wore. "Your dancing was so beautiful. I've never seen anything like it."

"And you looked silly," Okei laughed with a smile that made his heart melt. "You didn't do the crouch walking like the others. You didn't try to bend down."

Now Henry laughed. "Listen, these kinds of farm pants aren't made to do that kind of thing. They're stiffer than a washboard and too cramped in the wrong places."

Okei had to turn her face away before he could see the red warmth coloring her cheeks.

"Bandai-san!" a voice yelled out. The drums began pounding once more. The odaiko thundered. The food line and table seats were abandoned as people hurried to form a line encircling the lantern-lit area.

Before Henry knew it, Okei was pulling him by the hand to the top of the hill where the line of people was just starting to close the circle. They stopped and were facing each other. Even Schnell and Francis Veerkamp had joined in. The dining tables inside the formed ring were now totally empty.

"Aizu Bandai-san," Okei told him, "is our most famous folk song. It is a wish for good harvest and to show respect for the Bandai Mountain over our town. Follow me and I will teach you how to do the dancing."

"Ah, right." Henry found concentrating on anything but Okei's face and form to be very difficult. The long narrow hat that she wore and the beautiful figure-hugging silk kimono made her into a vision of slimness and femininity that he had never encountered before. His body felt numb and heavy next to her. He lost track of everything else that was going on around him, not even noticing the drum, flute, and shamisen music starting.

The older women and men from the colony had formed a small circle inside the larger one. There were some fifty people encircling them and watching from the outer ring, many of them local ranchers and their families completely ignorant of Japanese traditional dancing.

The dancers in the inner circle clapped as the odaiko boomed and the drums began a syncopated rhythm.

Okei clapped and Henry did the same. Her left hand rose up and all Henry could think of was how much the persimmon color of her long sleeve reminded him of the sunset he had seen that evening. He also noticed the darkness for the first time as evening had progressed into night. The soft glow of the surrounding lanterns barely illuminated the dancers far from the center tables.

"Hand up, step foot together," Okei gently guided him. Henry tried but doing both was too much, causing him to nearly trip over his feet. Okei's face remained emotionless despite his clumsy efforts.

"Other hand up, watch my feet."

The music seemed to be swirling around him. Shamisen. Drums. Flute. The sound was hypnotizing, but he could just not get into the rhythm. It was a syncopation that was as foreign as these people had been to him many months ago. Henry looked at the dancers below them to get some idea but the motions were too confusing to follow in the dim light.

"Do not be concerned about the others," Okei finally smiled at him and Henry felt like a child that had been given a reprieve. "Watch my feet. Keep arms close to body. Listen to music."

She swept her arms across her front as she went back several steps. Henry walked forward to stay with her. Just as suddenly she came forward and he had to scramble back to keep out of her way. Her arms both swept elegantly to the right, and then repeated to the left. She stopped with her arms extended, one foot slightly forward. She brought her hands together into another clap. By the time Henry could follow with his own hands, the dancing was already into the next step.

"Now repeat same pattern again."

"Repeat what?" It wasn't until the third or fourth time through that he began to sense familiar movements. At last he was moving his arms and following what Okei did. He moved his arms right then left. He extended his arms and he clapped at the same instant as everyone else. The music and dancing ended just as he was beginning to enjoy himself.

Okei hugged him like a star pupil who had learned well, but it meant more and they each knew it.

The tables were again filled with the noise of eating and talking. The moon had risen in full splendor to illuminate in its white glow what the lanterns could not. John Henry Schnell stood at the head of the central table and asked for quiet.

"Arigato gozaimasu, danke schoen," he began, turning toward the side of the table near him where Francis and Louisa and most of the Veerkamp boys were sitting. "I rise here tonight with a heart filled with much arigato and danke, but since we are in America, I think a simple deeply grateful thank you would work the best."

Kuni stood first and then Kintaro. They began clapping. Very soon, most of the other colonists joined in the show of appreciation. A glass of wine was given to Schnell and he raised it in front of him.

"People are beginning to appreciate the products of our hard labor. San Francisco was just the beginning and soon we will be known throughout California. I give a salute to all of you who came from Japan with little more than a dream and faith in me as your leader. I also toast all of you here in the Gold Hill valley who have welcomed us and contributed to our success."

"Even the Chilean miners?" someone shouted from the end table.

The laughter that followed made Schnell smile. "Why not, they are only a mere nuisance. We thank everyone and all the spirits and gods of California."

Schnell saw Okei stand as the others began to sit after applauding. He hadn't noticed the runner who had just come up from the house to deliver the news about Jou to her.

"Also I thank Okei for allowing us to borrow her favorite place for our celebration. We call this place "Okei's Hill" and it will be remembered from this time onward for the great happiness and togetherness that we are feeling tonight."

All the attention focused on her was more than she could bear. She shut out the noise of the clapping and voices shouting her name. She was able to bow briefly in appreciation. At the moment, however, she had other pressing matters to attend to.

"Jou is in final labor," she was able to say before Schnell could bring an end to his speech. "Mrs. Marquette has asked for Matsumoto sensei."

Okei, Dr. Matsumoto, and Schnell rushed off down the hill.

Yes, these were the good times that are still as familiar to me as if they had happened just yesterday. How could it be that I have been reflecting about what had happened more than 140 years ago? I don't know. I suppose time does not proceed in the normal way for a being such as I. What I know with great certainly is that these memories will endure forever within my heart and soul, or at least in all of the bits of silk and cloth and paper that comprise my being.

CHAPTER 11
Harder Times

The Japanese have always looked longingly across the Japan Sea towards China. Chinese poetry reading was considered a pursuit worthy of nobility and many samurai would alternate martial arts and battlefield training with peaceful moments reciting ancient Chinese writings. The basic Japanese writing system itself, the Kanji, was borrowed from China. It was altered to suit our needs; pronunciations changed here and there, sometimes even the meaning became different to better integrate it into our culture. The result of all the borrowing and changing was the creation of one of the most complex and difficult of all the languages in the entire world.

Along with Chinese poetry, the Confucian and Taoist philosophy also became a part of the Japanese mentality. Much of Shintoism is about these beliefs. One good example is the harmonious balance of Yin and Yang. Like light and dark, one cannot exist without the other. Waves in the ocean are huge only because of the great shallow in between. When the two merge, peace and tranquility are achieved. When there is imbalance, there is tension and stress, even when there is an appearance of serenity. I did not see it then, but now I realize that the period of hope and prosperity at the Wakamatsu Colony was a time of excess Yang. We had been blessed with success and lack of hardship for too long. It was only a matter of time before the Yin would arise to bring order and balance back to our world.

After a warm fall season, we prepared our farm for the coming winter. Neighboring ranchers had warned us that the rain could be severe and travel often blocked with several feet of snow. However, November went by with no storms. December had only several days where there was a light covering of snow on the trees. Only one storm came in January, leaving less than an inch of snow on the ground.

To many of the colonists, this did not seem like a winter at all. In northern Japan, they were used to large amounts of snow that would block the mountain passes sometimes for as long as a month. Storms were frequent even in the valley that sheltered the city of Aizu, and there were many days that the white covering remained on the streets to make travel difficult.

John Henry Schnell was concerned enough about this lack of rainfall that he brought the matter up at a meeting of ranchers in Coloma. Francis told him that it was not a matter to worry about. The other ranchers were confident that rainfall in spring would be able to meet the needs of their crops.

In March, the rainstorms began. After several continuous days of the wet weather, Schnell went outside and happily stood in it until he was thoroughly drenched by the welcomed moisture. It seemed that the many kami of the new homeland had only wanted to test our resolve, and once we had shown our fortitude, opened up the sky to quench our thirsty plants and animals.

The miracle rains of March saved our crop and resulted in a fair harvest of tea leaves and many boxes of silkworm cocoons ready to be spun. Although our production had been less than what we had hoped for, there was still great confidence that the harvest next year would be far better. In September, Schnell and two colonists went to Sacramento to exhibit at the California State Fair. Again our display was met with great enthusiasm and with a nice written article in the newspaper.

Even as I enjoyed sharing these times with Okei-san and the others whom I had grown to love, I could not contain the feeling of unease that lingered in my soul at night while the others slept. The balance of the Yin and Yang kept coming into my mind. Eee, if I could only close my eyes to sleep and not be bothered by this. My maker, Okei-san, should have drawn lines across my face for eyes, instead of my ever open vision of such a worrisome world.

My eyes, however, were also the pathways by which I witnessed the great beauty that sometimes occurs with life. I can recall a day in the fall that we had the Obon service. The Obon is a celebration of ancestors and in Japan mixes festive dancing along with prayers. Bright lights, dancing, and music help guide the spirits from their resting places so they can briefly rejoin the living for a festive and spiritual evening of thankfulness and forgiving.

This time, the dancing was done in the clearing between the house and barn. Besides the colonists, only the Veerkamps attended. One joyful folk dance mimicked the motions of dragging fishing nets to bring in the daily catch. Another song was from the mining regions in the Japan highlands, imitating the coal miners rhythmic shoveling of their load into ore carts.

Our Obon did not have the great joy of the American Matsuri. Most of the dancing was by the six women of the colony as the men chose to watch from their seats by the house porch. We only had a few paper lanterns hung on the side of the house to guide the spirits to us, so I doubt if many departed ancestors were able to find their way to our house.

Still, it was a celebration that we had long needed to bring us comfort in this new world. It was a way to tie the past to the present and bring closure to our yearning for the old life. When the altar that had been brought from Japan was moved into the family room, every colonist stood in line to wait their turn to worship their ancestors. There were many tears, such as at a funeral.

As the light of the day had begun to fade into darkness, we journeyed by wagon to the river by Coloma. The spirits of the ancestors would need to be shown the way back to their resting places. The Veerkamp family was invited, and Francis and several of the boys came to observe.

Okei led Henry in near darkness down the rocky embankment to the sound of the flowing river. In her hand was a small paper lantern attached to a lengthwise cut block of wood shaped as a boat. As Henry watched in wonder, she took a burning candle that was passed from one colonist to another and lit the wick of the lantern. Soon many small lights dotted the edge of the river. As the lanterns brightened, Okei knelt and placed her little boat on the water's surface, joining the others that glowed on the rocky shoreline with a multitude of colors of red, yellow, blue, green, and orange. Then, in unison, the colonists pushed them out into the river to be taken by the current. Tears forming in her eyes and thinking about everyone left behind in Japan, seeing the faces of her grandparents and a vision of her mother and father, Okei put her hands together in prayer, then gently pushed her tiny craft into the river's current to join the others that were already floating away.

There were perhaps a dozen of the little boats with lanterns.

In a moment they were in the middle of the darkened river, lights bobbing in the waves, their reflections still visible. Henry held tightly to Okei's hand. Far, far away, the colors of the different lanterns could still be seen: red, blue, yellow, and green, barely visible. The tiny light points were finally enveloped by the darkness. The spirits had returned to their homes in the world beyond the twilight.

By fall of 1870, the time of the Yang was already reaching its end. At first it had not seemed so. I did not mention that the second birth had occurred when Matsugoro's wife delivered a baby girl. Meanwhile, the Schnell's infant, Mary, was getting bigger and more rambunctious every day. All this seemed reason for future optimism.

John Henry Schnell decided that a record of our accomplishments needed to be preserved. He informed the colonists that he had arranged a visit to a Placerville studio to have pictures taken. The portraits were to recognize all of the colonists who had sacrificed and ultimately persevered to establish the first Japanese colony in America. Generations to follow would see the images and be able to admire the brave pioneers and their achievements.

I stayed back in the farmhouse with Jou, Frances, and little Mary. Mary had grown to become an energetic toddler who had to be constantly monitored. Jou was not up to the task, still anemic months later from the blood she had lost during the long delivery. Okei's workload had greatly intensified and she was surprised when Schnell told her to go with the group to Placerville. He assigned the wife of one of the carpenters to help Jou. Okei knew enough not to argue, although she couldn't fathom why her presence was needed for the portraits. After all, she was only the baby sitter.

I could not go, of course, now being the property of two little girls. I was able to sense Okei's thoughts long after their wagon had crested the rise to the south, but soon the distance had grown too far for my abilities. The emptiness I felt was unsettling, until I realized that her spirit had not left from an inner part of me. I had always wondered about this. Would I be able to function without Okei's presence? Would my soul vanish from this cloth body? I knew now that I was a real part of this world, a being onto herself, or itself, whatever that being is.

Later that day the girls had grown tired of placing me in

various parts of the house, and I found myself seated alone on a small chair. I suddenly saw a different room with a high vaulted ceiling and huge bright windows. At the same time, thoughts came into my mind, Okei's thoughts. She was wearing a strange and uncomfortable dress that she had trouble walking in.

Schnell-san had reassured everyone that the Placerville studio had nice clothes for the pictures and the colonists did not need to be concerned about what to wear. This turned out to be true, but of course the clothing was designed for people a good foot taller than the Japanese. The men found only one dark and one light-colored suit to wear among them. The women had two farm-style dresses to pass around. To make up for this lack of diversity, the group decided to change as many clothing accessories from session to session as possible. For example, the two available men's hats along with the two suits allowed for six different combinations, including some hatless portraits. Other items were used. A single blue vest. A pocket watch and gold chain. A bow tie. The women had a parasol that was handed off from photo to photo. There was also a broach and a belt.

A good-hearted argument ensued regarding the pocket watch. Kuni brought his own that he had purchased onboard the China and didn't want it to be upstaged by the studio's less exquisite timepiece.

"It doesn't even show the correct time," Kuni brought attention to the vastly different times that they showed.

"How do you know that yours has the proper time?" Matsugoro teased him. "It feels like is it five o'clock to me because I have begun to think about dinner. Your watch says four o'clock, which is over one hour too slow."

"Uso!" Kuni felt his face redden even though he knew that Matsugoro was just baiting him. "My watch has Swiss mechanism inside, the most accurate in the entire world. That thing that they have, why I have heard was made right here in the town foundry. They do them when they are not making plows and horseshoes!"

They all laughed at Kuni's tale but agreed to use his watch for the rest of the portraits. It didn't make any difference in appearance anyway, since the gold chain sticking out of the vest was the only part of it to show.

The colonists left Placerville in high spirits and talked among themselves of the many ingenious ways they had been able to overcome the lack of clothing choices. There seemed to be no doubt that the finished portraits would accurately reflect the first Japanese pioneers in America. Even Okei, the last subject and forced to wear her stiff and cumbersome borrowed gown for hours, had to agree that it had all gone well.

The package of finished photographs was delivered to the ranch several weeks later. After work was done that day, some of the colonists gathered in the dining room to examine them. They looked on with quiet contemplation at the eight small glass enclosed prints, about four-by-five inches in size.

"Your family looks very nice," Kuni told Matsugoro. In the photograph, he was in one of the dark borrowed suits. His wife stood beside him in the light-colored summer dress and holding their infant daughter in one arm and the infamous parasol with the other hand. "Very regal indeed. A hundred years from now they will see this and think that you are the famous Dr. Matsumoto himself. At the least this must be the most famous carpenter in all of Japan!"

"Yes, I have built the Great China Wall with just these two hands," Matsugoro smiled and laughed with Kuni.

Matsugoro then saw Kuni's image, and couldn't believe the

photo of the immaculately dressed and serious looking young man.

"Ah, what a striking young man this is! You can readily tell that this is the great samurai who held off the Imperial army so that the rest of us could reach the safety of the ship. I heard that he killed ten enemy with his sword before it broke, then he spit in the eye of the last rifle soldier before he was able to leap into the water to save himself."

"Ah, hontou desu." Kuni tried to keep a solemn tone to his voice, hoping he wouldn't be the first to break out in laughter. It was a losing proposition, however.

The four men had to back away from the table so their exuberance didn't sweep the small photos off the table. Kintaro noticed the image of Okei in the middle of the group.

"Oh, Okei-san would be very disappointed! The picture does not capture her beauty at all."

They all looked at the picture with her sitting in a chair and Umetaro's number two son standing beside her. It was true that the strange Western-style dress was too bulky to show off her petite, feminine figure.

"Kintaro, you just don't see a girl unless you see her in a shapely kimono!"

"No, it's her face. See, it looks swollen, like Umetaro's wife when she had the bad fever. I hope Okei-san has not gotten the miner's disease like the others."

They passed the photograph around and each of them examined it. Different sounds of concern were expressed. Finally, Matsugoro spoke.

"I will go talk to Okei. We should not get too worried, perhaps she is in her monthly period and she is just keeping too much water. My wife has had times like this."

Of course Okei said that she was fine, but no one knew then about the arrival of the time of the Yin. Several days later, Dr. Matsumoto was sent running to the barn as fast as his stubby legs could carry him. While gathering the morning eggs, Okei had collapsed and had not been found until the cook had become concerned that the breakfast was getting delayed. Okei was carried barely conscious into the other back bedroom of the house.

"Get my bag and the Peruvian bark powder, and hot water to mix it. We must hurry to break the fever." Dr. Matsumoto's obvious concern frightened several people into fast action. I do not have to mention that not much work happened on the Wakamatsu farm that day. The workers did not go out to the fields. People wandered around just waiting for news about Okei.

It was a true blessing late that evening when Dr. Matsumoto came out of the room and announced that her fever had broken.

"Everyone must drink the herb tea in the morning, no exception," he admonished before going up to his own room and shutting the door.

I was of course happy that I would continue to share this world with Okei-san. Even though I now knew that I had my own existence, I could not imagine proceeding into the future without her. She was my maker and also my best friend. Later that day, Frances carried me into the room where Okei remained in bed. I was shocked at how thin and frail she looked. I wanted to reach out and cry in her arms. Frances seemed to know this, and held me out for her.

"Do not worry your silly heart," Okei said as she held me out before her. "We have journeyed too far together for a small fever to end our bond. We have much work left to do. I have promised that I will never leave you."

Then she held me next to her warm body. I cried in my own, tearless way. Frances hugged Okei also, having real tears to shed for her.

There is one thing certain about the Yin. It is persistent. Only a short time after Okei's brief but worrying illness, another distressing incident occurred.

It happened after the nuisance of the Chilean miners at the head of Shingle Creek had grown to become a concerning problem. A vein of gold had been discovered along the bank and a stampede of miners had rushed into the area. They dug holes and built a small dam that decreased the water supply for our crops. Schnell went to the constable in Placerville and also placed a complaint article in the city newspaper. When the diversion of water continued, he ordered a wheeled water pump of the Chinese design be built to bypass the miner's obstruction. The work and the lumber to build the pump and a new quarter-mile-long channel had been costly in both time and funds, but we did not want a violent confrontation. The spell of the yellow gold often causes complete madness we were told, and it was best to avoid the miners if at all possible.

One evening on the way back from inspecting the pump wheel, Schnell's horse stepped on soil undercut by recent mining, sending both suddenly tumbling down onto the rocks in the creek below. He found himself under the horse that was still struggling to get up. Finally pulling himself free, he looked down at the animal and its foreleg that was hanging by just a few threads of tendons. Not until he tried to reach for his pistol did Schnell feel the throbbing ache on that entire side of his body. Briefly overcoming the pain, he willed himself to reach across with his other arm to raise the pistol and fire the shot that had taken mercilessly too long.

Matsu and Kintaro heard the gunshot and immediately rushed out from the field on plow horses. In short time, they found a dazed Schnell lying by the creek and brought him back to the farm. Dr. Matsumoto fortunately had some opium and was able to comfort Schnell's great agony enough to allow merciful sleep that night. After several weeks, our leader was able to resume management of the farm.

Schnell-san was never the same after that incident. He had apparently aggravated a battle wound suffered during the Ezo war. The arm and shoulder would forever after hang uselessly on his left side. His sword fighting days were certainly over, but this skill that was so highly valued in Japan meant little in our California life. I think this alone was not the cause of the change in the way that he now viewed this world. Rather, he was at last seeing a distressing pattern of ill fortune that was well beyond his capability to turn around.

That fall was unusually dry and warm, and November came with not a drop of rain. Even with the Chinese pump operating at maximum capacity, barely enough water flowed to feed our own thirst, least of all the plants. Many of the tea plants had lost their leaves early, and there was great fear that they would not revive for next spring. We lost several of our orange trees. Not until next year would we know how many of the dormant mulberry trees would survive.

There was a great feeling of apprehension when a meeting of all the colonists was announced in late November. Even before the meeting began, the changes that were happening at our Wakamatsu Farm were apparent. The number of empty chairs was starkly evident.

"Ara, where is Umetaro?"

"Okashii. I haven't seen him for the last week."

"His wife and child are gone too?"

"Eee. Come to think of it, Tanejiro has not returned since he decided to mine for gold on the river. That was four days ago."

Schnell came into the room from his bedroom office. Among the many thousands of days of his event-filled life, today had been one of the worst ones that he could recall. Even the sight of the many empty chairs before him barely registered in his mind. It was just another natural progression to the way that the orderly world he had envisioned was progressively slipping into disarray.

It was fortunate that the house had been empty a few hours before when Francis Veerkamp had come to inquire about the balance of the loan payment. Inquire was hardly the right word. He had come with no intention of listening to anything that Schnell had to say. He didn't care that the drought and the miner's water blockage had prematurely ended the tea harvesting. He even seemed to relish delivering the bad news from Sacramento that was just filtering to the other foothill farms. The legislature had terminated the silk subsidy program after less than three months. A state senator had declared that a "silk cocoon swindle" was occurring and tens of thousands of dollars had been paid with hardly any result to show for it.

"I need the balance of the $4,500 now, Herr Schnell," Francis had stood above him and glared down as he sat at his desk. "Because you are a gentleman of my own Prussian blood, I will accept a one week delay before I go to the court to foreclose on the deed. But I promise you I will do this, Herr Schnell. I have been far too lenient with you and your colony."

Schnell tried not to show emotion. "Francis, my good friend, you must know that I have been waiting for my Lord in Japan to send us more funds. A ship is arriving in January and I fully expect a representative of the Mikado to have full funding for me to continue my enterprise."

Francis laughed but not because of anything funny. "You do not know that your Aizu Lord was forced to give up his wealth? Ja, it was that or put a sword to his belly. He decided that he was yet too young to die."

"I have heard this news and know it is fabrication," Schnell immediately replied. "I have enemies in Japan who are spreading false rumors to undermine my success."

"But you have no success, Herr Schnell. For your sake, and for the sake of the good people who work for you whom I deeply admire, I implore you to see reason and terminate this venture before I resort to legal action."

Schnell stood up and faced Francis. "You and your wife, your sons, have always been here to help us. We have shown our gratefulness with a celebration to honor your family. All that I ask from you is more time to overcome hardships that we did not foresee. I assure you that we will overcome these. . . "

"Ja, Ja," Francis Veerkamp interrupted. "I am your friend but first I am a businessman. No businessman would be as lenient as I have been. You have your one-week warning. I must go back and tend to my ranch."

Schnell came from behind the desk and moved quickly to the door. "I have heard from others that you have always wanted a bigger ranch. They say you have always had an eye on this land. Perhaps this is why you are turning your back on all of us."

Francis pushed past Schnell and strode toward the front door. Once at the door, he turned and stopped Schnell who was following to catch him before he left.

"Look at yourself first before you cast judgment, Herr John Henry Schnell. I have done all that I can do for you. My boys have spent more time here than on my own farm. I only wish that you see the truth of what I have said before it is too late for you and your people. Auf wiedersehen, Herr Schnell."

He found himself staring at the empty chairs and a number of colonists seated in different areas of the room. They were staring intently at him and he met each of their eyes as he scanned the room. Knowing that many had already left the colony, he felt empathy towards these who were still here. There was Dr. Matsumoto seated beside Matsugoro and his wife and their baby. There was the brash Kuninosuke and pretty Okei. Kintaro was in the far back. Yana was still here. He counted no more than twelve from the original twenty-two who had sailed from Japan. There seemed to be someone missing that he hadn't anticipated. Matsu. Remembering that Matsu had gone to check on the water pump at least gave him some comfort.

"I have called for this meeting to inform all of you of our situation. Despite my best efforts, the sheriff of the county has not acted to stop the miners who have blocked our waterway. It has forced us to conclude our harvest one month earlier than anticipated. This has caused hardship and put at risk the trees we need to start next season."

While he spoke, he tried to find the words for the most difficult part of what he had to say. For the first time since they arrived, there would be no payment for their labor. The loss of the late crop had ended any hope of doing anything more than covering the supply costs for last month. He must ask them to forgo payment until funds sent by Lord Matsudaira arrived to save them. He didn't know when that would be. Despite what Francis Veerkamp had said, he was certain that the daimyo of their old homeland had not forgotten about them. Surely, he had not. Lord Matsudaira would not let their dreams die as long as there was still one breath of air left within him.

As Schnell looked around the room, there were sudden footsteps outside on the front porch and then the screen door burst open. Matsu took a few steps in, then abruptly stopped.

"Nishijawa-san has been hurt," he announced in an even controlled voice. "The water pump is destroyed."

Everyone stood at once and stared at Matsu with disbelieving looks. Matsu walked forward to stand before Schnell.

"They attacked him when he went to inspect the pump. They must have hidden behind trees because he did not see them until it was too late."

"Cowards! Did he not have his sword? Where is he? How is he?" The room was filled with many shouts and questions.

"He has bruises to his face and lower body. I took him to his house where he is now resting. He did not have his sword because we did not expect such a thing to happen in America."

Many faces began to turn to Schnell.

"We must teach them a lesson! We will take swords and guns and drive them all out!"

Schnell was as shocked as anyone. This dreadful day, which had begun with guilt for not being able to pay his workers' wages and Francis Veerkamp's threat of foreclosure, had unbelievably managed to deteriorate even further. It had become the worst day he could ever remember.

"Tell us what to do, Schnell-san. We must not let them do these things to us with impunity!"

Schnell was looking away towards one of the walls, out through a window.

"We will act, but not tonight," Schnell found that his voice was quivering with uncertainty. He fought to make it stronger. "They are cowards and they are already gone. We will let them think that we are afraid of them. When they come back, we will be waiting."

The shouting abruptly quieted. Schnell was never able to get to the subject of the late work payments.

Of the many memories retained within the fibers of my little body, two of the most stirring happened at the end of 1870. The first was the result of meticulous planning and execution. The other befell onto us with neither warning nor time for preparation.

First came the night when the samurai rose up to take revenge upon the miners. Even as our American venture had begun to spiral downward, the people of the colony were able to meet a grave threat with resolve and resourcefulness.

Schnell-san had been correct in assuming that the group who had destroyed the pump and injured Nishijawa would return to do more damage. Seven days had passed, more then enough time for them to believe that we had let our guard down once again. But they had not taken into account our patience or our determination to find justice for the cruelty they had done to us.

Of course, I was not there to see the battle. I was on a chair where Frances-chan had placed me, as every night before, when she went into her bed. Deep into the night, I heard the preparation in the large room. I heard the occasional sharp sound of iron and steel. There were some muffled voices, talking very softly. When I could no longer hear the sounds, the vision of our men leaving the farm came into my mind. Matsu, Kuni, and Schnell-san were mounted on plow horses, only they were no longer plow horses. Kintaro and Yana were on foot and held long lances. Last to leave, slower, walked Matsugoro and a limping Nishijawa. Dr. Matsumoto and Okei stood watching from under the glow of an oil lamp on the front porch step.

I think back upon these times, remembering those now long gone. Matsu. Kuni. Matsugoro. Schnell. Okei. They were all good people and they were all brave, and they were all my friends.

The miners hadn't anticipated the clash that would happen that night. They had left their weapons behind to carry digging tools to pull out the tea plants. Approaching low and cautiously under partial moonlight, they finally stood straight when they were within the shelter of the row of small trees. The leader gave a signal and smiled as he began to hack into the nearest plant with his spade. The others followed. The destruction they would inflict this night would be total and irrecoverable. The colony of Japanese would be forced away back across the ocean to where they belonged.

Hard at their destructive work, they barely noticed the animal sounds coming from three sides surrounding them. Was it an owl? Coyotes? Birds singing in the middle of the night? Finally the leader looked up when he thought he was hearing a human voice. A muffled sound coming from the miner closest to him diverted his attention. When he turned back, there was a large shadow just beyond the tea tree he had been digging out. He looked up, and continued looking up. He tried to shade his eyes from the glow of the quarter moon behind the figure, finally making out what seemed to be a sloping head with antlers or horns protruding out into the sky. Moonlight reflected intermittently off the head. It was an iron helmet! An arm covered with plates reached high above and the shadow of the long knife it held fell upon the miner's leader. The silhouette then screamed or roared, and the sound seemed to echo from all sides. Another giant figure appeared, then another. Strange looking armored men with long spears appeared from the trees at the sides. They all screamed and roared.

The terrorized miners let out frightened cries and dropped their tools. They ran away from the field as fast as their feet could carry them, tripping and falling in their dash over the uneven plowed terrain.

The victorious battle with the miners gave us much-needed morale boost during a time of fading hope. It seemed that the Yang had overcome the Yin, but of course that was not the case. The Yin, as I said, is persistent and takes many forms, sometimes even fulfilling dreams only to see them dashed into sharp rocks of even more cataclysmic failure. Most of us were aware of this by now. No one truly believed that the Wakamatsu Tea and Silk Colony would survive for very long into the next year. Still, it was human nature to appreciate any kind of victory.

Most satisfying to us was that it had been a unified effort by everyone in the colony, not just the men who had confronted the miners. With only days to prepare, there had not been enough time to make the iron parts for the samurai armor. They had been fashioned from local tree wood, even the helmets with their fearsome animal horns. The plates were gray painted roof shingles. The armor on the plow horses were just painted blankets. Ancient stone points found at the creek were used for the spears, so at least they were true weapons. Matsu, Schnell, and Kuni rode into battle with their swords, true samurai warriors ready for combat should that have been required. Gratefully, it had not.

⁂

CHAPTER 12
Torima's Revenge

It was Christmas Eve, 1870. With the guidance of Henry and William Veerkamp, a pine tree had been brought in from the forest and placed in the center of the parlor room. Everyone had stared at it in the beginning, wondering what could be its purpose. That was when Henry and the two younger Veerkamp sons started to hang various kinds of items on the branches of the small tree. Pine cones. Chestnuts. Even acorns. Dyed ribbons then began to give it color. Some of the remaining persimmons were added for their orange glow. Baked goods began to appear, cookies, brownies, even cake slices. As if by magic, they quickly disappeared.

Many of us knew something about the Christian tradition from one of the colonists whom the Dutch had converted to the religion before the Shogun's strict ban. We knew that Christmas was a holy time to celebrate the birth of the Christ child. We were not as enlightened about the need to make and give presents during that time, however.

When Henry Veerkamp came into the house nursery, he was surprised to find an older woman whom he did not know tending to the Schnell infants. He had difficulty trying to find out where to find Okei as this lady had absolutely no comprehension of the English language. Each time he tried, he spoke even slower and with fewer words.

"Okei-san, where she is, you know?"

Finally, he just said Okei, and pointed in all directions with a look of confusion.

"Ah, so desu!" she exclaimed with a smile, leading him to the door and pointing to one of the colonist's shacks at the end of the row.

"Arigato!" It was one of only a half dozen Japanese words that he knew. She smiled again in recognition.

The building was the last of five colonist shacks in a row to the south of the house. He found Okei inside the partition sitting on the wooden floor at a low table. She was working on a long piece of white cloth, about the width of the table. No one else was in the room.

"You are making a gift?" he asked before his eyes could adjust to the darker interior of the building. Immediately, he became acutely aware that he might have startled her with his naturally loud voice, but she did not flinch. Indeed, she kept her deep state of concentration as if he were not there at all.

She had a funnel shaped folded piece of paper in her hand and was leaning down with the tip of the paper on the wide cloth. On the fabric, Henry could vaguely see an outline of drawn patterns. The funnel deposited a thin line of creamy paste on the lines as she worked. He had interrupted Okei when she needed to focus all her attention on her work.

"I'll come back," he said awkwardly. "I came at a bad time." He was about to leave when she spoke in a very soft voice to keep her hands from wavering.

"Please stay, Henry-san. I will enjoy your company."

Henry tried to make himself comfortable on the floor but could not find any way to sit in the way that she did. His work pants were too stiff to fold his legs very much, and he also was wearing his work boots. Suddenly he noticed that she only had stockings on her feet. She had left her walking geta outside the entrance. Henry excused himself and half slid to the front door. It took a moment to undo the laces and kick the heavy shoes off his feet. A brief odor in the air made him wonder if he should also have removed his socks, or washed his feet.

Okei continued squeezing the paste onto the drawn lines as Henry quietly watched. Often her face was nearly on the fabric as she worked on small designs that required careful and intricate movement with just the tips of her fingers. Some of them were tiny flowers less than a fingernail width across, with infinitely smaller petals. There were clusters of minute elongated shapes that reminded Henry of schools of fish. Wavy lines looked like waves in the ocean. With no more than a suggestion of color, it was hard to tell. Finally, Okei rose up and took a deep breath. She opened the sliding door a little further to let in more light and held up the fabric before her.

Henry didn't know what to think. He recognized that this was just part of a long involved process for which he had no understanding.

"How do you say "gift" in Japanese?" he asked.

"Okurimono," Okei responded. "Why do you ask?"

"Well, it looks to me like you are making a gift for someone, being that tomorrow is Christmas."

"Oh, this is not a gift. I need a new kimono, and since it will take long time to make, I must start now."

Henry was puzzled. He had thought that it was some kind of tablecloth. Okei smiled when he saw his confusion.

"You were not supposed to see this yet, Henry-san," she went on. "It only has the preparation work done. It will not become beautiful until the colors are brushed on."

"It is not very wide to be a kimono," he noted.

"This is only one of four panels that I am doing. They will all be brought together to make the kimono."

Henry was taken aback. He had seen many kimonos since the colonists came but had no idea until now of the great amount of labor that it took to make just one.

"It's incredible. I always thought all the colors were just painted onto a piece of silk. I never realized all the work. . . "

"It is not just silk, Henry-san." Okei motioned him closer to her. She took his hand and placed it on the edge of the cloth. "This is shioze habutae silk, very light and finely woven. It is also very expensive."

The silk was feather light and cool in Henry's hands. It had a crepe paper feel but undeniable smoothness at the same time. It felt like the touch of linen when he had helped his mother hang garments on the clothesline.

Henry then saw what seemed like tents or teepees with long central poles drawn into the fabric. He was about to ask her how Okei knew about native traditions when she put down the fabric and went to the door entrance.

"Come with me," she simply said.

It was already getting dark on this winter evening but the full moon and mild temperature made the walk enjoyable. They went down the narrow road and came to the place where the memorable American Matsuri had happened a season and many months ago. "Okei's Hill," John Henry Schnell had christened the place. Okei's

Hill, it would forever be known. They passed under the big oak tree and into the clearing of the hill. Through the bright moonlight, the brighter stars were beginning to peer down upon them. To the west, opposite the moon, a brilliant Venus dazzled above the horizon. That was also the direction to Japan.

"Tonight, my mother and father, my brothers Otoshi and Miko, will be seeing this from the front yard of our house." Okei gazed as the last colors of the sunset faded below the horizon. "They will be wondering about me, as I wonder about them. Otosan and Okasan, Otoshi and Miko, I hope that all of you are well. Do not cry and worry about me. I am well and with my friends Matsu and Henry. They have helped make this land a new home for me, and I shall forever be grateful to them."

Henry put his arm around her, her body so small and with so little substance that her warmth was almost the only thing he felt. He sensed her melancholy, and tried to lift her from it.

"You can go back to visit, anytime," he told her. "I hear that steamships head to Japan almost every day now. Mom and dad, me, we can all help. . . ."

Okei surprised him with a kiss on the cheek. She dashed off into the shadow of some nearby trees.

A momentarily dazed Henry had to look around in a circle to see where she had gone. Finally he spotted the white of her dress reflecting the moonlight.

When he reached her, he wasn't expecting a hand to suddenly reach up to cover his mouth. He panicked and resisted for a moment but she showed unbelievable strength in holding onto him. Finally he heard her trembling whispering voice.

"There is something wrong, do not speak. . . "

Henry stopped fighting and began to listen. He heard nothing.

Again she was gone. Following the light sound of her footsteps, he found himself deeper in the brush and trees. He was beginning to have some real concerns about this entire matter.

Ahead of them were large shadows, darker than any previously. Henry heard the metallic sound of a bridle. They had come upon two horses under one of the trees. One of the horses moved into the moonlight but did not make a sound. Henry found himself trying to calm and steady the animal. Now he also sensed the danger and urgency surrounding them.

Okei had known for some time that something was not right. She had hidden the premonition from Henry because of a selfish desire to enjoy his company at all costs. But she could no longer be so selfish. Suddenly she remembered the wagon at the Aizu castle and the man who had peered steadily at her from beneath it. She remembered walking away with a hollow feeling inside her soul, recalling that face as a vision from the future, and the past. She felt his eyes on her back, watching, ready to order the soldiers after her, getting up and chasing her himself, short legs pumping, yelling madly and waving his hands with frenzied emotion.

The saddle on the horse was not of the western design but the low slung design she had seen in Japan. A large cloth bag hung from its short horn and Okei reached for it with a trembling hand. She had seen many of these black drawstring bags in Japan and knew before she turned it over what she would find. Emblazoned in gold leaf was the Imperial sixteen-petal chrysanthemum crest of the Emperor. Her premonition was realized.

"They have come for us, Henry," she was almost sobbing. "We must warn Schnell-san and the others."

Henry was in motion almost as fast as she was. "I'm going to my house to get dad's gun," he yelled as loudly as a whisper could be yelled, already dashing off in a different direction. Okei ran towards the farmhouse.

Running as fast as her feet would carry her, she struggled up the steep rise before seeing the lights of the farmhouse. Even from a distance, she could see a dark figure peering through the main house window. She saw the steel glint of the sword he held. Still running hard, she became frightened that she would fall on the darkened ground and not be able to warn them.

"Ninja!" she yelled out with every bit of breath that she had left.

The man stared at her for an instant in startled amazement. He seemed to take a step toward her, then quickly turned and sent himself crashing through the house window.

Schnell, Jou, and Frances were no longer seated on the long couch on the opposite side of the room from the window. They had started moving even before they had heard Okei's warning cry, alerted when the cat which had been laying contentedly on Frances' lap suddenly jumped sideways to the ground with a frightened yelp.

The ninja got to his feet in an instant, and ignoring the glass and debris around him, reached to his back to unsheathe his long sword. He smiled in satisfaction at the panic as people scattered away in every direction. Schnell struggled to get out the short sword that he always carried with him. He made a near fatal mistake of reaching with his damaged arm, realizing too late that it would not move.

Seeing his target immobile in front of him, the ninja raised his sword, shouted something guttural and incoherent, and charged directly at Schnell.

Matsunosuke Sakurai had been in the adjoining room. It is not known how he managed to get into the main room so quickly or why he happened to be wearing his katana that evening.

Though the sword is not heavy, it still is bothersome to have when there were so many mundane duties to do and danger seemed so far away. Maybe he too had a sense like my maker, Okei-san. I will never know. All I know is that he was there in this most dire of times.

The ninja's first realization of Sakurai's presence was when the downward arc of his sword crashed not into Schnell's neck but into an immovable object that sent a fiery jolt of pain through his body. A sword had appeared out of nowhere, denying him his rightful prize of the gaijin's head. He turned around and glared at Sakurai who was momentarily off balance from the great impact of the swords' collision. The ninja's swing at the samurai's back was barely caught by a backward maneuver of Matsu's sword hand. Now the ninja was off balance. Sakurai swung wide and the tip of the razor sharp blade caught the midsection as the ninja retreated, a fine spray of blood leaving a trail on the floor.

The situation would have been less frightful had the two other samurai, Kuninosuke and Nishijawa, been there to also fight the intruder. Surely they would have come to the aid of Sakurai-san and Schnell-sama. But Nishijawa was still weakened from the miner's ambush several months ago. All he could do was take Jou and the other women and children away to another room. Kuninosuke was not even present, and it would be a guilt that he would feel for the remainder of his life. He had found a woman in Coloma with whom he had been spending many evenings. He would not learn about the fight until several days later.

The ninja retreated only briefly before quickly turning with his arm cocked behind his back. "Shuriken!" Schnell yelled when he saw the long bladed throwing star in his hand. It flew so fast at that short distance that Matsu only had time to swipe his sword in front of him. A rattling metallic sound and a blue yellow flash filled the room. The throwing star thudded into the wall inches from where Schnell stood, while the momentum of Matsu's swing carried him away to nearly the center of the room. Undaunted, Matsu charged forward and was able to get a strong clean blow at the intruder with his blade. The ninja's head fell to the floor and began rolling before the rest of his body crumpled down.

The head rolled nearly across the room to where Schnell stood, stopping just as the front door opened. All anyone could do was to glance briefly as Okei entered. She had been running as fast as she could to the house the entire time all this had happened.

It was a scene that Okei could not readily comprehend. The ninja's body was lying on the floor closest to her. Matsu stood nearby with his bloody sword held downward in his hand. A long trail of blood led across the room to the head beside Schnell-san, whose wide eyes were eyeing the throwing star half buried into the wall beside his head. Jou and Francis were peeking out from behind the next room's wall.

Okei had been ready for grief and found it difficult to change her emotions. She brought her hands to her face and had to fight the deep need to burst into tears.

She only had time to half turn at the sounds that came from behind her. A strong blow to her back sent her flying forward and headlong to the floor. The man who suddenly entered through the door was dressed in a dark business suit but had the topknot on his head of a samurai. A longbow was in his hand. Quickly spotting Schnell, he lifted his arm and both grimaced and smiled as the arrow shaft was pulled fully back into his body. Torima would be proud because he was aiming directly at Schnell and could not possibly miss.

Then he seemed to pitch forward slightly. His eyes became glassy still. Something seemed to fly out of the chest of his neat suit, leaving tissue and red residue on the floor in front of him. His hold on the arrow and bow weakened and they fell to the floor just as the muffled boom of a rifle came from somewhere outside. He neither closed nor rolled his eyes. He simply fell forward to the floor.

It took a moment before Henry Veerkamp came running through the door. He held a rifle in his hand and had to lean on the doorframe to take several deep breaths before he could look up.

"Is everyone OK? Did I get 'em?" He looked around at everyone standing and at first missed Okei lying on the floor. Instinctively he went to help when he saw her but didn't notice the intruder's body just in front. Henry tripped and he and the rifle went crashing to the floor.

The completion of this eventful day that could have been so tragic but turned out so fortunate, was that Henry did not hurt himself and the rifle was empty and no further damage was done.

The small wooden shrine that had languished in the barn was brought into the main room of the house that night. All the people who remained at the Wakamatsu Tea and Silk Colony took turns worshipping at the altar. There now were eight, not counting Neko and little me. Frances held me before the small golden Buddha residing within the lacquered temple and put my immobile arms together with hers in gassho. Namu Amida Butsu, Namu Amida Butsu, Namu Amida Butsu.

With so many concerns in the world, why the Great Buddha should bother himself over a pitiful little being such as I, I do not know. I was thankful and grateful for this. Those whom I love will continue this journey with me. The story that I tell will go on, pages and pages into the future. Perhaps that was the Great Buddha's intention all along. A story untold is the tragedy of lives forgotten. The lives of everyone I knew. The Buddha works in mysterious ways.

On Christmas day, the sheriff from Placerville came out to our farm. He examined the two bodies and determined that they were celestials and probably had no family in this country. They could be buried anywhere on the property. They were, far, far away from all the buildings in the distant field, never to be seen or thought of again.

In the afternoon, we went to one of the Christian churches in Coloma. We were invited to attend by the Veerkamp family, and of course it would have been very impolite to refuse. Francis, Louisa, and all five sons were in attendance, along with Schnell-san, Jou, Frances and Mary, Okei, Matsugoro and his wife and daughter, and Dr. Matsumoto. I went as well. Only Matsu and Yana remained on the farm.

In the middle of the Coloma town, a large pine tree had been decorated with colorful ribbons and ornaments made out of metal foil. Even the hitching posts along the side of the road were wrapped with ribbons. The amount of work done for this Christian day was truly amazing.

"Is everyone in Coloma a Christian?" Okei wondered out loud.

"No, not more that half, I presume," Schnell responded. "But even non-Christians celebrate Christmas because it brings families and friends together. It is a good time to remember everything that has happened over the last year."

"It has been an eventful year," Dr. Matsumoto said thoughtfully.

Nobody was able to respond.

They sat in the church with the Veerkamps and prayed together, in the Christian and Buddhist ways.

※

CHAPTER 13
Schnell's Departure

The start of the new year of 1871 was not celebrated as we had done for the previous year. A year ago, we had made mochi and the wine and sake had flowed. There were almost thirty of us then. Now there were only twelve, counting all of the children. Of the able bodied young laborers who had toiled in the fields, only Yana and Kintaro were left. There would be no crop harvest in this new year.

It has to be remembered that Okei was still a young girl even though she had been forced to grow up so quickly. Because of her youth, she was unable to control her emotions when she saw the world around her beginning to collapse. She was beginning to feel that her life was collapsing, also.

She blamed herself for not knowing of the second intruder who had been just behind her that night. He had followed her into the house and only Henry's miracle long distance shot had prevented a terrible tragedy. She should have sensed him. She should have known.

It was because of the illness, she knew. The chills and fevers were more frequent now and lasting much longer. Oh, if only she could rid her body of the invaders that had snatched away her health. If only the Buddha knew of her dire condition and one day she would wake to a sunrise unburdened by this crippling sickness and her spirit free to soar once again.

But this would be a selfish and improper request of the Buddha. How dare she place her own welfare above millions on Earth who needed his compassion far more than she did? In time, she would pray to the Buddha when the suffering became too great to bear. She was confident that he would answer that prayer. Death was not an ending to be feared.

This morning, Okei was on her way to bathe in the small pond north of the house. She saw Matsu standing beside a horse next to the barn. The horse was sweating and Matsu was drying its neck with a towel.

"Matsu, you have already been into town?" Okei saw that he was wearing the nice dark haori jacket and one of his better fitting work pants.

"Yes, to Placerville. I had some business to attend to."

Matsu always had a serious expression on his face but now it seemed ever more so. Okei was curious about the "business" but didn't pursue the matter. He also looked different in some other way, and it took a moment before she realized that he did not have his short sword, the wakizashi, on his belt. Since the time when they had been surrounded by the angry mob in San Francisco, he was never seen without the wakizashi. Matsu saw Okei looking and immediately tightened the cloth belt over the haori to better cover himself.

Okei turned her gaze away. "I am going to bathe in the creek," she said, bowing just slightly.

Matsu bowed in return and watched her walk away.

He was a fool to think that he had any chance of deceiving Okei. She knew what he had done but had wisely recognized that he was in no mood to talk about it.

Matsu shook his head. He took a deep breath and stared for a moment at the ground. He felt the emptiness at his belt where the wakizashi had been. Soon he would have to go to his room and see the empty corner where he usually kept his katana.

Of all the self sacrificing acts he had done in his life, of which there were many, this had been the hardest and most demeaning for him. He had gone to the trading store in Placerville and bartered for the worth of his swords. The katana had been in his family for at least ten generations. It had been made by the twelfth-century master sword-smith Moritsugu, who made swords for many of the Shogun's family line.

The idiot storekeeper hadn't heard of Moritsugu and didn't even know who a Shogun was. He had no comprehension of hand-to-hand battles where sword skills and quality of the blade made the difference between life or death.

"It has saved my life numerous times," Matsu had argued. "I defeated superior samurai in armor because of this sword."

The shopkeeper laughed. "It's not a useful weapon here," he said. "It's only good for cutting firewood, and only very small branches. I'll give you thirty dollars for it and the short one you have on. Take it or leave it."

Matsu could barely hide the horror he felt inside, grabbing the wakizashi at his side. "Fifty," he said.

"Thirty-five dollars. No more."

He returned to the Wakamatsu farm having sold both his swords for thirty-five dollars.

Francis Veerkamp had reluctantly taken the money in exchange for a promise to let the colonists stay on the farm for another month.

"You are a good man, Matz," he had told him. "You are welcome to come work for me when Herr Schnell is here no longer. I have a cabin in back where you can stay."

Matsu was walking ahead without seeing and almost ran right into Dr. Matsumoto. The doctor was dressed in a light-colored business suit and wore a stylish light-brown derby hat on his head.

At first he just tried to get around Matsu without a word. Matsu saw a great deal of unease in the doctor's face.

"You are going somewhere?" he asked, not seeing any horses or wagons nearby.

"So, ne. I am going to Sacramento. I am almost out of some medicines and need to visit the Chinatown. Sumimasen, I must go now."

Matsu smiled but the doctor had already started away. Even more puzzling, he watched as Dr. Matsumoto went around the barn and disappeared beyond to the other side.

It was a concern of what might be happening that caused Matsu to go around from the west side of the barn. There at the back was a freight wagon with two horses. Jou held Mary on her lap on the front seat. Frances was standing in the back of the wagon and crying while John Henry Schnell tried to get her to sit down. Dr. Matsumoto held several luggage bags while waiting for Schnell to finish with Frances. Except for Frances, they all froze when they saw Matsu.

In a daze from the implication of what he was witnessing, Matsu slowly walked forward and stopped just before the horses.

"Matsu, I couldn't find you earlier," Schnell looked at him with his showiest wide smile. "I was going to ask if you wanted to come to Sacramento with us, but now Dr. Matsumoto is coming so there isn't room for you."

"I was in Placerville," Matsu said. "I had a business proposition."

"Well, yes, I do too, in Sacramento," Schnell continued his smile, trying to hide his mind's thoughts. "They wanted to see my family, you know, they don't just trust anyone."

"I see, Schnell-sama." Matsu noticed that the wagon and horses were different from anything on the farm. "You will be obtaining funds for our colony?"

Schnell was somehow able to make his smile even brighter. "Yes, Matsu. There is a bill in the legislature to support the kind of experimental agriculture like we are doing. If it passes, the government will pay for all our expenses next year."

"Ah, so ne." Matsu looked at the bags that Dr. Matsumoto still held in his hands, also noticing the number of boxes and a trunk in the wagon's back. Jou was dressed in a large full dress with ruffled patterns and wore a hat with a ribbon and feathers. They were the large feathers of an exotic large bird. A parasol was in her hand.

"I hope that you are successful," Matsu continued. "Too many workers have left to insure a harvest for this season."

Schnell came off the wagon and stood closely in front of him. "We will turn this around, Matsu. We are samurai from Aizu. You and I, we are used to battles of life and death, ne? Time after time we have faced far greater opponents with far fewer weapons. This is just about convincing people in Sacramento and signing papers. I know I can do this. The future of the Wakamatsu Tea and Silk Colony will be as bright as we had planned."

Schnell grabbed Matsu by the shoulders in his exuberance. Matsu tried to show his enthusiasm but found that there was little of it within him.

"Ganbatte!" Schnell exclaimed. "You will see, Matsu. When I return, we will plant new trees and get more silkworms. We will advertise in the best newspapers in the country. We will have so much business that they will have to change the stagecoach route to make a stop here!"

Matsu remembered the original vision they had of the colony back in the times past.

"The stagecoach will stop under our Aizu banner," he tried to bring the vision to life in his mind. "We can sell mikan and tomatoes, in the house will be silk kimonos they can buy."

"That's it, Matsu!" Schnell was so close that he could feel his heavy breathing. "I swear to you that I can still make this come true."

Schnell climbed up to the wagon seat as Dr. Matsumoto pulled himself into the back.

"When will you return, Schnell-sama?" Matsu had saved his most telling question for the end.

With the reins in his hands, Schnell appeared to be counting the days in his head.

"I don't know. At least a week. Maybe two, or three."

"So desu." Matsu shaded his eyes as he looked up at him.

"There are many people I have to talk to," Schnell said without looking down. "It will take some time to convince them. You will be in charge until I return."

"I will be waiting for you." Matsu hadn't realized that he was holding onto one of the leather straps of the horses.

"Schnell-sama?"

Schnell finally looked down at him.

"Do not go back to Japan," Matsu felt that he was pleading, but his voice did not show his emotional turmoil. "Torima will not rest until your blood flows like a river at his feet."

Jou must have heard, but she did not flinch beside him. Schnell looked ahead at the road for a moment before turning to Matsu.

"I am not a fool, Matsu. Japan and Torima are gone from my life. I will never go back."

Schnell nodded his head slightly, and Matsu bowed in return, releasing his grip on the strap. The wagon started and turned left onto the dirt road. It then disappeared around the house and soon the sounds of the hooves and wheels on the ground had also vanished.

The names of John Henry Schnell, Jou, Frances, and Mary, would never again appear on the pages of any known historical records. The question of their fate still remains the greatest mystery of the entire Wakamatsu Tea and Silk Colony story.

Of course those who record the history did not have knowledge of the little doll in the small bag labeled "Kodomo-no-mono" that was among the luggage in the wagon. They could not have known that a small and insignificant being such as I could witness what history had not seen, and retain within these fibers of cloth and silk and portions of paper fillings, the memories to complete the life stories that had been left unfinished.

I think this is why I am still here. No one else is left to remember. It is a responsibility that I humbly accept, and I am honored that the historic fate of so many has been placed onto my tiny body. The story of my friends, those who gave me existence and a reason to be, I pledged to tell without fail.

Now looking back, I realize how premature my promise had been. I could not have known how soon my integrity would be challenged. Shortly after our arrival in Sacramento, I suffered a serious injury that almost ended my existence. I hadn't even known until then that I could be harmed in any way. Eee, what other unknown surprises await in this world!

We arrived in the evening at the Sacramento river front district and Schnell-san went to find a hotel room for the night. Dr. Matsumoto went in the opposite direction to the herb shops in the China part of the city. Jou, the children, and I waited on a bench overlooking the busy river. Frances had asked to have her doll to play with and Jou had freed me from my enclosure. Although I could get images of my surroundings while stowed away, the clear vision that I had with my own eyes was refreshing and exhilarating. Boats with long billowing stacks spewing thick black smoke were everywhere upon the river. It was often difficult to see any of the water they floated on. Closer in front of the cluttered river was the loading platform of the new transcontinental railroad, complete with several long trains with locomotives partially obscured by swirling smoke. Indeed, the smoke would drift over and occasionally make us invisible to each other. Frances and Mary laughed as they played hide and seek. Jou coughed.

Schnell-san came back and found Jou staring out at the darkening river. He was anxious to get to the hotel where he had arranged a room, but decided that it was best to sit beside his wife in this instance.

"Did you find a good hotel, my husband?" she inquired.

"Hai, not far away. It will be adequate. We will be staying for only one night."

"Did you get the train tickets to the East?"

Schnell did not answer even though the tickets were in his hand.

"I did not like leaving as we did," Jou still didn't look at him.

"Yes, it was more difficult than I had imagined." John Henry Schnell sat back deeper into the hard bench, knowing that this was going to take some time. "I thought it over many times, but could think of no other way. The colony is finished and everyone knows this. They will feel pain at first, but they will move on with their lives as we move on. They are all strong and resilient people and will be successful where ever they decide to go."

Jou suddenly sat up and walked forward before realizing that there was nowhere to go but the river.

"I did not say goodbye to Okei," she shook her head and then wiped a tear from her eye. "I did not see Matsugoro-san. I never told Matsu-san how grateful I am for all that he has done for us."

Schnell went to hug his wife who did not resist him.

"Our dreams were so great, my husband," her voice was filled with sobs. "To leave them with this lie sickens my heart."

He stroked her shoulder. "I will send them money when we are settled in Boston." He felt like he was reassuring himself more than her.

Jou's trembling stopped but her voice was still filled with grief. "It will then be too late."

Schnell was up early the next morning but Dr. Matsumoto apparently had risen earlier. He was seated at a table in the hotel lobby and motioned for Schnell to come join him.

"This is the best coffee so far," he said as he put down the cup. "I cannot imagine how good it will be in the East where you are going."

Schnell normally would have had something to say in return to Dr. Matsumoto, but already his mind was filled with trouble and uncertainty. He hadn't slept at all. It had been one of the worst nights that he could ever remember.

He noticed the cloth bag on the table next to the doctor with kanji inscriptions printed on it. The meaning didn't make sense to him until he remembered that the doctor had needed to visit the Chinatown.

"Did you get the medicine for the colony?"

"Yes. I had wanted more but the supply was limited. However, our numbers are fewer at the farm and I think this will be enough."

Schnell fidgeted with a spoon that he had unconsciously picked up. He was finding it difficult to think clearly.

"Dr. Matsumoto, you know how much I value and respect your opinion. You and Matsu-san have been my closest friends and advisors."

The doctor put down his cup for a moment to listen.

"I need to know how you feel about what I am doing." Schnell thought about what he had just asked and realized that there were no answers that could truly fill the emptiness that he felt inside. It did not matter what others thought now that the feeling of guilt had permeated so deeply into his soul.

The only movement that Dr. Matsumoto displayed was the clenching and unclenching of his hands on the table. He stopped a waiter who was passing by not far away.

"Whiskey, please," he said. "One also for my friend."

He leaned back on his chair and looked directly at Schnell, who then stopped fidgeting with the spoon.

"I believe a man must follow his karma. It does not matter what other people say or think, because they will not always be there to comfort or criticize. In the end you will be alone to look back on what you have or have not done. Only you will be left to judge if your life truly had meaning."

The waiter brought the whiskey and Dr. Matsumoto raised his glass to Schnell. Schnell raised his and they both drained the liquid.

Schnell waited for his throat to clear of the potent liquid, then his eyes focused far into the distance. More uncomfortable moments passed as Dr. Matsumoto waited.

"I am going back to Japan," he finally said. "I did not know until this moment."

For the first time, the doctor displayed surprise. He had to close his eyes to think about what he had just heard.

"It will be suicide."

Schnell would not be dissuaded. He reached into the pocket of his shirt and unfolded a small piece of paper on the table in front of Dr. Matsumoto.

"I received this message a month after the ninja attack."

Dr. Matsumoto carefully read the note, all written by hand in kanji brush strokes. It took a moment. He didn't recognize Torima's illegible signature but the family crest stamp was unmistakable.

"This man cannot be trusted, Schnell-sama."

Schnell had thought long about this. "I am not a fool," he countered. "That is why I am sending my family on to Boston."

He shifted in the hard wooden chair and leaned closer to Dr. Matsumoto. "All that I ask of him is to have the funds to make the colony successful. We will have new trees and new silkworms. The Wakamatsu Colony will prosper and become famous. This is my greatest dream."

"How do you know that he will keep his word?"

"Torima has always fancied himself a samurai. He has no honor, but he wants the world to believe that he has. He will do this for my capture. He will send the funds to show the world what an honorable man he is. He will have more prestige and honor than ever before."

"And he will have you."

"Yes."

"You will never know if our colony succeeded or failed."

"You and Matsu, Matsugoro, those who are left, will not let it fail."

"You will have given your life in vain, Schnell-sama."

"I think not."

Dr. Matsumoto's mind was recovering from the shock of Schnell's audacious plan and only now began to think about other complicating factors. He now wished that he hadn't had the whiskey.

"What has Jou said? Surely she cannot approve. . . " Suddenly he was jolted by a stark realization that overcame all his other thoughts.

"I will need to trust you to insure the safety of my family," Schnell leaned closer to him. "I will need to get them on the train without me. I have a plan that I know will work."

Now Dr. Matsumoto wished that he had an entire bottle of the whiskey as he listened to Schnell's scheme of deception.

"This is a preposterous idea, Schnell-sama. I cannot approve. I cannot be a part of this."

That big bright smile that Schnell was famous for seemed to fill his entire face. He moved close enough to put his arm around the doctor's shoulder.

"It is my karma," he said close to his ear. "This is what I have lived my entire life for. The legacy of our people will endure, Matsumoto-sensei. This is what I will be remembered for. Ganbatte!"

The train would be leaving very soon and all of us entered into the madness outside the hotel. The riverboat, Delta King, had just reached port and hundreds were scrambling on and off. The giant ship towered over the train that waited just in front of it.

I viewed all of this with no comprehension of what was soon to become of me. Without Okei's vision or wisdom to help, all I could do was marvel at the fast paced world dashing by me. We had to cross several busy streets to get to the train platform at the wharf. Everyone seemed to be in a mindless rush to get somewhere. Jou carried Mary and Schnell held tightly to Frances' little hand. Frances held me in the crook of her arms.

At the first street crossing, Schnell stopped and appeared to be looking for someone. Jou had stepped onto the street but had to step back onto the boardwalk when he didn't follow. She tottered slightly from the weight of carrying Mary.

"Nan ka?" she asked, noticing his confused appearance. It was then that he let go of Frances' hand and began looking deeper into the crowd around them. Jou began to look also, although she had no idea what she was searching for.

Little Frances continued off the boardwalk and onto the dirt street. She looked in wonder at the large boat and the train cars and the great confusion of people and was eager to find out what all that was about.

Schnell heard the horse hooves and rumbling of a wagon closely approaching and reached down to find Frances. She was not beside him. He was bent down searching for her when Jou screamed. Schnell looked up to see the little girl striding with her tiny footsteps out in the center of the street. The horses and wagon were almost upon her. He only had time to shout out her name before a swirling cloud of dust enshrouded her.

CHAPTER 14
Gone From This Earth

It was like being born once again. I was staring up at the ceiling, seeing the rough boards and nails above but not aware of anything. My eyes had apparently fared better than my mind, which struggled in its search for the time and place in which I now found myself.

"You are back, Keiko-chan," a familiar voice spoke to me.

Okei? Is that really you?

"Hai. I am so grateful to the Buddha. I was afraid that you had been lost forever."

I began to see around me. I was on a table and Okei's hand was holding my body. She held a long needle with a thick white thread. I thought she was sewing a cloth but I soon realized that she was sewing my body. I began to feel the tightness and penetration of the needle.

"Something very big and heavy must have stepped on you," she said, as I cringed at the thought. "Your bottom part was almost cut from your body. The beautiful kimono I made for you is forever gone."

I sighed as much as an inanimate doll could sigh. I was just beginning to live, I thought, as much as an inanimate doll could live. Why had the great Buddha allowed this to happen to me?

What had I done wrong? Then I remembered Frances carrying me onto the street. Could I have caused her to be injured, or worse? Oh, no! It cannot be.

I then had the vision of a large and noisy object coming fast upon us and was wondering why Frances had put us into such danger. She was but a child, I realized, and knew that I had to do something quickly. But what could I do? I was just a little doll never meant to make changes to the world.

Okei picked me up and looked at me with her beautiful smile.

"You must have been so brave, Keiko-chan," she said to me. "I should not be so surprised, ne? A part of me is within you. Duty and honor is as important to you as it is to me."

I could not be placated, not even by Okei's soothing words.

Okei, I need to know about Frances-chan. I wanted to save her but I couldn't…

Okei continued to hold me, then brought me closer and hugged me next to her face and neck.

"A lady brought you back from Sacramento," she continued looking directly into my face. "She was very nice and was very concerned that she would find me. When she handed you to me, she told me a most unfortunate story."

Tears had formed at the corner of her eyes. One fell down by my side. She had to reach for a cloth that was lying beside her.

"Dr. Matsumoto was bringing you back to me. I am sure that he was excited to tell me about your heroic deed. But he was not able to do this. A terrible thing happened while he was returning to our home."

I looked on with my unblinking eyes, seeing her tears but unable to shed my own. I could not believe that Matsumoto-sensei was gone. He had been a part of my life for as long as I could remember.

"In his last moment he told the lady to bring you to me. He told her that Frances was safe and that you had saved her life."

I did?

"I wish I could tell you more, Keiko-chan. It is all so strange to me. Dr. Matsumoto. Schnell-san and Jou-san. Why did they take Frances and Mary with them? Are they not ever coming back? I cannot believe they would leave without saying good-bye to me after all of my service to them. Eee. If only I knew."

Okei cut the final thread and set me down. She left for a moment and when she returned she held up a silk fabric for me to see.

"This is one of the few silk cloths made at the Wakamatsu Colony," Okei said to me. "We did not know what to do with it because there was not enough of it to make a kimono."

It was of a brilliant orange red with many small dark red flowers. It was exquisite. I could readily see myself in it for the rest of my existence.

I am very small, Okei-san.

Reading my thoughts almost made Okei laugh, but the sadness of the day reduced it to a smile as Okei began to cut and shape the fabric. Within a few hours, I was wearing my new and beautiful kimono.

With my body now repaired, I felt almost whole again. Still, there was an emptiness in my life's past that needed to be filled in. I was hopeful that I could restore the memory of what had happened in Sacramento. After all, my physical body had been there, although in two pieces. My kami, though dissipated, had not ceased to exist. I had to put them together again and then I would remember.

I sat alone for many days. With Frances and Mary gone, that purpose in my life was also gone. Okei must have felt much missing in her life as well, because she spent more time at the Veerkamp house with Louisa and the sons. At the Wakamatsu farm, only Matsu, Yana, and Matsugoro and his family remained. One day, Okei took her bedroll and me to the Veerkamp home at the foot of the mountain. Henry and William would stay at the Wakamatsu house to make room for her there.

Then my memory returned one day as I sat on a small child's chair in Okei's bedroom. As each precious remembrance came into my thoughts, there came also a deep awareness that I was the only one remaining to know this story. I was left feeling humbled and also distressed. John Henry Schnell. Jou. Frances. Mary. I sensed that their kami had been extinguished from this world. Something had happened after they had left me. Oh, but what a terrible awareness to befall me!

I looked around for Okei but did not sense her nearby. I was desperate to tell her what I knew, but it would have to wait. Of course the more pressing matter of Okei's illness would soon occur and the story would have to wait even longer. Oh, but I could not have anticipated just how long.

Days turned into weeks, weeks into months, months to years. By now the history has been written in books and the books have been put away to dusty storage. Biographies have been completed. Stories have ended. I am filled with irreconcilable regret that I have taken so long to accomplish my duty. I ask forgiveness from all of you, the people I have known and loved. I waited and waited, hoping someday that the darkness would end, that the cover over me would be lifted and I would again see light, and I would be able to tell my story.

In an instant, the dust that rose up from skidding wagon wheels and four rearing horses enveloped everything in a choking red cloud. Schnell threw himself into it to where he had his last glimpse of Frances. The cloud lifted slightly just before he would have crashed into the stopped freight wagon. The wheels were massive and his dread grew.

"Dear God I just didn't see her!" the wagon driver was lamenting as he stood up in the seat and looked from side to side. Others who had watched in horror had also stepped forward to join in the search.

There was nothing under the heavy iron ringed wheels or the great hooves of the horses. In-between the wheels, directly beneath the center of the wagon, was a mound of red dirt. A tiny hand that emerged from it held up a small battered doll. There was a most mournful child's cry.

Schnell fell prone and his arm swept up Frances from under the wagon. He held her amid a cloud of red dust. He got up with the child in his arms. The driver smiled, nodded, and prompted his horses and wagon forward. Comforted bystanders nodded and continued on their way past.

Jou pulled both up to the boardwalk to avoid further possible tragedy. She busily dusted them with her hands, which also turned red from the dirt. She tried to take the almost severed doll from Frances, but the child would not allow it.

"Mommy, daddy, fix Keiko-chan," her little voice screamed between sobs. "Keiko hurt."

Indeed, the doll's upper part and lower part were only connected by several thin fiber threads. The kimono had been torn completely off. The head had split at a sewn seam exposing the fiber fillers within. The face and black hair were now caked with the red dirt.

Jou hugged both and Schnell let down a squirming Frances. It was then that Jou noticed Schnell's look of utter detachment. He seemed to be in shock instead of the child.

"Frances-chan is unhurt," she reassured him. "We are fortunate that the Buddha was keeping careful watch over us."

Schnell continued looking far away. Jou became distressed and began to feel around Schnell's head to see if he had been injured.

Finally, Schnell began to see the Jou's concern as she stared into him. He knew he should say something to reassure her. Could he tell her what he had seen, just before the dust from the wagon brakes had clouded his vision? He wasn't sure himself. Maybe his mind was making up an impossible sight for some unimaginable purpose.

"I saw something," was all that he could tell Jou.

Jou tried to smile and make a joke of it. "Will you tell me that you saw the Buddha's hand save Frances-chan?"

Schnell's silence made Jou frown. He could tell her that he saw the doll drop from Frances's arms as the wagon came closer. He could say that Frances had leaned down to pick it up just as the horses and wagons had crossed over the top of her. Had she not stooped down, Frances would certainly have been killed.

He could say all this to ease Jou's anxiety about him. However only part of it was true. Frances had leaned down. That had indeed saved her. But the doll had not fallen out of Frances's arms. It had jumped. He had seen it. He just couldn't say it. He wouldn't. He kept silent.

Schnell knew he had to act before Jou began screaming for help from people passing by. He got down on his knee to look Frances eye to eye. Frances allowed him to touch the damaged doll.

"We can't fix Keiko-chan, but I know someone who can." The smile on his dirt-reddened face was as cheerful and bright as it had ever been.

Frances' face brightened in recognition. "Okei-san!" she exclaimed.

"Yes! I will have Dr. Matsumoto take Keiko back to Okei. Okei will sew her back together and give her a new kimono. She will be just like new!"

Frances held out her doll for him. When he took it, she hugged him tightly and wiped the tears from her dirt-covered face. She again had a serious look.

"But daddy, how will Keiko get back to me? Can Okei come stay with us?"

Schnell hugged her once again. "I will go back to the colony as soon as I can. I promise I will get Keiko and ask Okei to come live with us."

Frances clung to his side as he rose to his feet. Jou looked relieved and Schnell felt a great weight lifted from him. After what he had seen, it seemed only right to give the doll the best possible care. That it was just an inanimate creation didn't matter. The universe was filled with many unexplainable things and sometimes there was nothing to do but to show his debt of gratitude. He only wished that somewhere before his journey's end he would find an honorable way to do this.

The crisis seemed to have passed when suddenly Dr. Matsumoto came hurrying toward them from the other boardwalk.

"Nan ka?" Jou said again in unbelieving surprise.

The doctor took a moment to catch his breath. "A rider has

come," he informed them. "He said that Schnell-san is needed immediately back at the farm."

Schnell stared emptily for a moment before he suddenly remembered his planning.

"We must be boarding the train," he was able to recite from his memory. "What does this concern?"

"The rider did not know," Matsumoto replied. "It must be urgent to send someone after us."

"We must all go back," Jou became fearful for what might have happened. "Okei may have the fever sickness again."

John Henry Schnell struggled to remember how all this was supposed to play out. He turned to Jou.

"I will go and see what has happened. You must take Frances and Mary to Boston as we had planned. We do not have funds for another journey. My brother Edward will meet you there and take care of you. I will follow in a few days once I take care of this."

Jou looked like a defeated child. This day of all days just couldn't seem to end soon enough.

"I cannot care for the children by myself," she pleaded. "I will be alone on the train."

"People will help you, I know they will," Schnell knew he should have made better plans. Then he felt Frances tug at his leg.

"I will help mummy," the child said. "I will help take care of Mary."

Schnell looked down and felt a huge surge of guilt. This was the greatest lie he had ever concocted. What was left of his honor seemed to have vanished with the dust into the wind.

Gratefully, Jou composed herself and bowed before him on the wooden plank boardwalk in Sacramento. A train whistle blew in the background.

"You must do what your heart tells you," she said as she returned his dazed stare. "We will be waiting for you in Boston. Sayonara, my husband."

She took Frances' hand and rearranged her arm hold of Mary. She breathed deeply, turned from the men, and began to walk toward the train platform.

Schnell and Dr. Matsumoto watched the figures until they could no longer be seen in the crowd of people. For an instant, Schnell saw himself running after her and putting an end to this dishonorable scheme. He put his arm around her and kissed Mary and Frances and pledged his loyalty to them for the rest of their lives. Instead, he looked at Dr. Matsumoto who recognized his look of despair. The doctor was looking down at the badly damaged doll in his hand.

Schnell gazed at it and again the vision of the doll jumping from his daughter's hand flashed into his mind. Perhaps the Buddha himself was trying to send him a message. Perhaps he was trying to make him realize how precious his family was and that his quest to find dignity and honor in Japan was utterly selfish. How would they survive without him? What does dignity and honor mean when one is dead?

"Schnell-sama?" Dr. Matsumoto looked into his confused face.

But this wasn't about dignity or honor he tried to tell himself. He could not care less what others thought about him, especially after his death. It was about helping people at the colony, the ones who had remained faithful up to the day that he had left them.

Everyone had worked hard for him and never questioned his leadership. They had such great dreams in the beginning. The dreams could still come true. Now was the time of trial and no true warrior would surrender.

Schnell was able to raise the hand that was holding the doll. He watched as Dr. Matsumoto took it from him.

"It needs to go to Okei-san. I promised Frances…"

"I know, Schnell-sama. I too saw what it did."

He was too confused to understand what had been said. He saw the doll in the doctor's hand and realized that his last duty for his family was done. There was nothing more left to do except to begin the journey on his chosen path.

Matsumoto bowed low in his direction.

"Sayonara, Schnell-sama. Douzo o-tassha de."

John Henry Schnell could only bow and smile weakly as the doctor turned and began walking away.

The stagecoach was crowded and bumpy. Dr. Matsumoto sat in the middle of the seat facing backward because he had let the other passengers take the better window and forward-facing seats. He had ingested several of the Chinese herbs before departure and knew that he would not be experiencing the nausea like the others certainly would.

However, he was far from comfortable. His mind wouldn't stop thinking about the Sacramento world he had left behind several hours ago. When he tried to silence one troublesome thought that would come into his mind, another would rise up to take its place.

He had tried to chart the course of this day using all the courage and honor that his forty-seven years of life could provide. If only he were more certain that this had been enough. Being a physician used to the battle between life and death hadn't prepared him to face the consequences of what he had done on this day. The injuries that he might have caused could be just as fatal as a botched operation or incorrect diagnosis.

If only he knew what he had done was just and correct. His punishment, he sensed, was that he would never know. Whatever path he chose, the guilt was certain to hang over his head for the rest of his life.

His most bothersome and recurring vision was of Jou seated in the train car heading to the East. She would be in the aisle seat to allow the children to look out in wonder at the passing countryside. She would remember the letter that he had given to her that morning. He had told her that it was a note of gratitude from the members of the colony and should only be opened later. He didn't know when she would read it. Perhaps it was best that he should never find out. History would just have to sort out the final outcome.

Matsumoto went over the letter in his mind, silently mouthing the words,

Jou-san,

You have always honored me by your enduring trust. You have always known me as a truthful friend. It is because of your belief in me that I must tell you what follows.

Schnell-sama is among the bravest men that I know. What he has done I believe is in sacrifice for the people that he loves. He is giving up everything meaningful to insure that the dreams they envision will become the reality.

Please do not judge him harshly. He believes it is for the

benefit of everyone he loves. I have been honored to have known him.

Matsumoto

He couldn't stop wondering about the moment when she would read it. What would she do? If the train had yet to depart, would she grab her children and bags and dash out the coach door? If later, would she have the train stopped so she could pursue him?

He pondered over it for hours as the Coloma stagecoach bounced its way toward its destination. During one treacherous stretch of canyon road with nothing but curves for miles, he finally came to a satisfactory answer.

Jou will find Schnell at the ship and they will go to Japan together. Jou, Frances, Mary, and Schnell-sama. This was a thought that left him feeling great inner peace.

The woman seated to his right by the window was looking strangely at him. He felt embarrassment because he had probably been babbling aloud in a language foreign to her.

"Excuse me for my intrusion," she said to him. "Did you say that you are going to Japan?"

Dr. Matsumoto stared in surprise. He hadn't been aware that this new world had ingrained itself so thoroughly into him to cause him to speak his vision in English.

"No, I'm so sorry. I was just talking to myself." He thought his answer would satisfy her and that would be the end of it. He was wrong.

"I have always wanted to go to Japan," she continued on.

Dr. Matsumoto decided that he should be polite and turned his attention to her. She was a middle-aged woman who wore her age well. Her hair was tied back with a yellow ribbon and she wore a white flock-lined blouse with a short tan-colored coat. Her skirt was long and brown.

"I'm Drucella Matson. I'm just headed to Coloma, not nearly as far as you are going I'm afraid."

He had to smile. He had never talked to an American woman before.

"I am Dr. Matsumoto. I am returning to my farm in Gold Hill."

"From Japan?"

Now he had to laugh. "Please excuse my mindless talk. I have been greatly preoccupied."

"I have noticed. I was just going to leave you alone until you started talking about Japan."

"I am from Japan, but my home is Gold Hill."

"The Japanese Farm! I have heard that there are samurai warriors there that make beautiful silk kimonos."

For the first time in his life he had to bury his head in his hands to keep from breaking into uncontrolled laughter. The woman was enjoying the improvement of the temperament.

"Samurai don't make kimono."

"I know. I was just trying to make you smile."

Matsumoto sat back in the hard seat and began to relax for the first time. This might be a pleasant journey after all.

He had been dozing on and off when he felt the stagecoach lurch to a sudden stop. The sound of great commotion came from outside. One of the women passengers screamed. He heard loud demanding voices through the window.

The door flung open and a tall man in a large sweat-brimmed hat stood outside. He held a large pistol in his hand and demanded that everyone exit the coach.

There were two other men with him. One pointed a rifle and the other was holding onto the reins of three horses. The stagecoach driver had his arms in the air. Dr. Matsumoto thought it best to raise his arms, also.

All of the men and the horses also were caked with dust from hard riding. There was a growing tenseness when no one spoke or moved.

"Empty all your pockets and purses," the leader of the bandits finally demanded. "We'll shoot anyone holding anything from us."

The other robber began to collect valuables as they appeared in trembling hands. Dr. Matsumoto froze when he had heard the demand, realizing that he would not be able to comply.

The leader noticed the man standing stoically still. He pointed his pistol directly at him and pulled back the trigger.

"The chink over there better start emptying his pockets real soon! I don't care if he don't understand me!"

The other man approached Dr. Matsumoto, wheeled, and then hit him across his face with the back of his hand. The doctor staggered from the impact.

The robber found the bag in his coat pocket and held it up for the others to see. He dipped his finger into the white powder inside and gave a yelp of joy when he tasted its bitterness.

"China white!" he declared. "One hundred percent grade. The chink was trying to hide his stash!"

The leader realized that he had finally hit the jackpot. He could cut it and sell it in all the Chinatowns throughout the gold country. He was destined to be rich beyond his wildest fantasy.

Dr. Matsumoto knew he had to speak up. His voice sounded tiny and he tried to make himself louder. "It is medicine for my colony. It is Peruvian bark powder to treat the relapsing fever. Please, I need it back!" He began to step towards the man holding his bag.

A thunderous gunshot was followed by smoke and the sound of a falling body. The leader holstered his gun knowing that nobody else would dare to challenge him now.

"Chinks all the same, God damn it," he mumbled but everyone heard him clearly in the ringing silence after the shot. "They take your money and take your women and don't even bother to say thank you. Serves 'em right, damned fool."

The robbers stepped around the body to gather up their booty, mounted up, and soon disappeared around the curve in the road.

People in shock stood around long after the robbers were gone. Those who assumed Dr. Matsumoto was already dead stepped over the body that was directly in front of the stagecoach door.

Drucella was the first one to come to his side. The twitching of his nostril showed that he was still alive. He was trying desperately to say something to her. His voice was very weak and she had to lean so close that his blood stained her white frock blouse.

"There is a doll in my luggage," he said in a quivering voice.

"Japanese doll. It saved life of child, Frances-chan. Hard to believe, ne?" He coughed blood and she had to pull away for an instant.

"Believe. It is true." His voice was getting weaker and more garbled. "Promise me you take doll to Okei-san at farm. Okei-san has magic to fix doll. Good as new. Please promise…"

Drucella listened and felt too much turmoil to be able to find her voice. She was aware that he was fading fast and she could not let him go without letting him know.

"I promise to take the doll…" That was as far as she got before she realized that he was gone. "... to Okei-san," she finished as she rose to her feet.

Some of the luggage had been scattered by the robbers and Drucella had to search hard to find Dr. Matsumoto's bag. Finally she found one of a peculiar black woven design and opened it. The feeling of a silk shirt told her that this was his bag. There was an oblong cloth wrapped object towards the bottom. Immediately she knew this to be the doll. She unwrapped it and saw Keiko for the first time.

Drucella sat on one of the trunks on the ground and held the doll before her. It was clothe-less, battered and a sorry sight. The wounds and dust seemed only to hint of what had happened to it and what it had done.

You must have a miraculous story to tell, little doll, she thought in her mind and held it to her red-stained chest.

I sat in the child's chair in Okei's bedroom and could feel the wetness of the blood on Drucella's shirt. I could smell the lingering smoke of the gunshot and then could hear Dr. Matsumoto's last request to her. I wondered if knowing that I was now safely with

Okei would comfort his spirit, wherever it was now. I prayed that he knew that his death had not been in vain.

Though I always wondered about the Schnell's fate, other concerns soon occupied my attention. I didn't think any more about it until one evening many years later as I sat on a shelf in Matsu's small cabin. The shelf was empty except for a white smooth stone and a whiskey glass. I was alone and had not seen anyone for many days. A disheartening void was in my heart where there should have been the kami spirits of the ones I had loved. With little to stimulate my mind, I began thinking about little Frances. I missed her and wondered about her. She became more and more clear in my mind until I could truly hear her speaking to me.

It was a thought sent out by a brave little girl who had departed all of the worlds that she had ever known. She had wanted me to know so that my soul could rest in peace when my own time ultimately came. It had taken that long to reach me.

Do not worry, my little Keiko. We are all together. We are all going home together.

CHAPTER 15
Running Out Of Time

It was spring and I felt boundless new life and energy. Perhaps Okei's hand had given me more of the magic that had first created me. All of our time now was at the Veerkamp farmhouse. The Wakamatsu farm seemed a world away even though it was only a short walking distance down the road.

As my energy increased, I sensed Okei's strength waning as a result of her illness. Still, she would not let it deter her from her duties to her adopted family. She helped Louisa with breakfast in the morning, not an easy chore with so many large hungry mouths to feed. She got milk from the milking cow and eggs from the laying hens. She watered the gardens and picked the ripening fruits and vegetables. In the evening, Louisa would spend time teaching her needlework and sewing techniques on the treadle Singer machine in the family room.

She kept herself busy with chores even after dinner. When everyone was asleep at night, she would continue her work on the kimono. Her limited energy often left her exhausted by the time she was able to sit down at her worktable.

Louisa lightened her load and insisted that she rest whenever possible, but Okei would not hear of it. Working for the family was necessary to show them her gratitude. It was not their fault that her illness was keeping her from fulfilling all of her obligations.

The kimono had become an obsession. I think she sensed that her time on earth was quickly diminishing. The kimono would be the final achievement in her life and she would not be denied its completion.

Louisa and sometimes Francis came in to watch her work under the glow of the oil lamp. Louisa marveled at the painstaking and rigorous procedures that had been developed in Japan over thousands of years. The paste resist had to be applied. Then came hand painting of intricate designs. Then more paste to protect the new paintings after which the paste had to be washed off to begin again.

The important time soon came to do the main background dye for the kimono. Okei was granted an entire day free of her chores. She got the blue dye from the Wakamatsu farmhouse and spent hours diluting and mixing it to the proper pale shade. She went to the back laborers' shed where a rack had been built but had never been used. Then, without a break, she applied the blue dye with a wide fine bristled brush to each of the four panels of the kimono on the rack. It took nearly two hours of constant work. By sunset, it was done and hung to dry. Okei was so exhausted that she was barely able to drag herself back to her bedroom at the Veerkamp house.

A small tin shed at the back of the ranch house was converted to a hothouse with help from Henry, who helped stoke the fire. The steam was needed to set the colors. Henry marveled at the beauty of the unfinished fabric when he finally got the chance to admire it. The pale blue color reminded him of the sky opposite that of the setting sun.

"It is water," Okei chided him. "Fish do not swim in the sky."

"Well, I heard there are fish that can fly."

"Uso!" Okei brushed aside such nonsense and grabbed Henry's

hand. They began to walk towards Okei's Hill. Okei stopped for a moment at the keyaki tree as they were about to pass in front of it.

Henry had gone by it many times without seeing how much the small tree had grown. It was now as tall as he was. When Okei remained silent, he decided to speak up.

"I suppose it will just keep getting bigger and bigger. I wonder how old they get."

"There is a great tree in Aizu over 1,000 years old." Okei made herself look skyward as if the little tree already towered over them. "It will be here long after we are gone."

Henry couldn't help being aware of Okei's melancholy mood. He was determined to bring more happiness into her life.

"Then a hundred years from now the tree will tell those people about us. They'll gather here and listen to the stories about Okei, and Matz, Kuni, and my folks."

"And you too, Henry-san," Okei had to add.

"Ah, nothing much good that it could say about me."

"Uso. You shot the Imperial samurai who attacked our home. You have helped all of us at the colony, and, and. . . "

Henry waited as Okei hesitated. "And what?"

It was then that she got up on her tiptoes and kissed him lightly. "And you have always been my friend." She began walking away and left Henry stunned beside the tree. He had to run for a moment to catch up.

Their walking slowed considerably and the sun had set before the last climb to the top of the Okei's Hill. The evening star shown brightly to the west along with another, fainter star. Gradually as they watched, the crimson tinge of the sunset darkened and more stars began to appear. They sat on the hill together and the jewel-box sprinkle of stars of the Milky Way shown overhead. The land was black compared to the sky's glowing blue-gray.

"My father told me that each speck of light is a world like the Earth." Okei tightened her grip on Henry's hand without realizing it. Henry didn't mind. "On some worlds there are people looking at the stars and wondering about us just as I am."

"They probably think they are alone," Henry said. "They have no way of knowing that we are here looking at them."

Okei moved herself closer to him. "But they know that they are not alone, Henry-san. Look how many stars there are! There are more than the grains of sand on Earth. Surely among so many, someone is looking back and wondering. It could be a world just like here. I could be the one looking up at the sky and looking down at myself."

Without realizing it, Henry had put his arm around her. She held him around the waist.

"In that world, Henry-san, you are with me, and I am not sick. In that world, there is a future for us."

They held each other tightly. Henry could feel the wetness of her tears on his arm.

"You will get better," Henry said as if it were a wish upon the stars.

Okei left his side and stood at the spot that would be her final resting place. She closed her eyes and did not move or say anything. After several minutes, Henry decided to reach out to her.

"I didn't want to disturb you if you were meditating." He felt like holding her but sensed that she wanted solitude with the glittering stars.

"I was not meditating. I was sending a message to myself up above." She again felt Henry's touch upon her shoulder.

"What did you say?"

Okei continued gazing skyward. A meteor flashed a trail of light overhead.

"I told myself to value each precious moment of life. I prayed that she would never get this sickness."

I remember that it happened on an eventful day in May, nearly two years after the beginning of the Wakamatsu Tea and Silk Colony.

Okei had hoped that a night of rest would refresh her. In a dream she had awakened in astonishment to realize that the fever was gone. Immediately she prayed her eternal gratitude to the Buddha and promised her lifelong devotion. Once again she was free to think about her future. How wonderful it was to see the distant horizon and feel the desires and hopes stirring within her soul to reach it. Thoughts of time with Henry came into her mind.

It was not to be. Instead, she woke up shaking from a feverish chill. Her feeling of fatigue was greater than ever before in her life. It would have been easy to sink further into despair and not make the effort to start another day. She could have succumbed to self-pity and regret and asked the Buddha why she had to be the one to have to face such an unconquerable foe. She could have felt such total defeat, but she did not.

Gradually, she gathered what little remained of her inner

strength and pulled her aching body from the bed. Leaning from one wall to the next, she made her way down the hallway and at last found Louisa sitting by her sewing machine. Louisa immediately jumped up and grabbed hold of her.

"What do you think you are doing, young lady? You can't be roaming all over the house in your nighties. The boys might see you and get improper ideas!" She began taking Okei back to her bedroom but Okei protested.

"Louisa-san, I need to show you how to do the gold thread stitching on the kimono."

At first, Louisa tried to steer her the other way but Okei was determined to get to her worktable. Knowing how much the kimono meant to her, Louisa relented and helped hold her up by the shoulders until Okei was seated.

"I have drawn the lines on the fabric," she said, pointing to the curled ripples made in lead pencil. "These are swirls of the river. There and there. There are many. They need to be of the thick gold thread." Okei showed her the golden wound spool on the adjacent desk. "You must secure them with this thin thread."

"Yes, it is called couching," Louisa wanted to reassure her that she was up to the challenge. She kept watching intently, however.

Okei pointed to the objects that Henry had thought were drawings of Indian teepees. "These are fishing nets," Okei told her. "It is a very famous fishing scene in Japan, very beautiful at sunset. The waters reflect many colors off of the nets. Blue. Red. Green. You must thread it with many colors. Use imagination."

Louisa laughed. "I have a good imagination, believe me!"

Even to smile was difficult for Okei but she summoned the strength to do just that. It lasted barely an instant, however. Tears begin to fill in her eyes. Louisa noticed when they began to flow down her cheeks and she bent down to gently hug her shriveled body.

"I am so sorry that I am a burden to you. I do not know why this has happened to me."

Louisa kissed her on her tear-streaked cheek.

"I am sorry to make another request of you," Okei looked back at her. "It is most difficult to put into any kind of words."

Louisa pulled up a chair that was near by and moved as close as she could to her.

"I have never said this to Henry, or anyone. You must especially not tell Henry."

Okei was having difficulty gathering her thoughts and Louisa had an idea of what might be on her mind.

"It is a special kimono," Louisa said for her, starting as a question then deciding that it wasn't. "It is a wedding kimono."

"Yes. You have known this?"

Louisa decided that she had. "Yes."

Okei found the strength to turn to face her. Their eyes searched to find hidden answers in each other's minds.

"I know it is not a proper thing. I have asked myself many times why I do this, why I cannot stop my feelings," Okei hung her head down and seemed to close her eyes.

Louisa sat back for a moment and took a deep breath. She remembered the first time Henry had mentioned his fondness for her.

"I tried to blame Henry at first. I had to be an old world fool, I guess. But I realized Henry didn't care how I felt. He only saw a beautiful girl he loved and it didn't matter much what world she was from. Then I decided that it didn't matter to me either. You just can't hold love back. You just don't."

Both sat facing each other but with their heads bowed down. Louisa could sense that Okei had more to say and needed a bit of time. The only sound was the ticking of the large clock on the mantelshelf.

"It was never meant for sadness," Okei said, glancing at the beautiful silk kimono before her. "I do not want to be buried in it. Promise to use my older kimono." She held up the fabric to her cheek, feeling its luxurious smoothness.

"You have my promise."

Louisa had come with her husband by wagon across thousands of miles of prairies and deserts. She had raised six sons and buried two daughters. She had been the unrelenting force that had kept her family together for more than twenty years. In all that time, she could not remember a more poignant, heart to heart conversation than what happened on this day in May.

"You have been a blessing to me, Okei-san." She had to work hard to keep her voice from fading to nothing. "I lost two daughters before I could see them grow and only had the boys to look after. I think the Lord took pity and sent you to me. I can only guess that I must have done something right in my life, because you have been the greatest gift that I could ever have received."

The young pioneer girl from Japan and the matriarch mother of a pioneer-farming dynasty locked in embrace in the empty room of the house where they were alone. Francis and all the boys were out scattered in the vast fields of both the Veerkamp and Wakamatsu lands. There was no one to see this and now there is no one left to remember, except for a small and insignificant being sitting on a bedroom chair at the far side of the house, who saw and heard all. Me.

Matsu put his hoe down when he saw the horse and rider stop in front of the house. He smiled in recognition and quickly strode from the side of the barn where he had been working.

"Kuninosuke! I have not seen you in months!"

Kuni stepped down and the two men embraced in the western way of friendship.

"They would behead us in Japan to see two samurai hug each other," Kuni laughed.

Matsu tried to look serious. "Ah, if there are any samurai left."

Kuni tied his horse. "Yes, I heard Emperor Meiji decreed a new period in Japan. It is called the Meiji Restoration. The first thing those in power did was to take swords from all samurai and terminate the entire samurai class!"

Matsu was visibly shocked. He had not known that such an outlandish thing had happened in the old homeland.

"So, Matsu, if you were ever thinking of going back to Japan, you should take that hoe and shovel because you would be the lowest common laborer."

Matsu shook his head, realizing there was nothing he could do about a world so many thousands of miles distant.

"You must have come to see Okei. She would be very happy to

see her old admirer."

Kuni didn't smile and Matsu knew that he had just come from the Veerkamp house where she was in her sick bed.

"She is worse than I had thought. I was just glad that she could still recognize me."

Matsu could think of nothing else to do but pick up the hoe that he had dropped on the ground. He began thinking about the long road they had all traveled to get to this day.

"I always thought that Okei would outlast all of us," Kuni was also thinking about their long path. "We fight, we break our backs in the fields. We drink too much and don't take care of ourselves. Eee. Why a sinful man like me can keep going and she cannot is not fair. The Buddha in his infinite wisdom is not fair." Kuni mounted his horse.

"How is the married life in Coloma?"

Kuni laughed loudly. "You should try it, Matsu-san. There is nothing like a lady to take care of your needs every night. It keeps you satisfied until the next night."

Matsu smiled weakly then waved. "We did not know it would turn out like this," he said.

The horse wheeled and Kuni had to bring it back around.

"Yes, losing Dr. Matsumoto, soon Okei. Schnell has gone. All the tea and plants that we worked so hard for will soon be dead. There does not seem to be much good to come out of this."

Matsu looked at his old friend. "We are still here."

"The survivors!" Kuni laughed. "But we have failed,

Matsunosuke-san. Our resolve was simply not strong enough to make the farm successful."

Matsu had thought about this for some time before. "We had unquestionable resolve, Kuni-san. I think our aspirations were too high, our dreams too grand."

"So, it is still the fault of all of us."

Matsu disagreed. "No one is at fault. Sometimes great dreams are necessary to inspire action."

Kuni held tightly to the reins as the horse was bent on rushing home to awaiting hay and pasture.

"You have changed much, Matsunosuke," Kuni looked down upon his old friend. "You have become a true American." He saluted then whipped the horse's rump. He was gone in a cloud of dust.

Matsu watched Kuni leave then pointed himself back to the barn. Something had been said that had stuck in his mind. Instead of walking forward, he looked at the hoe in his hand and dropped it to the ground. He turned around and rushed into the house and then up the stairs to the room Dr. Matsumoto had shared with Nishijawa many months ago.

The doctor had taken his medicine bag and much of his possessions when he had left for Sacramento so the room was almost empty. A heavy black trunk tied with straps remained in the far corner of the room.

Matsu wasted little time untying the straps and then diving his arms into the open trunk. He felt no shame or guilt rummaging through the man's possessions since the doctor had died many months ago. He might even be somewhere above encouraging him to find what he was looking for. The only problem was that Matsu wasn't sure what he was trying to find. There were underwear and pants and shirts, Western-style and Japanese-style clothing. There was a derby hat. He reached deep down to feel what was below. Just more clothing. Matsu sat down beside the chest and decided that he had to put his mind to better use. When he closed the chest, he noticed the arched top of the lid. He pulled the trunk away from the wall. On the floor in the back was the very thing he was seeking.

It was a small empty cloth bag with Chinese kanji characters on it. The writing was similar enough to Japanese that Matsu could read it. Kusuri. Medicine. The smaller Chinese characters written by hand were more complicated but he had a good idea what it said.

Henry heard Matsu's shouting from several hundred yards away where he was planting new pear trees on the land that had previously grown tea plants. There was great urgency in Matsu's running and Henry began a fast walk in his direction.

"Kusuri! Kusuri!" Matsu kept shouting. Henry had no idea what the samurai was talking about. They finally met in the middle of the field. Henry was breathing as heavily as Matsu because he had suddenly realized that he been out in the field for many hours. Okei had been sleeping peacefully during his last visit. Not wanting to disturb her, Henry had come back outside in a daze, picked up a shovel, and headed out to a distant part of the ranch. Now he felt the crushing anguish of having abandoned her, of not having been at her side when she had urgently needed him. He expected the worst possible news.

"I am an imbecile for not thinking better," Matsu spoke fast in broken English as Henry struggled to try to understand him. "Dr. Matsumoto was bringing the medicine back from the Sacramento Chinatown when he was killed." He held up a small white sack in his outstretched hand. "I found this empty bag in his room. It is for curing the fever! Okei's fever!"

Henry's heart was suddenly thundering in his throat. The idea that any hope existed amid such impossible despair jolted him like a lightning bolt crashing close by.

"You mean we can help Okei? She don't have to die, Matz?" All the muscles in Henry's body seemed to be twitching with energy, relieved not to be helpless anymore.

"Hai. Sacramento Chinatown. We must get medicine, soon as possible!"

Matsu was still not sure if Henry fully comprehended what he had said when Henry suddenly snatched the bag out of Matsu's hand. Henry was already striding quickly towards the Wakamatsu farm where the Veerkamps kept their horses in the large barn.

"I'm a better rider than you are, Matz," he yelled behind him. "I'm going to get the medicine. You take care of Okei and tell her to hang on until I get back!" In an instant, Henry was running. Matsu headed for the Veerkamp house.

Louisa was coming out of the house as Matsu quickly approached. She asked if he had seen Henry.

"Henry is going to Sacramento to get medicine," Matsu stopped and tried to gain control of himself before talking to Okei. "The medicine could save Okei."

Louisa looked distressed. "I don't think there's much more time left. Henry should be here. Okei's been asking for him."

The samurai bowed and went to Okei's bedroom. He could hear her voice even before he entered. He sat down on one of the chairs beside the bed. He wanted to let her know that Henry would be bringing the medicine soon, only she wouldn't let him. She was talking in a feverish pitch. It was something about Schnell. She seemed to be talking to him. She was asking why he had left with Jou and the children. She wondered why they had not asked her to go with them. In her mind she seemed to be running frantically to try to catch up as they left, yelling behind them. "Schnell-san! Schnell-san!"

Louisa came in to put a cool, creek-soaked towel on her forehead and she quieted considerably. Because of Okei's feverish dream, Matsu now found himself thinking about Schnell. Didn't Okei understand that their leader had intentionally abandoned them? Could he tell her that Schnell and his family had been seen boarding a train to the East Coast of America? Eee, what good would it do now?

Matsu was about to speak, but unbelievably she silenced him.

"Matsu-san! I am so glad that you are here." She turned her head to look at him.

He was left speechless. He hadn't anticipated a conversation with her. He didn't know what to expect because he hadn't seen her in days.

"I have had to work," he said guiltily. In truth, he had avoided seeing her because he could not bear to watch her suffer. So much for samurai bravery.

Unbelievably, her gaze and voice became steady. "We were lovers once," she said to him. There was a faint smile as she saw Matsu's cheeks turn red with embarrassment.

"I was just a child. You were older, and always looked after me, like a big brother."

Matsu could feel his heart tremble and cloudiness was beginning to dim the corners of his vision. He had completely forgotten about Henry and the medicine.

"I made a promise to your family to protect you." He couldn't believe how weak his voice sounded. "I deeply regret that I have not been able to fulfill my obligation."

She closed her eyes for a moment as another chill swept across her body. He thought that she would have to rest now, but instead she managed to reach out her hand to him. It burned from the fever.

"You take blame for so many things, Matsu-san. I have wondered how you can ever stand up when you place such great burdens on yourself."

He couldn't believe that she squeezed his hand.

"It is my nature," Matsu answered her. "I cannot change."

She clinched her teeth from unimaginable pain. She seemed to motion him closer to her.

"You must promise…"

Matsu moved in even closer. He couldn't miss her last words. She was then still. He began to shake.

Then her eyes opened again. She turned and lifted her head slightly to look directly into his eyes.

"Promise me that you will let me go. I cannot be in peace until you do. Please have only good feelings about me, just good feelings."

It had taken every last ounce of energy and spirit that she had. She laid her head back down on the pillow and closed her eyes.

Matsu stood and didn't know what to do. Should he call Louisa? Henry would be back very soon. What was he going to say to him? Matsu soon noticed Okei's very shallow breathing. She then took a last deep breath, and seemed to answer his plea.

"…and tell Henry that I love him."

The days were longer as summer approached and the sun was still several hours from setting when Louisa heard the rider approaching. She immediately rushed to the front door.

Henry had jumped off the horse and was in such a rush that he almost ran over his mother. It took a moment of trying to go around before he finally noticed her in his path.

"It's over," she said simply.

"I got the medicine. I need to get Okei the medicine!" Once more he tried to get around her but she kept moving to block him.

"Henry, she's gone! She died a couple of hours ago."

He no longer moved. He kept looking at the small white bag he held up in his hand, as if trying to think of some other way to get the drug to Okei. Getting by his mother did not, however, seem to be the problem.

"I went as fast as I could," he said.

"I know you did. You did everything anyone could have done."

"Not fast enough…"

Louisa was standing on the first step but even then Henry was a good head taller. She hugged him but knew that he barely felt her.

"Needn't blame yourself, Henry," she looked him in the eyes. "Should have got the medicine weeks ago when the fever was first getting bad. I'm to blame as much as anyone for not thinking of it."

Now Henry just stood motionless, even when Louisa stepped away from the door. He looked so defeated that she almost had to push him into the house.

Once inside, he didn't seem to know which way the room was. Louisa had to direct him like a guide leading a blind man. She held his hand then felt it slip away. He had stopped following.

"I just can't, Mom. I can't see her like this."

Louisa again took firm hold of his hand.

"Henry, you have to see her! You need to do this for her. She would want you to tell her goodbye."

They approached the room and Louisa could just see the still form on the bed. Henry went in with his head bowed down. The bedcovers were pulled back and Okei was dressed in the light blue kimono with fishing designs all about it, the one he had watched her create over the last several months. Her face was as serene and peaceful as the beautiful motif of the kimono.

"I finished the last embroidery and had just stitched it together," Louisa said from behind. She found that she had to steady herself against the doorframe. "I wanted to show it to her, rushed in to let her know that it was complete…but she was already gone."

Henry stood beside the bed, towering over Okei's body until he sat on the chair Louisa had placed alongside. She needed to leave him alone with her. She remembered something.

"Okei wouldn't let us bury her in it. We'll have to change her to the other kimono. She had been saving it…" Louisa suddenly hoped that Henry had not heard her. She didn't know. She held her hand over her mouth as she closed the door behind her.

It took Henry a long time to trudge up to Okei's Hill. His mom had said that Matsu would be there, digging the grave. Henry carried a shovel.

The evening on a late spring day was mildly warm. There were a few clouds in the sky, not enough to mean anything. All that the clouds did was to give a nice sunset-color to the west, toward Japan.

He could see Matsu on the hill after he crossed the road. The samurai looked small and insignificant along the panorama of the rolling ranch land. Henry, however, could see nothing else. Matsu stopped digging as he approached, acknowledging him with a brief bow as he held the shovel beside him.

"Henry-san," he said. He was sweating from the work, which seemed about half complete.

"I've come to help you, Matz," Henry said, showing his shovel. "I didn't know what else to do."

Matsu smiled and they walked to opposite sides of the hole. He had chosen the site just slightly below the knoll where Okei had sat during many contemplative sunsets. As he looked across the ground below him, he noticed the orange glow of light all around.

Henry noticed, too. They both turned to the west and shaded their eyes.

"Ara," Matsu said and got down on his knees. The clouds had cleared and the blazing red sphere of the sun was hanging low just above the saddle on the side of Thompson Hill. The world was awash in its glowing colors. It was a sight Okei had beheld many times, prayed to many times, sang children's songs to many times. It had been the center of all her unfulfilled longings, hopes, and dreams.

Henry sat down beside him. Together they watched the sun slowly descending into the horizon line below it, dipping its edge, a quarter, a half, the warmth of its light fast fading.

Finally only a glowing luminescent line of light remained, then it descended into the next world beyond.

"Sayonara, Okei-san," Matsu whispered.

"Goodbye, Okei-san," Henry said.

CHAPTER 16
The End Of The Beginning

Okei-san's death hadn't been the end of the Wakamatsu Tea and Silk Colony. The Colony had effectively ended several months earlier, before the spring had even begun. When John Henry Schnell had left with the balance of the loan unpaid, the land was foreclosed and soon changed into the Veerkamp's hands. The Veerkamp boys who had spent many hours helping their neighbors were now grown young men working on that land as part of their father's property.

For Matsu, working for the Veerkamp family was an easy transition. Much of the land was still the same, only now he took his orders from Francis Veerkamp and not John Henry Schnell. No one asked him what he thought of his former boss and he never volunteered to talk about him. He kept himself busy and never discussed matters of the larger world. He seemed content to be where he was at this stage in his life.

Henry Veerkamp decided to leave the ranch to marry and raise a family in Amador County. He would later return to help his brothers on the Veerkamp farm.

Matsu moved to Coloma in 1880, living with Nishijawa for a time. Shortly after he moved, Francis invited him to dinner with his family. Feeling his age more and more, Francis wanted to delegate all of the farming responsibilities that had both burdened and enlightened him for nearly thirty years.

"Matz, you are now the distribution manager," Francis told him while raising a glass of German beer. "My son Louis will do the east and the mountains, and you will manage everything from Sacramento to San Francisco."

⁂

From 1872 through 1900 the Veerkamp enterprise was one of the most progressive and productive farms in California. They grew then distributed their fruits, vegetables, and grain the width of the state from San Francisco in the west and Bodie and Nevada border towns like Reno and Carson City to the east. Miners and residents especially found their carefully packed boxes of fruits and vegetables irresistible. In the Wild West town of Bodie, peaches often sold for five-dollars each and watermelons commanded twenty dollars. It was hard work taking the loaded wagons across the mountain passes over rocky, twisting roads, but the profits from these ventures helped to establish the Veerkamp farming dynasty that would last for over 140 years.

For almost thirty years, life for me was a changeless routine. Matsu-san kept me on a shelf above other more utilitarian shelves in his one room cabin that sat towards the creek from the first old Veerkamp home. I shared the shelf with a white smooth stone he had found in the mining tailings and later with a whiskey glass that had come from a drinking bar in San Francisco.

The story about the glass is that Matsu had delivered a wagonload of produce to San Francisco clients and then went out on the town to celebrate his success. Matsu had not limited his indulgences that evening and by nightfall patrons had to carry him back to his wagon. No one seems to know how he managed to get back home from that eventful outing. This was his only breach of samurai etiquette that anyone could ever recall.

With only the white stone and the whiskey glass to keep me

company on most days, I had time to reflect on the course of my journey since I had first found existence. I tried to remember that day in the castle I was made and wondered what date it had been. This birthday had been important to all of my human friends and I wanted such a date to celebrate also. It had been April, I think. How about April 15? Henceforth my birthday would be celebrated on April fifteenth.

Of course, no one else would know this. Okei-san was no longer with me to share my thoughts. Matsu did his best and was good to me, keeping dust and spider webs off my space on the shelf. Once in a while he would pick me up and move me to the small multiple use table in the center of the cabin. He would stare at me long into the night. We both shared the enormity of Okei-san's loss and would deeply miss her forever.

The funeral had been on the evening following her death. Henry had tracked down Reverend Cool in Greenwood and had him preside at the service on Okei's Hill. Francis, Louisa, and most of the sons attended. Several local ranching families sent representatives. Of the twenty-two colonists who had come with John Henry Schnell, Matsu was the only one present. I was not able to go, but Matsu spent time with me that night to tell me about it.

It had been short and respectful, and of course, sad. Bittersweet was a new feeling for me, remembering the times of joy and reflection, the many times that I had sat on the top of that hill with Frances and Okei-san, listening contentedly as they sang songs while the sun settled gloriously into the dip of Thompson Hill. That it was now the final resting place of my best friend and my maker, was immensely hard to accept.

A wooden cross was erected over the burial stones with Okei's name written across the horizontal board. Over the years, grass and brush grew to cover the gravesite. The Veerkamps remembered Okei but they were converting from an agricultural farm to a cattle operation and didn't have time to reflect about the past. At least with the cattle, Okei's Hill was not a lonely place.

After a record-successful farming and ranching season in 1885, Matsu was given time off to attend to a task he had been contemplating for fifteen years. With the help of several farm hands, brush that had overgrown Okei's Hill was cut down and the grass trimmed. Then a wagon came from Coloma carrying a white stone monument. Matsu supervised every aspect of its precise placement. Though the wooden marker had long ago weathered away, he knew exactly where to place the stone.

Matsu returned that evening, just as the sun was setting in the saddle beside Thompson Hill. He hadn't realized until then that it was nearly the fifteenth anniversary of her death.

He read the words that he had the mason carve into the stone,

"In Memory of OKEI, died 1871, aged 19 years. A Japanese Girl."

On the backside were the same words written in Japanese.

"I am sorry that fulfilling my duty to you has taken so much time," Matsu spoke not to the new stone but to the spirit that had been lying under the earth for fifteen years. "I could not collect funding from all of the colonists as I had planned. Most have disappeared into the wind. I found Matsugoro and Yana who were in San Francisco. Kuninosuke made a small donation, all that he could afford."

Now fifty years old, Matsu gingerly lowered himself to the ground to rest his weary legs. His back hurt. His shoulders hurt. More than fifteen years of farm labor had taken a great toll on his body. He had probably planted a thousand trees. He had plowed the hundreds of acres many times over. In all that time, he hadn't swung a sword since decapitating the ninja in the farmhouse so long ago. Matsu flexed his shoulders, realizing how far in the past his samurai days were. Of course it didn't matter anymore if he could wield a sword, since all he had now resembling a weapon was a serving knife.

Matsu sighed and bowed forward as far as he could.

"You will never be forgotten, Okei-san," he whispered to her. "The stone will last for a thousand years to let those who come here know of your brave spirit. This is my sacred honor for you. Rest forever in peace."

He got back up to his feet and did his gassho. "Namu Amida Butsu. Namu Amida Butsu. Namu Amida Butsu." Slowly he trudged home towards his cabin.

Matsu's final day came in 1901. Mary Veerkamp, the young wife of Egbert who occupied the old Veerkamp homestead, knew that the loyal Japanese worker had not been doing well for the past several weeks. For the last several days he had not been able to come up to the house to obtain his meals. Mary had her seven-year-old son, Adolph, take steamed rice to his cabin several times every day. Sometimes she stirred in bits of meat in hopes of improving his health but the old samurai seldom ate those. One day, young Adolph came running up the hill from the cabin shouting for his mom. Mary met him half way, holding him by the hand and walking back to the small building. She closed Matsu's eyes for the final time.

The bent old Japanese man had been a fixture in the small Sacramento River town of Colusa for many years. The small group who saw him passing by the barbershop tried to guess when any of the townspeople had first noticed him.

"Saw him in the Jap town about ten years ago," one patron said.

"Nah, more like five years. It was the year my sister got hitched."

Kuni waved and they waved back at him.

Since he had left his family in Sacramento, he had been doing any kind of work he could find to eke out a living. When his health was better, he was a woodchopper and made good wages during the fall. Now in failing health, he found that fishing the river was about all that he could do. Years ago, he had owned a fish store in Sacramento and went out on his boat every evening to fish in the strong currents of the Sacramento River. Now with the store gone and boat fishing a distant memory, he simply cast his line out from the shore.

It was 1915 and he was sixty-six years old, the same age as Matsu was when he had died in 1901. How he had managed to live this long was baffling to him. He drank to excess. He had been a smoker until he could no longer afford cigarettes. He ate only sporadically, and couldn't remember the last time he had eaten fruits or vegetables. Exercise was something unknown to him.

As he headed out to the river with his pole and tackle box, he saw the group of school-age kids coming towards him. He sighed but would not alter his path for them.

"Lookie at the old Jap," one boy said, stopping and slanting his eyes and mouth with his fingers. The others started shouting gobbledygook that was their interpretation of an oriental language.

Kuni stared with thin weather worn eyes and maybe a faint trace of a smile on his crease-filled face. Like all the times before, he would let them have their little fun at his expense. They were just too ignorant and immature to know that the man before them had lived the rich and fascinating life of an immigrant pioneer. They could not comprehend the fact that he had once been a samurai in the last samurai stronghold in Japan, or that he had crossed the ocean and been a member of the first Japanese colony in America. They could not know that he had raised a family and could speak four languages and had been a court interpreter in Sacramento. In his carpentry days, he had been able to construct anything from raw lumber and had helped build several hotels, stores, and churches. He had opened the first fish market in Sacramento.

"Pa says all you Japs oughta go back home to where you came from."

Kuni's slight smile faded.

"America is my home, just like it is your home," he said. "Each of us has come from someplace else."

"Pa says your kind of people aren't even human."

It hadn't taken long for Kuni to lose his patience. He began to swing out his pole like a samurai blade, the heavy lead river sinkers and sharpened hooks arching wider and wider around him. The boys yelled and scattered off in every direction, not to come back again on this day.

Kuni continued down to the river, finding his favorite tree from where he heaved out his long fishing line. The splash was half way across the wide flowing river. He was surprised how far he could still cast out. Maybe he should have kept his samurai sword and given the local kids a real fright.

Sitting under the tree, he tried to lie down and relax but his congested lungs would not allow it. His heart began to hurt and it continued until he sat up and was able to take some deeper breaths.

It has been a long journey that is coming to an end.

No longer with a family, barely able to make a living, now a loner with few friends living in a dilapidated boarding house in

Colusa, it seemed that his life was ending in a downward spiral. It seemed that it had all been a total waste.

Kuni kept watching the pole for signs of a bite. Even though he had caught nothing for the entire week, he remained confident of a change in his fortune. Deep inside, apparently, the pioneer spirit of hope never dies.

There would be no regrets when his time came to leave this world. He had used up all the karma and kami endowed at his birth within the life that he had led and would not change anything about it.

He thought about Okei, Dr. Matsumoto, Matsugoro, Schnell, and Matsu. He thought about the hopes of the colony in the beginning and the despair towards the end. He wondered who was still alive, who had stayed and who had gone back to Japan. If only there was some way to know.

The many unanswered questions had driven him to return to the colony in the fall last year. He hadn't been back to the old farm since he had moved his family to Sacramento in 1889. That seemed so incredibly long ago, since he hadn't even been to Sacramento or seen his family in the last five years.

He recalled wandering near the old Wakamatsu farmhouse when a young man dressed in farm overalls spotted him and walked over.

"You must have been one of the colonists," he said and shook Kuni's hand. Kuni soon realized that the young man was a Veerkamp son who had not even been born when the colony had ended.

At the back of the house, Kuni came to the keyaki tree that had been planted in a ceremony at the colony. Schnell had spoken about a new beginning and Tanaka had given a short prayer. In the place of the small sapling that had barely come up to Schnell's hip now was a thirty-foot high adult tree that could not entirely be seen without straining his neck.

How could it have grown so big in so short a time? Of course, it hadn't been that short of a time. They had come as pioneer-settlers from Japan in 1869. Now he had returned in 1914, more than forty-five years later.

Looking up at the tree had made him feel dizzy, and this feeling of disorientation remained even as he began walking the dirt road to Okei's gravesite. Old memories were reaching out to him from all over, trying to divert him from his path in the present world.

He walked past the barn, now rebuilt and different. The old structure had been destroyed by a tornado in 1897. Getting his feet wet in the creek along the road brought back more memories of times gone. Once he had seen Okei and other women bathing there, a vision that he had tried to keep fresh and clear in his mind over the years. Alas, even that pleasurable memory had now faded.

Reaching Okei's gravesite, he knelt down before the stone in prayer. He asked forgiveness for not having attended her funeral. There had been no excuses. He had been thoughtless and disrespectful.

"I thought that you would never die," Kuni confided to her in his prayers. "You were the special brightness and like the sunrise I assumed you would never fail to shine." If Okei was not immortal, then how could anyone else be, least of all an old broken-down alcoholic fisherman?

He said his gassho, "Namu Amida Butsu" three times then did a long parting bow. He would never again return to this place.

The final stop on his reflective journey back into a life long-past had been the Coloma Cemetery just down the hill on the Coloma Road. He had left the visit for last because it had been his primary reason for undertaking this long and tiring journey from his Colusa boarding house.

Past the open gate, he went by many grave markers on a steep hill. Some were freshly dug with shiny stones but many of the wooden markers were already weather-worn and indecipherable. Once at the top of the hill, Kuni began to look around. He carried a paper-wrapped oblong object under his arm. Then where the hill began to slope downward again, he spotted the small wooden board posted on a moderate sized oak tree. "Matz Sakuri," it was barely readable in fading and chipped blackened print. "Died 1901." Beside it on the sloped hillside was a small-leveled area covered with years of twigs and crinkled up leaves.

Kuni knelt down and clasped his hands in front of him. In them he held his juzu prayer beads. He bowed further down, touching his forehead to the earth, not moving for many moments. He said his gassho and then painfully rose back to his sitting position.

"My old friend," he said in flawless Japanese diction, still his native tongue after many years in the American land. "We have journeyed far since Tsuruga Castle, ne? We came as pioneers to a strange land with only hope to guide us over innumerable obstacles. I was impulsive and carefree and did many foolish things. You were the stoic samurai always trying to do what was right. I always wondered which one of us would find success in the new land."

Kuni gazed around the leaf-covered ground, his hand clearing off part of the grave that he could reach. He listened for birds but on this autumn day there was only the barely noticeable background noise of the wind rustling leaves on a distant mountain.

A smile came to his lips as he thought aloud. "We did not become rich, ne? But I think we each persevered, and achieved our own success. I lived and will die a vagabond, as I wished. You lived and died with the courage and honor of a samurai, as you wished."

Kuni got up but could not fully extend his permanently crooked body. At the side of the tree he picked up a small round rock and produced a nail from his shirt pocket. He unwrapped the wooden board he had brought and spent a moment nailing it to the tree below Matsu's marker. Kuni stepped back and gazed at the Japanese words written in his hand,

YOKU KITA NE

It didn't bother him that most people who came up this hill could not possibly understand what it said. Even translated, the English did not capture the full meaning; *you came here well*. The deeper essence of the words was something only a Japanese pioneer would be able to understand. Maybe only a samurai.

As he slowly descended the cemetery hill, his footsteps crunching on leaf covered earth began to change to the different sound of steps over river sand. He held his fishing pole in his hand and wore his straw hat to shade him from the burning sun. His eyes, slit-like to see in the blinding light, saw the way back to the Colusa boarding house alongside the river where he would spend his final days. The tears that dwelt in them didn't help his seeing.

EPILOGUE
Echoes Of The Past

"This is Henry Veerkamp," the young docent began, making sure she was making eye contact with the people in her tour group as she had been told. "This picture was taken a few years prior to his death in 1934."

On this April day, a group of perhaps twenty were in the dining room of the old farmhouse where photographs of the Veerkamp family hung on the walls. The Conservancy had only recently purchased the land from the pioneer family and had first planned to do several months of cleaning and restoration work. However, articles appearing in the local newspapers, a TV news report and the beautiful spring weather had combined to cause a flood of public interest. The first public tour of the Wakamatsu Tea and Silk Colony Farm was quickly scheduled.

The earlier start to the season also meant less training time for the docents conducting the tours. Donna was the youngest of the three assigned to the task today. She tried her best to ignore the feeling of apprehension that felt like a cramp in the middle of her stomach.

The old black and white photograph was that of an aging man standing in his farming bibs and heavy work boots. His head was bald with a deeply furrowed forehead. There was just a brush of white sideburns and below his chin was a full scraggly white with black-tinged beard. His narrowed eyes gazed at something out of view in the distance.

Donna had a momentary lapse and struggled to remember what she had learned. Gratefully, her memory came back very quickly.

"He was the first of six sons of Louisa and Francis. After working on the farm for several years, he left to work in Mendocino. He returned many years later to help the family's agricultural enterprise."

She felt that her delivery was uneven and made it a point to speak slower and more clearly. Encouraging, however, was that all the eyes were intently watching her and the photograph.

"Henry is important because he was the first person to tell historians about the Wakamatsu colonists from Japan. Without him, this story might have been lost like so much of history has been lost before. He had known Okei-san, and Matsu, Kuni, and Schnell. He had lived and worked among them, shared their dreams and failures, and would not let his memory of them be forgotten."

"Did Henry and Okei love each other?" someone asked.

She worked hard to keep the smile on her face. Of course there had not been a chapter on colonist's love stories in her docent information sheet. How could she know the answer to such a personal question about people gone for over 140 years? Just at that instant she remembered a quote from Henry Veerkamp she had read in the study material and the words came to her lips,

"Okei was bright and when she wore her kimono, she was very beautiful. She learned sewing and cooking from my mother, who was very fond of her."

"If they were in love, we just don't know. History does not answer that question."

When she finished her presentation, the group moved to the next room where another docent would be taking over. Several people lingered behind to ask more questions about Henry and the Veerkamps. They also thanked her for her wonderful insight into the Veerkamp and Wakamatsu colonist story. That compliment was enough to brighten the entire remainder of her day.

The three docents remained after the tour to gain some volunteer hours by cleaning up the house. They searched the main floor for something to do as Carl, the docent leader, went to the front door to let in some fresh air.

"Oh, what is this…?"

"Carl, did you just say something?"

"A cat just walked in!"

They all turned to look and sure enough a fairly large black and white cat had stepped in through the front door. With slow, regal strides, it went to the center of the room and sat on its haunches staring at them.

"Sorry, but you're kind of late for our tour," Carl told the animal. "Also we don't have any cat food on the menu at this time."

It didn't seem hungry, however. More than anything, it appeared to be curious about the visitors.

"You're welcome to help us sweep the house," said Wendy, who was the third docent in the room. However, when she approached the cat, it nimbly moved away. Finally it took some long strides into the other room, kept going, and then quickly climbed up the back stairwell.

"Well, just great. We can't lock the house until we find it."

They decided to go upstairs, bringing brooms, dusters, and pans with them. They could find the cat and also do some much-needed cleaning in the bedrooms.

The cat was sitting in the center of the far upstairs bedroom.

"He seems to think he belongs here," Wendy observed, determining in some esoteric way that it was a male. "I wonder if the Veerkamps owned him."

"Not very likely. No one's lived here for the past twenty years."

They decided to split up to clean each of the three upstairs bedrooms. Wendy volunteered to do the larger room because she loved cats and it would be good company. The furry creature seemed to be watching her every move with keen interest.

"You probably have a name, you must," she talked as she swept with the broom. "I'm sorry I don't know it. If you promise to stick around here, maybe I'll give you a new name."

The cat kept looking at her, apparently letting her know that it wouldn't be going anywhere anytime soon. She stopped sweeping to gaze at it.

"So, OK. You need a name. Perhaps a historic character that lived here? How about Schnell?"

The cat sat further back on his rear as if getting more comfortable for a prolonged stay.

"No, not Schnell. Not Okei." Wendy did not bother to check if it was a male, as she had first thought. She stood with her arms crossed looking down at the cat. She began to think of something in Japanese, since it seemed to possess a samurai-like regality in its manners.

"Neko. That's cat in Japanese. Your name will be Neko."

The cat simply kept staring at her with the same keen interest.

Wendy looked at her watch, remembering that the tour had only been a part of her day. She hadn't eaten lunch yet. There were other places to go. She quickened the pace with her broom, carefully working around the cat that had now decided to curl up in the middle of the old wood flooring.

She went searching for the docents in the other bedrooms but they had apparently gone downstairs. She returned to the bedroom to gather up her tools. The center of the room was empty. The room was empty. Neko had disappeared.

Where could it have gone? Had it somehow managed to dart by her while she was looking into the other bedrooms? This didn't seem possible. She had been watching to see if the cat would follow her. Down that hallway was the only way for it to have escaped.

She remained perplexed as she gazed around the empty room. The windows remained closed, probably unopened since the last occupants had left more than twenty years ago. The wall panels were slightly warped but there wasn't a crack or hole.

A small area on the floor cleared of dust remained in the center of the room. There were outlines marks made by tufts of the cat's fur. She turned herself in a circle. The only possible hiding place was a shallow closet built into the far wall but it had no doors. Obviously nothing was inside, just a platform in the middle probably put there for reaching the upper shelf. Or maybe it was a seat. Then she noticed that the top of the platform overlapped the bottom panels like a lid. The edges were ornately carved. It was a lid. Sitting in the closet unnoticed for who knows how many years was an old trunk or locker. Suddenly she forgot about the cat.

Wendy went to the door and shouted for the others before coming back to kneel in the closet. Her hand reached under the lid and lifted. There was a resistance until the old paint began to crack, then a bit of the inside darkness appeared. She closed it again when she heard the others approaching.

Carl and Donna came rushing in thinking the worst: that Wendy had stepped on a rusty old nail or fallen through an age-worn floorboard. Maybe the cat had attacked her. Seeing her kneeling transfixed at the opening of the empty closet was the least of their expectations.

"Where's the cat?"

"I don't know. He disappeared," Wendy kept staring at the trunk.

"It's gone? Where did it go?"

"He disappeared."

They finally saw what Wendy was seeing.

"Oooh, God...what is that?"

"It's a locker or a trunk," she said. "Someone painted over it when they painted the walls...they didn't realize that anything could be inside."

"It could have been here since this part of the house was built."

"Open it!"

"Don't everyone get so excited," Carl cautioned, the senior member who had seen many dashed expectations in the past. "The Veerkamps would have taken anything with them. Those Germans wouldn't leave anything valuable."

"Unless it was forgotten. It was painted over a long time ago."

"Well, open it!"

"Shouldn't we call our director?"

They looked at each other, sensing hopeful anticipation that just could not be denied. They decided to open it.

Wendy lifted again and more of the old paint that had sealed the box began to crack. Other impatient hands reached over her to push the lid all the way back to the wall.

Peering into the dark interior, at first they could see nothing. No one reached inside, cautious of skeletons and lurking slithery things seen in horror movies.

"We need a flashlight."

"No, I'm beginning to see." Kneeling, Wendy's eyes were closer than the others. "There is something inside."

Closing her eyes, she bravely reached into the darkness and lifted out a small wrapped bundle of cloth. Her other hand searched around the flat bottom. Thankfully, there were no skeletons or mummified mouse carcasses. Regretfully, there was nothing else.

"That's it? Just a bit of old laundry?" Their vision of gold coins, jewelry, and wealth beyond description dissipated like the dust from inside the trunk.

Lying on her side and feeling as let down as the others after such high expectations, Wendy began to unwrap the small bundle. The cloth had once been white but had yellowed from years of starching and existence. It still retained some of its stiffness. The fabric had been carefully folded many times over by someone to protect whatever was inside.

With more unwrapping, a reddish orange color soon began to

show through the cloth. As the others gathered closer to watch, a slender shape became evident. A pair of little white fabric arms stuck out through openings of the cloth. Then little white fabric legs.

The covering cloth was laid back. The little kimono still had its brilliant red and orange colors and was as beautiful as the day Okei had first stitched it together.

The doll saw light for the first time in over one hundred years.

"Konnichiwa," Keiko said.

APPENDIX

Characters And Notes In Order Of Appearance

Boshin War (1868-69)

The Boshin War was a north versus south civil war in Japan fought shortly after the American Civil War. Southern forces, mostly from the Choshu and Satsuma domain, were incensed that the Shogun's isolation policy and negotiations with foreigners had weakened Japan. They took control of the Emperor's Imperial Court and then defeated the forces of the Shogun and his close supporter, Lord Matsudaira, in a series of bloody battles fought with swords, lances, rifles, and cannons. This ended nearly 250 years of Shogun rule and began the Meiji Restoration. One of the first edicts of the new government was to ban the carrying of swords, effectively eliminating the samurai warrior class.

Tsuruga Castle (Crane Castle)   **Page 1**

The castle was the stronghold of Lord Matsudaira in Aizu. The heavily damaged castle was torn down after the Boshin War, then rebuilt in 1965 and is now a major tourist attraction.

Keiko   **Page 1**

The doll was discovered in 1985 in a trunk that had belonged to Mary Veerkamp. Mary had helped care for Matsunosuke Sakurai during his final illness. Her descendants donated Keiko to Wakamatsu historians Henry and Sally Taketa. Sally donated the doll to American River Conservancy (ARC) in 2014. Despite the author's many efforts to learn more information about the doll, its origin remains unknown and mysterious.

Okei Ito (1853?-1871)   **Page 1**

Her family lived near John Henry Schnell's mansion in Aizu. She was only seventeen-years old when she was recruited to help care for Schnell's infant child when he set off to America. Okei-san has achieved legendary status for many Japanese in the U.S. and in Japan. Bound by duty and honor, she persevered in a difficult situation in a strange new land.

Satsuma   Page 7
Satsuma was a southern Japan domain. The Satsuma area historically resisted governing efforts by the Shogun in distant Edo (Tokyo). One of their greatest leaders and warriors, Saigo Takamori, has often been called "The Last Samurai."

Matsunosuke Sakurai   Page 15
Matsunosuke was a samurai in service to Lord Matsudaira and a friend of Okei. He spent fifteen years collecting funds to purchase an enduring headstone for Okei's grave. Known as Matz, he remained to work on the Veerkamp farm for thirty years, becoming a foreman in their agricultural enterprise. He died in 1901 and is buried in the Coloma Pioneer Cemetery. ARC is hoping to find and mark his final resting place.

Aizu   Page 18
Aizu is the historic domain of Lord Matsudaira in northern Japan, in present day Fukushima prefecture. Aizu was the last stronghold of the Shogunate forces. After the Boshin War, many citizens were purged from their homes and the name of the town was changed to Wakamatsu. In 1955 the name was again changed to Aizuwakamatsu. Residents are prideful in its recognition as a "Samurai City" and many reminders of those historic times remain.

Tokugawa Shoguns   Page 18
Tokugawa Ieyasu ruled Japan from 1603 to 1616. He consolidated power in a time of feudal unrest with a series of sweeping military victories, unifying Japan and resulting in rule by succeeding Tokugawa Shoguns until the Boshin War in 1868. An isolation policy imposed during this time, called the Edo Period, limited travel and access to and from Japan. The Edo Period is regarded as a time of cultural enrichment, offset by economic and military regression.

Lord Katamori Matsudaira (1836-1893)   Page 18

Lord Matsudaira was the daimyo, or ruling head, of the Aizu domain. Related by marriage to the Tokugawa Shogun family line, he stubbornly held out in his castle against the Imperial forces until 1868. He became a priest after his life was spared.

John Henry Schnell (Hiramatsu Buhei)   Page 19

He came to Japan from Prussia as a teenage adventurer and made his fortune selling surplus U.S. Civil War armaments to Lord Matsudaira. He was rewarded by being made a samurai, owning a mansion, and being allowed to marry the daughter (Jou) of a samurai family. After the Boshin War was lost, he persuaded Lord Matsudaira to fund a colony in America as an escape from persecution by the victorious Imperial forces. Their second daughter, Mary, is regarded as the first Japanese born on American soil. When the Wakamatsu Gold Hill Colony faltered in 1871, Schnell, Jou, and their two daughters left the remaining colonists behind, Schnell promising to return with more funding from Japan. They then disappeared from the pages of history.

Yaeko Yanamoto (Niijima Yae) 1845-1932   Page 24

Yae learned gunnery skills from her samurai father and with her Spencer repeating rifle, helped defend the Aizu castle during the Boshin War. She was one of a number of female defenders of the Aizu homeland. She became a nurse during the Russo and Sino Japanese wars. She received several commendations and honors from the Japanese government.

Kotoshi Torima   Page 33

Torima is a fictional character created to represent one side of the East verses West friction in the second half of the nineteenth century in Japan. While many who opposed the Shogun in the Boshin War did so to try to save old traditional ways from foreign onslaught, others like Torima saw business opportunities and personal profit by increasing ties with the West.

Blacks Ships of Commodore Perry   **Page 34**
Commodore Perry's four gunships arrived in Japan in 1853, pouring black smoke from their stacks. He intimidated the Shogun government into signing trade treaties, ending nearly 250 years of isolation from the rest of the world.

Kuninosuke (Kuni) Masumizu (1849-1915)   **Page 56**
He was a carpenter with the colony. He married then moved to Sacramento where he used his language skills to help new immigrants and also acted as a translator in the court system. He fished the Sacramento River and opened one of the first fish markets. A loner in later life, he died in Colusa where he is buried. Reports that his descendants once possessed his sword and other samurai items are the basis for his portrayal as a ninja in my story.

Dr. Goro Matsumoto   **Page 73**
California newspaper articles mention a physician with the colony named Matsumoto who could cure many ailments with natural products and herbs. He does not appear on the 1870 census and his fate is unknown.

Matsugoro Ofuji (?-1890)   **Page 81**
He was a carpenter who also learned winemaking and food preservation skills while in California. When he returned to Japan around 1876, he established the first food canning process in Japan and then helped install the first wine fermentation equipment in Yamanashi. His descendants have been in contact with the American River Conservancy.

Emperor Norton (1819-1880)   **Page 85**
He became eccentric and proclaimed himself Emperor of the United States in 1859 after losing a fortune in the rice importation business. His decrees abolished the national political parties and congress, calling them frauds and corrupt. He printed his own money that was honored at many city businesses. He once saved a group of Chinese from an angry mob by reciting the Lord's Prayer, the basis for one of my San Francisco scenes. San Franciscans generally

accepted his idiosyncratic nature and upon his death it is said that 10,000 people participated in a two-mile long funeral procession.

Reverend Peter Cool   **Page 116**
The town of Cool, just north of Coloma, might have been named for this man of religion during the Gold Rush period. He is often portrayed by a local citizen at Coloma festival events.

Henry Veerkamp (1851-1934)   **Page 125**
The first son of Francis and Louisa, he is credited with revealing the story of the Wakamatsu Colony when historians came to the farm to interview him late in his life. He showed them the location of Okei's grave and still remembered the times of his youth he had shared with Okei, Matsu, and the other colonists.

Francis and Louisa Veerkamp   **Page 125**
They arrived in Gold Hill around 1852 and began a pioneer farm and ranching dynasty. When the Japanese colony came to an end, Okei and Matsu found refuge with the Veerkamp family that took over the land. Descendants of the six surviving Veerkamp sons continued the family's agricultural enterprise up into the 1980s. Over many years and across many generations, they maintained Okei's gravesite and memories of the Japanese colonists. After nearly 140 years of farming and ranching, they sold their farm to the America River Conservancy in 2010.

Aizu banner and sword   **Page 133**
A beautiful silk flag and intricate tanto sword that belonged to John Henry Schnell resides in the California Archival Collection alongside the California State Constitution. Schnell may have left these as collateral before he disappeared. On special occasions, such as important festivals, these items are brought out for display in the old Wakamatsu farmhouse. The display is carefully monitored by State Park Rangers.

Peruvian bark powder   **Page 173**
Peruvian bark powder is derived from the Cinchona trees that grow in South America. It was known to cure certain fevers before

the parasite that caused malaria was discovered. Quinine, the first effective anti-malarial drug, was derived from Cinchona alkaloids.

Okei's kimono   Page 184

Among items donated to the American River Conservancy was an old brown-toned photograph of man holding up a robe. The caption under the photograph stated "Okei's quilt." Further study of enlarged images showed that the quilt was actually made up of segments of a kimono that had been stitched together. The design of a fishing scene with nets, schools of tiny fish, small flowers, and intricate waves and reflective patterns was revealed. The author spotted a kimono with a similar design at the Asian Art Museum in San Francisco. The colors and complexity of the fabric design was as breathtaking as I presume Okei's kimono would have been.

JAPANESE GLOSSARY

akachan	baby
amigasa	half moon shaped woven hat
arigato	thank you
arigato-gozaimasu	thank you very much
asagohan	morning meal
asoko	over there
-chan	honorific for children, pets
douzo o-tassha de	Godspeed
gaijin	foreigner
ganbatte	persevere, good luck
gassho	Buddhist act of prayer
geta	walking sandal-like footwear
gomennasai	I'm sorry
hai	yes
Hana-matsuri	festival to honor Buddha's birth
hontou-desu	that's the truth
ikimasho	let's go
ikinasai	go
itadakimasu	gratitude expressed before meals
kagami	mirror
kaminari	thunder
kanpai	toast
katana	samurai long sword
kodomo-no-mono	child's things
konnichiwa	hello
kusuri	medicine
matte	wait
migi	right
mikan	mandarin orange
nihongo	Japanese language
nori	dried seaweed
oba-chan	grandmother

Obon	festival to honor one's ancestors
odaiko	large Taiko drum
ohayo-gozaimasu	good morning
oka-san	mother
okashii	funny, strange
ri	measurement of distance
-sama	honorific suffix for one of higher class
-san	honorific suffix after person's name
-sensei	honorific title / name suffix for one with greater knowledge
seppuku	ritual suicide by disembowelment
shimbun	newspaper
Shina-machi	Chinatown
shuriken	ninja throwing weapon
sode	sleeve
sukoushi-dake	just a little bit
uso	a lie
wakarimasu-ka?	do you understand?
wakizashi	samurai short sword